ONE YEAR AFTER YOU

SHARI LOW

Boldwood

First published in Great Britain in 2024 by Boldwood Books Ltd.

Copyright © Shari Low, 2024

Cover Design by Alice Moore Design

Cover Photography: Shutterstock

A CIP catalogue record for this book is available from the British Library.

Paperback ISBN 978-1-80426-892-6

Large Print ISBN 978-1-80426-891-9

Hardback ISBN 978-1-80426-893-3

Ebook ISBN 978-1-80426-890-2

Kindle ISBN 978-1-80426-889-6

Audio CD ISBN 978-1-80426-898-8

MP3 CD ISBN 978-1-80426-897-1

Digital audio download ISBN 978-1-80426-894-0

Boldwood Books Ltd
23 Bowerdean Street
London SW6 3TN
www.boldwoodbooks.com

ON THIS DAY WE MEET...

Odette Devine, 69 – Grand dame and star of the Scottish TV show *The Clydeside* for over forty years. Married four times, now single.

Calvin Fraser, 58 – Odette's ever-patient manager and friend. Most of the time. Has been known to claim that working for Odette is like handling bees but without the natty white overalls.

Carl Newman, 38 – Director of *The Clydeside.*

Elliot Banks, 40 – Documentary producer/director shooting a chronicle of Odette's life.

Mitchum Royce, 56 – Former Edinburgh banker, gambling addict, Odette's fourth and final husband.

Tress Walker, 43 – Widowed one year ago when her husband, Max, died in a car crash, she's now single mum to their child, Buddy, aged one. Recently took up a position as set designer on *The Clydeside.*

Rex Marino, 34 – Ruthlessly ambitious, way-too-handsome actor who plays Odette's son on *The Clydeside.*

Nancy Jenkins, 67 – Tress's next-door neighbour, happily engaged to Johnny Roberts, her late husband's childhood friend, whom she met again a year ago at a school reunion. Retired school dinner lady, head of Neighbourhood Watch, force of nature.

Val Murray, 67 – Nancy's friend since they met at Weirbridge Primary School a million years ago. Married to Don, the love of her life, and heartbroken that her wonderful man has Alzheimer's disease.

Noah Clark, 36 – Paediatrician at Glasgow Central Hospital, divorced from ex-wife, Anya, after the car crash that killed his best mate, Max, also exposed his wife's affair with his friend. Now he's helping Tress raise Buddy, while dating...

Dr Cheska Ayton, 36 – Head of A&E at Glasgow Central Hospital and Noah's girlfriend of the last few months.

Keli Clark, 29 – Noah's sister, a nurse on the elderly ward at Glasgow Central Hospital.

Yvie Danton, 34 – Keli's friend and a nurse on the same ward.

Gilda Clark, 64 – Noah and Keli's straight talking, ever-loving, no-nonsense mother.

PROLOGUE

Odette

I'm very aware that life can change in a heartbeat. In a minute. In an hour. In a day.

Forty years ago, I was working in a school canteen in a village on the outskirts of Glasgow, despairing that my dream of becoming an actress would amount to nothing more than another clichéd story of failed ambition and grudging obscurity. Then a twist of fate presented the opportunity to get everything I ever wanted, but I had to do the unforgivable to claim it. Now, the fame, the fortune and the glory are being stripped away from me and I'm going to be left with nothing and no-one. And I can't help wondering if I'm paying the price for the sins of my past.

Tress

I'm very aware that life can change in a heartbeat. In a minute. In an hour. In a day.

One year ago today, I was heavily pregnant, only three weeks before my due date, when I waved my husband, Max, goodbye and told him I'd miss him, even though his business trip would only take him away from me for one day. At least, that's what I thought. I had no idea that he'd be dead by nightfall. A car accident. And it came with a devastating twist. He wasn't alone. He was in the car with his mistress, my friend, Anya. It was a betrayal that was so close to home, so brutal, so calculated, that I'm not sure I'll ever get over it. How will I ever teach our son how to trust someone with his heart, when I don't think I'll have the courage to let anyone into mine again?

Noah

I'm very aware that life can change in a heartbeat. In a minute. In an hour. In a day.

A year ago, I had a lifelong mate who was closer than a brother. I didn't know that Max was sleeping with my wife, Anya, until I found their car overturned in a ditch, both of them close to death. I switched into doctor mode, and tried desperately to help them, but I couldn't save Max. Anya survived, but the wounds of her infidelity with my best friend were fatal to our marriage. It flatlined. Since then, I've forced myself to love again. Now I'm at the precipice of a new life – but am I brave enough to jump?

Keli

I'm very aware that life can change in a heartbeat. In a minute. In an hour. In a day.

I used to be proud of who I was. Honest. Hard-working. Head screwed on and big plans for my future. But that was before I met him. Before I slept with him. Before I got caught by the oldest lie in the book – I'm yours. Turns out he didn't even love me for a second.

And yet, despite that, I've honoured my promise to him that I would never tell anyone about our relationship. Not a soul. So what do I do? Do I expose his lies and spill his secrets? Do I save my dignity and walk away? Or will a blue line on a pregnancy stick make that decision for me?

FRIDAY 9 FEBRUARY 2024

8 A.M. – 10 A.M.

1

ODETTE DEVINE

February in Glasgow. There was frost on the streets outside, so, of course, someone in the maintenance department at *The Clydeside* studios had overcompensated by turning the heating up too high and now Odette could feel tiny beads of sweat pop from the pores of her freshly made-up face. Damned incompetents. It had been set in stone for the last forty years that her dressing room be kept at a steady sixty-two degrees. Fahrenheit. None of this centigrade nonsense.

Odette considered explaining this to the production runner who'd just popped into her dressing room with a fresh vanilla cappuccino, but the girl looked about twelve and she had the thumbs of someone who spent way too much time scrolling on her phone, so there was always the worry that any perceived slight, criticism or display of divadom would result in a disparaging post going viral by lunchtime. Odette had already discovered how quickly that kind of thing changed public perception. Until her last day on earth, she would believe that the viral clip of her disdainfully binning her lunch after some hopeless assistant had brought her the wrong order for the third day in a row had been the first brick taken out of the wall of her career. A wall that was getting its final kicking and crumbling to rubble today.

She subtly blew some air up onto her lip, hoping that the camera that was only three feet away (again, none of that metres nonsense) wouldn't pick it up. The documentary crew had been following her last month as one of the stars – some, including her, would argue the *biggest* star – on the set of *The Clydeside*, the thrice-weekly Scottish soap that was as much part of the cultural identity of her generation as bagpipes and Billy Connelly. The show aired every Monday, Wednesday and Friday, and pulled in over a million viewers a week – although, granted, that was down from three million in its heyday. The TV network had pitched this fly-on-the-wall film to her as being a tribute to her life's work, the chronicle of the swansong of a Scottish acting icon, but Odette knew the truth of it. Nothing was more dramatic than witnessing a demise, a good-bye, the end of an era, and they were hoping that she'd give them a meltdown or controversy that would make it must-see, car-crash TV. Well, she wouldn't give them the satisfaction. She was going to glide out with elegance and grace, because that was all she had left.

'That is the face of a star who is thinking evil thoughts,' Calvin chided her playfully, as he glanced up from his laptop. He'd been her manager since the early nineties, and friend too, and she was all too aware that he could read her like a well-worn, ancient old book. And that went both ways. She knew that in his head he had one raised eyebrow of disapproval, even if he couldn't show it, thanks to his last round of Botox. He'd had it topped up because he knew he was going to get screen time on the documentary. She also realised that he was giving her a subtle heads-up that she wasn't giving her best face to the camera, so she immediately turned on her famous, mega-watt cheeky grin. In the old days, that smile had been pure gorgeousness. Now it looked like she was advertising denture cream. Which was probably the only option open to her now that the curtain was coming down on her acting career.

'Och, not at all, Calvin,' she chided him jokingly, hoping that she was giving 'relaxed and relatable' to the camera, as opposed to the 'bloody furious, irritated and devastated' that she was feeling on the inside. This was a more strenuous test of her acting skills than the episode where she found out that her screen husband was having an affair with the postwoman. Or even the scene where it was revealed that her long-term nemesis was the sister she didn't know she had. It was probably up there on a par with when eco-terrorists stormed the town hall meeting and held the townsfolk hostage in protest against... Actually, she couldn't even remember why. It had been such a ridiculous storyline that she'd made sure the writer who came up with that nonsense only lasted one series. That was when she'd had power. Now her opinions meant nothing. 'I'm just thinking about all the wonderful writers I've worked with over the years, and all the drama that it's been a gift to put on screen,' she warbled on, face to camera. 'I just hope I've done it all justice.' Humble. Grateful. Calm. Talking down the Clydeside eco-terrorists had been a breeze compared to this.

The director of the documentary, Elliot, was in his late thirties, handsome and obliging, in a Hugh Grant *Notting Hill* era way. He would never have been her type. Odette had always had a penchant for men with a hard edge, a touch of arrogance, the ones that had a presence when they walked into a room. The same men who inevitably turned out to be chronic arses, who swaggered out of her life, taking her heart and her bank balance with them. She knew the type so well because she'd married four of them. Four husbands. Four splits. No children. The last one had robbed her blind. Taken every single penny she had. But she would be six feet in the ground before she'd admit that to anyone. She hadn't even told Calvin the extent of it, so she sure wouldn't be flashing her dirty laundry to the probing camera of this wannabe Scorsese here.

Elliot took that moment to throw in a question. 'So, Odette, it's your last day on set after four decades of playing Agnes McGlinchy on *The Clydeside*. Tell us how you're feeling.'

How was she feeling? Bloody furious. Enraged. Lost.

One last day. This was it. She had a final scene to shoot, and then a lame lunch soirée with the cast and crew, dinner with her manager, Calvin, tonight and then...

She had no idea what would happen after that.

She would wake up tomorrow morning and what? Stare at a wall? Watch old recordings from a time when she mattered?

Odette didn't miss a beat. 'Just ever so thankful. How many actresses get to spend four decades playing the same part? Agnes McGlinchy and *The Clydeside* have been my whole life and I've adored every day of my career.'

If she had been linked up to a lie detector, the needle would have fired across the paper like a serial killer denying he had anything to do with the bodies in his freezer. Her declaration of love for her life on the show was perhaps true of her first three and a half decades, but the last five years had been a battle. Diminishing screen time. Ever-changing writers. Directors who thought they knew better. The buggers had got her now though. A new team of producers, directors and writers had come in a few months before and they'd told her six weeks ago that they were 'going in a different direction'. And their new direction was sending her to Destination Unemployment.

'The people that really matter, though, are the fans. I hope that all my lovely Devine Believers...' Yes, she had a fan club, and yes, that's what they called themselves. People really had to get out more. '...will look back on these years with love and keep me in their hearts, even when I'm no longer on their screens.'

Cheesy nonsense. Her toes were curling inside her Louboutin stilettos (her own – wardrobe was too cheap to go designer and Agnes McGlinchy rarely wore anything other than slippers these days). But Calvin's subtle smile and nod told her that was the right answer.

Elliot wasn't done. 'And how will you spend your days now, Odette? Do you have plans for your retirement?'

Good question. And one that made her stomach flip.

For the last forty-odd years, her days had been structured, giving her whole bloody life to this show. Five, sometimes six days a week, she'd grafted long hours, leaving her too exhausted to do anything more in her time off than marry losers, sleep and binge-watch the other soaps. *EastEnders. Coronation Street. River City. Emmerdale.* Throw in the odd true crime show, and sleepless nights spent glued to the overnight TV shopping channels, and before she knew it, it was Monday morning and time to do it all over again.

If she didn't have her work, then what did she have?

Sure, she had friends. Kind of. Perhaps they were more acquaintances. Colleagues. Fans. Although, she would bet her last pound that they would scatter when she was no longer the celebrated actress and star of the small screen. Dame Judi Dench and Dame Maggie Smith might still be landing roles in their eighties, but Odette was irrevocably typecast. To the TV-viewing world, she was Agnes McGlinchy. And Agnes wasn't about to give up her role as the serial busybody on *The Clydeside* and start doling out missions to James Bond, or swap her Glasgow brogue for a cut-glass accent and spend her twilight years firing off words of sarcastic disapproval in an aristocratic country estate in 1921. Nope, she was doomed. Over. Finished. Maybe only a life insurance or a stairlift advert between her and the crematorium. In fact, that might be another opportunity. A crematorium advert in return for a free funeral. That was the level of her career expectations right now.

'There are so many things I plan to do now. Of course, the most important is to spend time with the people I love.' Odette didn't mention that they were in short supply. Her most consistent relationship was with the delivery guy who brought the packages she'd ordered from her late-night TV shopping habit. 'And then I want to travel, perhaps to Asia, to America. I've been thinking of renting a convertible and driving across Route 66. Maybe spend some time in Los Angeles. I've had some very interesting calls from that side of the pond, and I might just dive into some other opportunities.'

The imaginary lie detector just started beeping like a reversing bin truck. Hollywood wouldn't know her number if someone spray-painted it on the Walk Of Fame. And if she was going to go travelling, she'd need to use her Government-issued, over 60s, free bus pass because she was broke. Skint. Cleaned out. Her last husband, Mitchum Royce, had been a former Edinburgh banker (with a 'w'), who had schmoozed her until she'd married him on holiday in Vegas in 2015. The reality of who he was couldn't have been clearer if it had been plastered on a flashing billboard on The Strip, playing 'Viva Las Vegas' on a repetitive loop, but she'd been too blinded by love or lust or loneliness to see it.

Gambling addict. Compulsive liar. Not a faithful bone in his body. She found out later that just days before their wedding he'd agreed to quietly resign from the bank after they found out he'd been misappropriating client funds (a move kept confidential to save the bank's image). Their marriage had lasted two years, before he'd taken off with a cocktail waitress half his age that he'd met on yet another trip with his cronies to Sin City. Only afterwards did Odette discover that before he'd left, he'd systematically drained her bank accounts of over two hundred grand, every penny she'd saved since her previous divorce, while racking up tens of thousands of pounds of debt in her name. She'd been paying it off ever since, keeping it secret from the world, because she hadn't wanted to look like the sad fool she'd become.

Now all she had was her re-mortgaged home, her shoes and her name, because, thankfully, she'd been smart enough to keep it through four marriages, realising that when it came right down to it, it was all she had. And it wasn't even real. She'd become Odette Devine when she'd landed her big break, saying goodbye to Olive Docherty, her moniker for the first twenty-nine years of her life. Another secret. And yet another one that she wasn't giving away to anyone, including the documentary director who was like a wasp buzzing beside her ear. One she wanted to swat.

Elliot was still standing to the side of the camera and nodding thoughtfully now. 'And I have to ask... do you have any regrets?'

On any other day, she might have been able to brush seamlessly over that sucker punch to the gut, but as she opened her mouth to speak, her vocal cords seemed to have gone in to some kind of state of paralysis. Did she have regrets? In the words of Frank Sinatra, probably too few to mention.

In fact, only one.

One forty-year-old regret.

Back when she was just plain Olive Docherty, working as a school dinner lady, barely covering her rent with her paltry wages, there had been a split-second, sliding-doors moment. She'd manip-ulated a situation, told a lie, stolen something from a friend. That one act of duplicity had transformed her life, delivered her dreams, and given her the career and the stardom that she had craved. But at what cost?

Her life was now a wreck. Other than Calvin, she had no one in it that she cared about. She was deeply lonely. Damaged. Destroyed. Washed up. Devoid of joy. Staring down a barrel of nothingness until she keeled over, and then she'd have a funeral attended by no more than a handful of Devine Believers and a few hawkers who would probably come for a nosy and some free sausage rolls at the wake.

Karma had caught up with her. This empty life was her punishment for taking what should never have been hers in the first place. Justice. Fair play.

Sometimes she wondered if there was any way to go back and fix it, but it was impossible to give back what she'd taken. She had snatched a friend's opportunity right from her hands, been too damn selfish to do the right thing. Instead, she'd just kept on moving, left her old life, and her friend behind, and she'd never looked in her rear-view mirror. Until now. And that was only because the road in front of her was cutting right through a barren wasteland and there wasn't much tarmac left before she would fall off a cliff.

Elliot was still gazing at her expectantly, waiting for an answer.

'Regrets?' she mused. For a split second, she was tempted to lay it all out. To get real and honest and truthful. To let the world see what a horrible bitch she really was and to make some attempt to fix what she'd broken.

But the moment passed, and before she could come up with some fluffy, bullshit answer about doing nothing differently and loving her life, there was a knock at the door and another production assistant who looked about twelve popped her head in.

'Ms Devine. They're calling you to the set. Are you ready?'

'I'm ready.'

No time to answer the question. Odette pushed herself up from her make-up chair. For the last time. Checked her expertly applied visage. For the last time. Pulled back her shoulders and slipped into character. For the last time. And then, followed by Calvin, Elliot and his cameraman, who was catching everything on film, she made her way out of her dressing room and onto *The Clydeside* set. For the last time.

Tomorrow she would go back to being plain old Olive Docherty.

Today was the last day that she would be Odette Devine. And she was going to put on a show to remember.

2

TRESS WALKER

Buddy timed his assault perfectly. The minute the doorbell rang, he took advantage of Tress's distraction. As soon as she raised her eyes to gaze at the kitchen clock and murmured, 'That'll be Val and Nancy – they'll let themselves in,' her one-year-old son flicked a spoonful of Weetabix directly at her, then giggled as it landed with a splodge on the sleeve of her freshly ironed, crisp white shirt. At the other end of the reclaimed wood planks of the kitchen table, her friend, Noah, took a bite out of his toast and Tress knew it was to camouflage his amusement.

She grabbed a baby wipe and began to scrape and dab. 'It's okay, you can laugh. It was a rookie error. I knew I should have waited until after he was done before I changed into my work clothes.'

'Agreed. Although, your Power Ranger pyjamas might have been the most alluring sight I've ever seen. I've no idea why you're single.'

Laughing, Tress chucked the wipe in Noah's direction, but he was already on his feet and it missed him completely. This was why she'd never made the netball team in high school.

Noah headed to the coffee machine with his mug, but on the way past his godson, he leaned down and kissed the top of Buddy's blonde curls. 'Great shot, Buddy. As soon as you can talk, tell Mum you want birthday cake for breakfast next year.'

Tress was pretty sure her son had no idea what his godfather was saying, but he gazed up adoringly anyway. Her son had four favourite people in the world and his god-father, the man he was named after, was one of them. The forename on Buddy's birth certificate was actually Noah, a decision she'd made with her husband, Max, as soon as they knew they were having a boy. Ironic. Max loved his friend, Noah, so much that he wanted to name his son after him. Yet, at the same time, he was having an affair with the person Noah loved most. Just one of the many contradictions that made Max Walker impossible to understand. Even in death. And the whole 'Until death do us part' thing had come way too soon, before he even got to forty.

Max Walker had been the driver of a car that had overturned as he'd raced back to Tress after he got the call to say she was in labour. Unbeknownst to them all, he had a mistress, Noah's wife, Anya, and she was in the passenger seat. Anya survived, but Max died later that night, only hours after his son had been born in the same hospital.

Tress had loved Max with her whole heart and she'd lost him twice. The first time was when she'd found out that he'd been having an affair with Anya for years. The second time was just hours later, when he took his last breath. Now, one year on, the pain had dulled to a gnawing ache that she managed to ignore a little more with the passing of time. She had to. Her son deserved to grow up in a warm, sunny house with a happy, positive mother. It was the least she could do to compensate for the actions of his dad.

It would have been easy to crumble, to fall apart and convince herself that love had never existed, but Buddy was her reminder that it did. On the nights when she'd been unable to sleep, and in the days that she'd struggled to get out of bed, Buddy was the one reason that she'd kept going. She wouldn't give in to the sadness because then his little life would have been tainted by even more heartache. No. She wouldn't allow it. So every day for the last twelve months, she'd put a smile on her face, she'd taken strength from the special people in her life and she'd loved her son enough for two parents.

However, having two males called Noah in their little unconventional family had soon proven to be confusing, so they'd switched to the nickname that they'd used for her boy since he was only a day old. Just hours after his father had died, a tear-stained, heart-broken Tress had stared into her new-born son's face and whispered, 'Well, buddy, it's just you and me now, but don't you worry because I've got you, today and every day.'

That was it. Officially, on paper, her son was called Noah Walker, but to everyone in his world, he was Buddy. And Buddy Walker was the absolute love of her life. Even when he was weaponising Weetabix.

There was a hoot from a party blower, followed by a 'Happy Birthday, gorgeous boy!' as Val, right on cue, burst through the kitchen door, clutching a life-size stuffed octopus. 'I tried to wrap it, but I gave up on the third arm. There isn't enough wrapping paper in the world for this bugger.'

All five foot of Nancy came right behind her, wrestling a giraffe that was at least a foot taller.

Shrieking with laughter, Buddy put two arms up to welcome his new furry friends, side-swiping his breakfast right off the tray of his highchair. Any irritation Tress could possibly have felt was squashed by her son's cheek-splitting grin at seeing both an eight-armed sea creature, an outlandishly long-necked safari animal, and two of the other people who reigned supreme at the top of his love list.

Nancy was her beloved next-door neighbour and Val was Nancy's closest friend. The two of them had become self-appointed aunties to her and Buddy, and they had seen her through every sad time and happy moment in the last year. They also pitched in with childcare while Tress was at work, except on Noah's day off, when he eagerly hung out with his godson for the day, and Fridays, when Tress usually worked from home.

Not today, though. Today she'd been summoned to the studio for the grand farewell to the legend that was Odette Devine.

In her previous life, Tress Walker BC (Before Children) had been a freelance interior designer, working for individual clients who wanted bespoke decor on a budget. After Max died, the luxury of self-employment was no longer an option. Max's life insurance had given her enough to pay off her mortgage, but she still had to cover all their other bills and needed set hours, a fixed salary, paid holidays and sick pay if required, which, thankfully, it hadn't been in the six months she'd been in the job.

If someone had told her twelve months ago that she'd have to give up the business that she'd grown from scratch, she'd have been devastated, but on the scale of life's upheavals in the past year, changing career barely registered. Besides, surprisingly, she thoroughly enjoyed her job. Working on a TV set didn't have the glamour or glitz that she'd imagined – half the sets were built in a panic and held together with gaffer tape and prayer, but she loved the variety of it, and it was nice to be surrounded by people every day. Even those prone to a touch of the divas, like Odette. Tress found it all fascinating and a welcome respite. A solitary occupation had been fine when she was married, but now she came home to a house where the only male was a year old and his conversation skills didn't yet stretch to words with more than one syllable – even if his cuteness made up for it.

Val and Nancy serenaded Buddy with 'Happy Birthday', finishing with more blasts on their party hooters, which sent him into raptures of giggles and squeals of delight. Tress was ambushed by a distinct dampness in the cheek area and dabbed away her tears of gratitude. Buddy didn't have a dad, or grandparents, or real aunts, uncles, or cousins, but he had two adopted aunts, his godfather, Noah, and a mum who adored him, so he lacked nothing in the love department. Every day, not just his birthday, was a happy one, but there would be an extra special sprinkling of joy this weekend. Buddy's official first birthday party was planned for Sunday, when everyone had the day off and Tress was determined to make it the most special day for him. She'd bought balloons, streamers, party bags, ordered food, arranged a bouncy castle, and invited all their friends and neighbours. There was definitely a part of her that was relieved that his party wasn't happening today, on his actual birthday. There were already way too many emotions to deal with. She immediately chided herself. This was the first and last time she'd allow herself to feel a shred of sadness on his birthday. From now on, all negative connotations about today would be banished and it would only be about celebrating her son. Even if he was way too young to understand what was going on and why there were giant stuffed animals in their kitchen.

Songs and cheers over, Buddy got busy trying to feed his octopus some mashed banana, while Tress poured two fresh cups of tea from the pot in the middle of the table, then slid them across to where Val and Nancy were clambering onto the bench on the other side.

'In the name of the holy hernia, can you not get chairs for this table instead of this bloody bench?' Nancy muttered. 'I'm going to do myself an injury climbing over this plank one of these days. I'm trying to hold out a while yet before my first hip replacement.'

Tress didn't like to point out that the dining set was an artisan piece, crafted by a local carpenter from reclaimed railway sleepers. And yes, it was heavy, but the whole industrial vibe had been her obsession when she'd designed this room.

Val had an opinion, which she delivered to Nancy while spooning half a sugar into her tea. 'You're more likely to fracture something at Zumba.' She turned to Tress, to impart more context to the statement. 'Last night, they introduced a new routine to a Shakira song. Honestly, my pelvic floor hasn't clenched like that since the eighties.'

Tress loved how Noah just accepted these conversations without batting an eyelid – probably because the two older women made no secret of their absolute devotion to Dr Noah Clark, whom they'd known since he was a kid climbing over the fence to Nancy's house next door, to get his ball back after Max had booted it too hard for the hundredth time.

Tress and Max had bought this house, the one her late husband had grown up in, from his parents, after they had retired and moved to Cyprus. When she'd met Max, Tress has been on a work trip to Glasgow from her native Newcastle, but she'd been happy to be the one who relocated. Her mum had passed away, she'd never known her dad and she was an only child, so she had no strong ties left to the North East. A fresh start, in a gorgeous old house in a beautiful Scottish village, with her new husband, hadn't been a hardship. Tress had spent the next couple of years renovating it to make it their forever home, with no idea that Max wouldn't make it to forever.

'Eh, Noah Clark, did you have a sleepover here last night?' Val asked him, one eyebrow raised in suspenseful optimism.

Tress rolled her eyes.

'Yep...' Nancy and Val's eyes lit up like strobe lights until he went on, 'I was in Spiderman pyjamas, Tress wore Power Rangers ones, and we played video games all night because we're twelve.'

Val's shoulders sagged as she realised he was joking.

Tress didn't have time to point out that elements of that were true, before he laughed and went on, 'No, I didn't have a sleepover. I popped in to have breakfast with the birthday boy and my *friend,* Tress, and now I'm off to work, where I'll no doubt see my *girlfriend* if she's on shift too.'

Indignant, Val only unpursed her lips to have a sip of her tea. In the last couple of weeks, she'd suddenly started dropping hints about the possibility of Tress and Noah getting together romantically. Tress had no idea where it was coming from, but it was so ridiculous, they just laughed it off.

'I'm just saying...' Val went on. 'I watched a documentary about that Shania Twain...'

'I saw that!' Nancy blurted, but there was a knowing amusement in her voice. 'You know, that lassie, Shania, is not far off our age, and she hasn't got a line on her face, and from what I could see, her boobs still point forwards. The aging process is a selective bugger, it really is.'

Val brushed right past the commentary. 'Anyway,' she said pointedly, 'Shania Twain's man and her pal had a secret affair and took off together and you know what happened? Shania and the pal's husband got together and they've been madly in love ever since. Just saying.'

Tress grinned. 'You mean, *hinting*?'

'As if I ever would.'

Noah pulled on his jacket, the corners of his mouth turning up as he winked at Tress. 'Of course not. That might be only the...

what? Third? Or maybe the fourth time we've heard the Shania story?'

'At least,' Tress agreed, playing along. 'But she's definitely not trying to influence us. Absolutely, totally not.'

Val refused to succumb to the teasing, mostly because, Tress knew, she really thought it was a great idea. They all loved Noah's girlfriend, Cheska, but the A&E doctor had made it absolutely clear that, much as she and Noah had a great relationship, her medical career came first, and she had no intention of prioritising her personal life. Not even for the total catch that was Noah Clark. While Noah was perfectly happy with the terms of their coupling, Val and Nancy had apparently grown restless for a happy ending, and for the two aunties, that happiness now seemed to be Tress and Noah getting together. Loose ends tied up. The big fat fly in Cupid's ointment was that Tress and Noah just didn't think of each other that way. They were friends. Joint survivors. As close as brother and sister. But romantic? No. There was way too much baggage for them to even think like that. Their spouses had been having an illicit affair for years behind their backs. The thought of that betrayal, that dishonesty, that brutal secret that ended in tragedy, had a way of knocking the hearts and roses right off any romantic possibilities.

And besides... Tress felt her face flush and hoped that Val and Nancy's eagle eyes wouldn't spot it. She wasn't ready to share yet, because it was probably nothing. No big deal. Just a guy at work, who had asked her out. Someone who had no shared baggage. Someone who could become so much more than just friends. Six months ago, she'd have immediately refused his invitation to go on a date. Two months ago, she'd have considered it for a moment, before politely declining. Now?

Today was her son's birthday. It was the anniversary of the day she'd found out the most unfathomable truth about her husband.

And it was the day that Tress was going to stop living in the past and start building the kind of life that would make her jump out of bed in the morning. With or without her Power Rangers pyjamas.

Today was the day she was going to say yes to starting something new.

3

NOAH CLARK

Noah poured some more coffee into his travel mug and leaned his six foot two inch frame down to kiss Tress on the cheek, then did the same with Val and Nancy before giving Buddy a high five. He'd spent weeks teaching him that and the little one now had the waving, the high fives and the fist bumps down to perfection, all of which gave Noah the same level of thrill as his favourite football team winning the league. 'Right, I'm heading into work.'

'Weren't you supposed to be on a late shift tonight?' Nancy asked him. She had his schedule memorised.

'I was, but I took the day off.' He didn't need to say why. The truth was, he just wanted to be free to be around if Tress needed him. 'And then I had three patients who couldn't make my clinic yesterday, so I agreed to see them today. I only need to go in for a couple of hours or so, then I'm planning to grab a late lunch with Cheska. You know, my *girlfriend*. Please apologise to Shania for not following her blueprint.'

'You're a huge disappointment, Noah Clark,' Val tutted. 'Apart from, you know, the successful career as a paediatrician, the lovely personality, the big heart, and that handsome face. But apart from that, nothing going for you at all.'

'I was thinking the same thing,' Nancy concurred woefully. 'All that perfection is exhausting. I mean, I said the same to George Clooney last time I met him in Aldi.'

That set the two of them off, while Tress met his gaze, grinning as she shook her head. 'Run while you can. Save yourself.'

He returned the smile. 'I'm running like the wind. I'll give you a call later and see how your day is going.'

An innocuous statement on the surface, but he knew that Tress understood that it was so much more than just a flippant comment. For the last twelve months, they'd been through the wars and they were still standing, mostly because they propped each other up whenever the grief or the regret became too consuming. That happened less and less now. This was their normal. They'd come out the other end.

Part of him wanted to stick around Tress's kitchen, because as long as he was there, with Val and Nancy blasting his eardrums with hooters, his mind wouldn't wander to the sad stuff. Today was the anniversary of the best and worst things that had happened in his life. Buddy's birth was at the top of the miracle list, and he was grateful every day that the little guy had made it into the world, even though it was in the worst of circumstances.

That night, Noah had made the hardest decision of his life, when he'd resolved not to tell Tress that Max was hovering between life and death in another ward in the hospital, until she'd safely delivered the baby. He'd held Tress's hand in the delivery suite as she'd moved to the late stages of labour, before bringing her boy into a family that had been turned upside down.

Focusing on Tress and her newborn that night had distracted Noah from the bomb that just exploded in his own life. In the midst of the heartache and trauma was the discovery of the affair between his best friend and his wife, Anya, that had destroyed their marriage. She had been the love of his life, his partner of almost twenty years, his wife for eleven, and he'd adored her. Even now, a year later, it was tough to say what hurt most. Her betrayal. The fact that it was with his best friend. Or the realisation that he'd been so wrong in believing that they were solid, that they would never hurt each other, that he'd promised forever to someone who could lie to his face.

Afterwards, he and Anya had half-heartedly tried to fix their relationship, but the damage had been terminal. As a doctor, he'd seen people overcome heart-crushing pain and devastation, and for a moment he'd thought they might be able to do the same. But no. The affair was carnage enough, but the consequences were insurmountable. Heartbreak. Death. Grief. Rage. Resentment. It was too much.

Months after the accident, Anya had packed up and gone back to her parents' home in New York. They'd communicated a few times on legal stuff, but other than that, the woman he'd loved with his whole heart since he was twenty-one years old had become a ghost. And he was glad of it. Especially today, when everything that had happened to them seemed a little more vivid.

Today, just like every day, Noah had two choices: dwell in the pain of the past or be grateful for the good stuff. And today, like most days, he chose the latter.

He'd just jumped into his car, started the engine and reversed out of Tress's drive when his phone rang and MUM flashed on the screen. He answered straight away. 'Hey, Mum, how are you doing?'

'I'm only on for a minute because I've got a million and one things to do. It's crazy in this office today. Her royal highness is on her high horse about something and we're all hearing about it. Thank God I finish early on a Friday.'

Noah smiled, envisioning his mother's cool, calm exterior in the face of crisis, but knowing that inside she'd be calling her boss choice names. He could hear a very faint trace of her childhood Ghanaian accent – always a tell that she was under pressure. His dad, Leo, worked for the council, while his mum, Gilda, was a legal secretary and personal assistant to Helena McLean, a fierce, no-nonsense legend in the legal world, regarded as one of the top criminal defence solicitors in the country.

'Anyway,' she went on, 'I know it's a significant day today, so I'm just making sure that you're okay and checking that I don't have to get your sister to pencil you in for a session on her couch.'

All three of his sisters were in the medical profession. Keli was a nurse, Amelie was a carer in a nursing home, and Bria was a counsellor specialising in trauma and PTSD. He had one brother, Dylan, who had bucked the family trend and worked as a freelance photographer.

'I'm fine, Ma. Really. I've just left Tress's after Buddy's birthday breakfast and I'm on my way to work. Thanks for worrying about me though.'

'Always, my love. If it's not one of you, it's another. If you see Keli at the hospital today, can you check in on her for me? I've not been able to reach her for a couple of days and that's not like her. Ignoring the world usually means she's having a great time or a terrible time. I just want to make sure she's fine and that she's coming for dinner tonight.'

'I'm sure it's all good, Mum, but yes, I'll check on her.' It wasn't a chore. His sister was one of his favourite people and he'd been thrilled when she'd joined him at Glasgow Central Hospital, albeit at the other end of the age spectrum. He was in paediatrics and Keli was a senior nurse on the elderly ward.

His mum began to wrap up the call. 'Right, I need to go. And you're still coming over for dinner later too?'

He knew better than to resist, understanding that Gilda's need to care for her adult children through emotional challenges and hard times took the form of phone calls and feeding, sometimes both in the same day. 'Of course, Ma. Not sure what time I'll be there though – can I keep you posted?'

'Of course you can.'

'Great, thanks. I'll see how the day plays out and how Tress is doing later.'

There was a pause at the other end of the phone, and he briefly wondered if they'd lost the connection, before his mum spoke again. 'You know, son... I watched a documentary about Shania Twain last night...'

'Ma, I'm just about to lose you, but I'll buzz you later. Love you, bye!' Noah hung up, aware he probably wouldn't go to heaven now because he'd just bold-faced lied to his mother. Then he decided that no jury would convict him under the circumstances. Shania Twain's romantic history was having an increasingly irritating impact on his life. It was nothing personal against Ms Twain or her music. He didn't mind admitting that he knew all the words to 'You're Still The One'.

He distracted himself from his feelings of parent-centric guilt by placing his next call to Dr Cheska Ayton, head of A&E at Glasgow Central Hospital. She had been an old friend from their time as junior doctors, but somewhere in the last few months, their relationship had progressed to something more. Not that they'd ever put a label on it. They were more than friends, but less than a full-blown, committed relationship, and that suited them both. Cheska had slotted perfectly in to their 'framily' group. Her research thesis had been on Alzheimer's, and Val's husband, Don, was in the latter stages of the disease, so Cheska had been a steady support to Val too. She was someone special. And it made it her even more special that she put no pressure on him at all to define their relationship. No ties. No pressure. Her first love was her job and he was totally fine with that.

She answered on the first ring, and he immediately kicked off with, 'Hey, gorgeous, I missed you last night.'

They slept over at each other's homes once or twice a week, but Cheska had stayed at her own place last night, because she was going straight from a 10 p.m. finish to a 6 a.m. start. '*Grey's Anatomy*, but with less make-up, more sleep deprivation, much lower budgets and no sex in the on-call rooms,' was how Cheska described working at the hospital, and she probably had a point.

Cheska answered his greeting with a very formal, 'Dr Clark, I concur with that diagnosis, but I'm waiting for scans. Can I get back to you?' Code for yes, I miss you too, but I'm with someone at the moment and can't talk.

Noah let out a low chuckle. 'I love it when you talk doctor to me.'

'I'll be sure to keep you informed. Are you still available for the meeting we'd scheduled today?'

'I wouldn't miss it.'

'Excellent. I look forward to it. Goodbye, Dr Clark.'

There was a click as she hung up first. His Carplay system automatically reverted to his music selections, and he felt his shoulders relax as Usher's voice flooded his car. It was short-lived. His neck muscles spasmed back to stressed when the memory that he'd been dodging all morning finally barged into his brain. A year ago, Noah was in this same car, speeding down to Loch Lomond after he'd discovered his wife was in a hotel there. Anya had left that morning, saying she was flying to London for a business conference with Max, who worked for the same company. It was only after she was gone that Noah had realised she'd left her laptop behind, but when he'd called her office to track her down, he'd learned there was no London conference. Some more detective work had pointed him in the direction of a Loch Lomond hotel, but he didn't even make it that far. He was almost there when he encountered the local police at the site of an overturned car, and inside... It was the worst thing he'd ever seen. His wife. His best friend. Both of them gravely injured.

The song changed, snapping him back to the present in the company of Beyonce. There were worse ways to pull himself out of the dark shadows of his memory. Bey serenaded him with her Renaissance album until he pulled into the hospital car park. It took the usual ten minutes to find a space, but he finally squeezed in between a Skoda and a Porsche.

As always, something about being on hospital grounds focused his mind, and his thoughts went to this morning's clinic. In a normal clinic he'd see up to fifteen patients, usually a mixture of existing patients checking in for follow-up appointments, sometimes six monthly or annual reviews, alongside new referrals that required investigation, but today's special clinic was just for three patients he'd been treating for some time. Paediatrics was one of the most rewarding disciplines, but it could be the most heartbreaking too. The best he could hope for in any given day was that the wins outweighed the losses. Most days they did.

Head down, Noah was almost past the woman walking the same path to the hospital entrance, before she cleared her throat pointedly.

'Just as well you didn't become a detective because your observation skills need work.'

Noah stopped, grinned, and threw his arm around his sister. Keli was ten years younger than him, the baby of the family, born six years after his younger brother and a surprise, given that Noah and his other three siblings had all come along in rapid succession.

Like the rest of the family, she was tall, around five foot nine inches and had been the most athletic of the girls. Bria was the dreamer, Amelie was the bookworm, but Keli was the track star, the basketball player, the tennis champ. They all thought she'd opt for a future in the sports industry, so it had initially been a surprise when she'd decided on a career in nursing, but she was made for it. She'd worked in a hospital in the nearby town of Paisley for many years after she qualified, but she'd moved to the elderly ward at Glasgow Central the year before and Noah loved having her in the same building.

'You just saved me a job,' he told her as they walked.

'I did?'

'Mum told me to hunt you down and do a welfare check. Says she hasn't spoken to you for a couple of days. If I don't give her a progress report by end of day, she's calling in a SWAT team.'

Keli sighed. 'I'm glad she's not dramatic or prone to over-reacting.'

'Only where we're concerned and just because we're lovable,' Noah joked, sensing an edge of irritation in Keli's tone that surprised him. She was usually the most laid-back and easy-going of them all and being the youngest, she had an especially close bond with their mum. Must be having an off day.

Keli didn't skip a beat. 'You're not wrong. I'll give her a buzz this afternoon. I've just been stacked with work and...'

'Dating websites?'

She elbowed him in the ribs. 'Definitely not dating websites.'

'You've met someone new?' Noah asked, with a hint of teasing. Keli had always shared the stuff that was going on in her life but she'd been surprisingly coy lately. Over the last few months he and Tress had been sure she was seeing someone, but Keli had refused to confirm, deny or elaborate. Noah had just accepted that she'd tell him when she was ready.

'No. Yes. It's a long story.' She promptly changed the subject.

'Anyway, sorry, why are we talking about me today? How are you doing? How's Tress?'

Noah paused to allow the automatic doors at the staff entrance to the building to open. 'I think she's okay. I popped in this morning to have a birthday breakfast with Buddy. That kid is amazing. He definitely helps us all keep it together and focus on the good stuff.'

Keli went through the door first into the foyer. 'I have a birthday pressie for him so I'll call Tress or I'll bring it over to you later. I take it you're still going to Mum's for dinner?'

'I'm not sure I have a choice in the matter,' he said, grinning. 'So yeah. How about you?'

'Two birds, one stone. It stops Mum hunting me down and we get great food. I'd be a fool to refuse.' Keli pushed her arm through her brother's as they crossed the reception area. 'Anyway, you didn't tell me how you're doing. Today can't be easy...'

Noah's shoulders sagged a little. He wasn't going to lie, but at the same time, he didn't want to acknowledge the anniversary of the accident. Not here. Not now. Preferably not ever. Two pills of denial, taken with water, and he'd be feeling better in no time. 'I'm just doing a really good job of trying not to look backwards. As long as I don't think about it, I'm...'

'Noah?' The voice from the sofa over in the staff rest area cut right through his thoughts, and for a second, he thought he'd imagined it. Maybe misheard. Perhaps it was mistaken identity. Another woman with an American accent that had a twang of Scottish brogue because she'd lived here for years. Yep, that was it. He must have mistaken another half American, half Scottish woman for his ex...

He turned his head to see, and the answer was there. No mistake. Definitely his ex-wife. Anya was sitting on the edge of the sofa, hands clasped on her lap, looking at him with a mixture of trepidation and something else. Hope?

She stood up and walked towards him.

'Oh shit. Oh shit. Oh shit.' That came in a hissed whisper from Keli, followed by, 'You don't have to speak to her. Say the word and I'll tell her to go.'

In any other setting, Noah would be touched that his little sister was trying to bail him out, but right now he was too shocked to process the words, so he didn't have time to reply. His gaze was locked on Anya until she reached them and stopped right in front of him.

'Noah, can we talk?'

He'd thought that today was going to be the day that he put the past behind him.

Now he saw that it was going to be the day that his ghosts came back to haunt him.

4

KELI CLARK

Keli had told herself that she wasn't going to think about it today. Today was such a significant day for Noah. It was little Buddy's birthday. It was the anniversary of Tress's heartache. Yet, just like every other day for the last week or so, it had been the only thing on her mind since the moment she woke up after another fitful night of sleep.

Her mother's psychic powers were scarily accurate as always. Keli wasn't okay. She was so far from okay. And she had no idea what she was going to do about it. For a moment, she'd thought about saying something to Noah, asking him for help. There was no doubt that he'd do anything for her, but she couldn't, *wouldn't*, add more onto his shoulders than he was already carrying. And besides, her former sister-in-law, Anya, showing up had just detonated a bomb in his life that he could do without. She had desperately wanted to stay downstairs by Noah's side, but he'd made it clear he needed to deal with Anya on his own. Keli made a mental note to check on him when she got off shift, to make sure he was okay and find out what Anya wanted. As if she hadn't done enough damage. Anya's actions had devastated them all. She'd been another sister to Keli and the loss had stung, but she'd put her own feelings to one side and focused on supporting Noah, just as he would do for her. So no, she wasn't going to add her own sister drama to his woes now. She had to deal with this herself. And right now, the way she was going to do that was by filling her day with distractions and trying not to think about how her whole life was on the brink of falling apart.

Keli changed into her uniform and made her way up to her ward, half an hour early, so that she could grab a green tea and get her head into work mode before starting her shift.

In the staffroom, her friend Yvie, queen of multitasking, was simultaneously making tea, eating a biscuit and humming to the Taylor Swift song that was playing on the radio. Keli waited until the end of the chorus before interrupting, with, 'Not sure Taylor Swift has ever sung "Cruel Summer" while eating a Hobnob.'

Gorgeous, voluptuous, huge-hearted Yvie swung round, grinning. 'Well, more fool her. I highly recommend it.' Still multitasking, she carried on dancing and stirring her tea, while asking, 'I thought you were off today? Did you get your days mixed up?'

Keli shook her head. 'No, Sima called me at eight o'clock this morning and asked if I could cover her for a few hours. She's on ten till six, but Karim has a dentist appointment she completely forgot about, so she'll be in after she drops him back at school.' It was one of the reasons she loved working on this ward. It was a great team that went above and beyond to support each other. 'I was happy to help out. I wasn't doing anything today anyway.'

'You mean other than fretting, beating yourself up about your choices and generally questioning the rest of your life?' Yvie replied, perceptively close to the truth.

'Yep, other than that. Thanks again for coming over last night. I appreciated the company and the chat.'

'No worries. Did you get any sleep?'

'A few hours.' Keli joined her at the kettle, flicked it back on and pulled her mug and her box of herbal teas from the kitchen cupboard above it.

Yvie lowered her voice. 'Did you do the test?' She didn't even have to wait for an answer – Keli's face said it all. 'You didn't.'

'I didn't,' Keli conceded, flushing with the admission because she knew how ridiculous it was. She was an adult. A nurse, for God's sake. She was also a focused, smart, independent woman. And yet all of those things seemed to have gone into hibernation for the last week, ever since her period didn't arrive and she'd started to suffer from unexpected and frequent bouts of queasiness. 'I was too busy. After you left last night, I texted him, then stared at the phone for the next four hours hoping he'd reply. He didn't. I'm pathetic. I know this.'

'Morning, ladies,' a male voice interrupted them and Yvie immediately spun round with a beaming grin. Dr Richard Campbell, head of the ICU was in the doorway. 'Nurse Danton,' he addressed Yvie. 'I'm looking for Dr McVitie. Any clues?'

'Radiology. He's down there chasing up overdue scan results. If you listen carefully you can hear the thunder roar.'

Dr Campbell nodded with mock seriousness. 'I thought it was the air conditioning playing up. Thanks, Yvie,' before retreating and going on his way.

During the exchange, Keli had carried on making her tea, completely disengaged from the conversation, a point that wasn't lost on Yvie.

'Oh no,' Yvie whispered, gazing at Keli intently.

'What?'

'It's him. It's Dr Campbell. Bloody hell, I can't believe it.'

Keli stopped her right there. 'Yvie!' she exclaimed. That got her friend's attention. 'It's not him. He's married. He's about twenty years older than me. He's a doctor. One red flag equals disqualification. Three is a ten-foot bargepole.'

'Oh thank God, because I know his wife, Liv. She works over in palliative care and she's lovely. If you hurt her, I'd have to kill you and then we'd be short-staffed here.'

Despite every bone in her body being crushed by the weight of the world, Keli laughed. She'd only known Yvie for the ten months or so since she'd transferred to Glasgow Central, but they'd immediately clicked. She was warm, she was funny, and she had a great line in gallows humour. It wasn't difficult to love her.

'Anyway, you said you'd stop asking...'

An uncharacteristic sheepishness shadowed Yvie's face. 'I know. I lied. My dignified, understanding side wants to respect your privacy, but my insane curiosity is in charge today. It's only because I love you that I'm not getting offended that you won't tell me who he is. Honestly, my imagination is running wild. Last night, I decided it was Lewis Capaldi. Then I thought, no, because when we saw him at Glastonbury, we were stuck up the back. If you were doing the naked stuff with him, we'd have been down the front. So I'm back to thinking it's the bloke in the canteen because I'm really hoping I'll get free pies out of this.'

Despite the ache in her gut, Keli smiled, but there was more than a hint of an apology in there. 'I know. I'm sorry. You know I'll tell you when I can, but I promised him and it's...'

They both said, 'Complicated' at the same time.

Keli hated all the subterfuge, but even if the man she'd fallen for wasn't keeping his promises to her right now, that didn't mean she was going to break the promise she'd made to him.

On the first night they'd got together, he'd told her how important his privacy was to him and she'd understood. In his line of work, he had to protect his personal life, and there were a hundred complications to going public, so when he'd asked her to keep their relationship completely confidential until he was ready to share it, she'd agreed. For three whirlwind months, they'd kept their meetings under the radar, never venturing out, staying away from anywhere they'd be spotted. Keli hadn't minded. She was naturally private and all the subterfuge had added to the excitement and the exquisite intensity of the time that they did have together. She'd fallen hard, fast, he'd told her that he had too and then... nothing.

Out of nowhere, about a month ago he'd stopped answering her texts. Stopped calling her. She knew he was alive because he was still posting on social media and it looked like he was living his best life, so the question that kept her awake at night, that made her fluctuate between confusion, anger and hurt was... why? Was this just a game that he played with women? Had she read him wrong? Was the guy she'd thought that she was falling in love with actually a heartless bastard who had just picked her up and dropped her? And if that were true, how the hell was she going to handle her very real fear that she might now be pregnant with his child?

'Tell me what I can do to help?' Yvie asked her, sympathy oozing from every word.

Keli wrapped her in a hug of gratitude. 'Nothing. That's the thing – it's all down to me and I'm too much of a flipping coward to face it. I met my brother on the way in...'

'Tell me he's finally single,' Yvie begged, lifting her mug over to the white Formica table in the middle of the room. 'I'd give up my fiancé and both Ben & Jerry for that man.'

'Still not single, sorry.' Keli followed her to the table and pulled out a chair, folding one leg under her as she sat down. As she did, she felt a tug of tightness around the waistband of the trousers of her scrubs that made her stomach lurch.

Yvie slipped into another of the blue plastic chairs. 'Sorry, I made that about me there. Okay, let's go. Let's talk through your options, but start with telling me why you still haven't taken the test.' They'd had this discussion a couple of times over the last few days, but Keli had waved off that question with a vague excuse, then changed the subject. This time she answered honestly.

'Terror,' she blurted. 'I always thought I was pretty brave. Spider in the bath? I'm in there like a shot. Hard conversations with patients? I can handle those too. Turns out my courage draws the line at finding out whether my womb is occupied.'

'You know it makes no sense to wait, right?' Yvie said gently.

'I do. I just... Aaaaargh.' Keli dropped her head down onto the table. 'How did this happen to me? I'm twenty-nine years old and I may or may not be pregnant to a man that has been ghosting me for the last month. How could I have got it so wrong, Yvie?'

Yvie shrugged, and answered the question with a sad smile. 'Because you're human. And because life sucks sometimes.'

'I just can't believe I didn't see it. Didn't see who he was.'

'Sometimes we don't. Did I ever tell you about my sister, Zoe? She fell madly in love. Turns out one of my other sisters had a thing for the same guy, but that's another story. Anyway, Zoe is the most switched on of us all, the one who has her head on straight, yet she married this bloke, then discovered he was an absolute tosser. It lasted four weeks.'

'Four years?' Keli asked, thinking she must have picked that up wrong.

Yvie took another bite of her biscuit. 'Nope, four weeks. A one-month marriage. It was a nightmare. Thought she'd never get over it, but the point is, she did. Look, no matter what, I'm here for you. And we have a group meeting at lunchtime today, if you think it would help to vent or talk more about it.'

Yvie ran a weekly hospital group for staff or patients who were struggling with anxiety or who just needed conversation and human connection. Every session was packed.

'Thanks, but I wouldn't take up the group's time. I'm planning to drown myself in work, combined with a solid schedule of burying my head in the sand. I might even send another futile text or stalk his social media. I feel that's the mature way to deal with it.'

'Good plan. Or, you know, we could take lunch at the same time, nip down to the pharmacy for a test kit, do the test, then you'd know one way or another.'

The suggestion immediately made goosebumps pop up on Keli's arms. Yes. That would be the right thing to do. But then, what if...

She paused the thought to let the sudden wave of nausea pass. What if she were pregnant? That would make it real and change her whole life, her whole world. She'd worked on elderly wards since the day she'd qualified, and she used to think that it was all she would ever want to do. Lately... well, lately she'd begun to think it was time for a change and maybe a break from nursing. A new chapter. She'd been contemplating perhaps travelling. Maybe working for a charity abroad. But if she was indeed pregnant, she could kiss any hopes of doing that goodbye. And she'd have to tell her parents...

She got stuck on that thought. Her parents. She'd have to lay it all out to them. That made her want to put her head back on the table.

After a brief pause for another bite of biscuit, Yvie carried on with her plan. 'And then you – or we – could go force this bloke to see you, to face you, and tell him everything that's happened. He's fifty per cent involved in the potentially life-changing pregnancy question, and a hundred per cent dickhead for ghosting you. No matter what, you need to have a conversation to get some sense of closure.'

Closure. Keli knew she was right. This wasn't a one-night stand. It had been love, or close to it, at least on her part. And he told her he felt the same – right before he checked out of her life and stopped responding to her for no apparent reason at all.

The thoughts, the possibilities, endless awful scenarios began to overwhelm her, so she stretched up from the chair. 'I'll think about it, but right now, I'm going to stick to the burying my head in the sand thing, and go say hello to Freda and then you can fill me in on everyone else. Did she have a good night?'

Keli frequently struck up a special bond with a patient, and this week that was Freda, a lovely lady of eighty, who'd broken her hip after a fall, and who'd had no visitors in the week she'd been here. She'd told Keli that she had friends in the clubs that she went to a couple of times a week, but no family left in Scotland. Her adult daughters both lived in Canada, and she didn't want to let them know what had happened to her because she didn't want to trouble them. Keli had spent as much time with her as possible, some days staying late after a shift to sit with her. She'd tried her best to change Freda's mind about contacting her family, but so far, no success.

'She did,' Yvie nodded. 'She's been lined up for surgery day after tomorrow, but she's not keen. I think she needs some more reassurance.'

'Okay, I'll go talk to her. And, Yvie, thank you. I appreciate your support, I really do.'

'No problem. I'm always here. No matter what, we've got you.'

Keli felt tears prickle the insides of her eyelids and she blinked them back. 'You're really going to have to stop being so lovely. Do me a favour and be a complete cow to me for the rest of the day because that makes me less emotional.'

'No problem. You're a daft boot and an indecisive tit. How's that?'

'Perfect. Thank you. Keep up the good work.' Keli managed a smile, and kept it on her face all the way to the ward.

Freda shared a room with three other patients and right now, Vera and Janet in the beds opposite were fast asleep, and Emily, who was in the bed next to Freda, had been taken to the day room to watch her favourite morning show. It was one of those ones that involved lots of people arguing with each other, so they didn't put it on here on the ward for fear of disrupting the morning peace.

As always, the elderly lady greeted her with the widest of smiles. 'Good morning, lass. It's a treat to see you.'

'And you, Freda. You're looking stronger today.' Keli pulled up a chair and sat next to her. 'How are you feeling?'

'Aye, well, I'm still breathing. Always a plus,' she said in her soft Highland lilt. She'd explained that she'd moved to Glasgow from Inverness after her husband died, because her daughters had been at university here. When they'd graduated and moved abroad, Freda had stayed. 'I learned a long time ago that sometimes that's all you need to do. Just keep breathing until it all gets better.'

That kicked Keli right in the heart. She'd been dumped and ghosted by a man she'd thought was her future, and now she was fairly sure she was about to have his child. She didn't feel equipped for that. For any of it.

But today? She realised she had two options. She could take Yvie's advice and confront her problems, or she could listen to Freda and just keep breathing until it got better.

And it was time to make her choice.

10 A.M. – NOON

5

ODETTE

'Gorgeous Odette. Are you ready for our final act of family disfunction?' Rex Marino greeted her as she walked with regal deportment on to set, stopping only to swap her Louboutins for Agnes's threadbare furry slippers. In the storyline, Agnes had fallen on hard times, after she'd been conned out of all her money by telephone scammers posing as the staff of her local bank. She'd agreed to send them everything she had, believing their story that her bank account had been hacked, and she'd followed their instructions to transfer every penny she had to a new account. The money was never seen again, and in this scene, her son, Hugh, played by Rex Marino, had just found out and he was about to burst into her home in a rage.

'I was born ready, darling,' she answered tartly, while withholding the urge to add, 'you arrogant pillock'. This guy had the world fooled, but not her. Sure, he was attractive, if you liked the whole Henry Cavill vibe. Well over six foot tall. A jawline you could break a nail on. Perfect white teeth. Dark hair and the bluest eyes this side of Paul Newman. He'd been playing her long-lost son – given up at birth and reunited as an adult – on *The Clydeside* for the last two years, but she'd bet her last furry mule that he wouldn't be here much longer. This guy had his sights firmly set on Hollywood. On the big time. He wanted to follow Gerry Butler, Sam Heughan and Richard Madden to the land where they loved the twinkly eyes and the gruff accents of Scottish actors. Odette didn't doubt for a second that he'd try to make the leap, but she really hoped he'd fall on his arse, because there was just something about him that set her Untrustworthy Git Radar up at high. But then, she hadn't realised that all four of her husbands would turn out to be feckless shits, so maybe her radar was in need of recalibration.

Off to her right, she saw that Elliot was watching her and the documentary camera was still running, so, naturally, she put on a show, taking both Rex's hands. 'Let's make this the best goodbye ever,' she told him, loud enough for the camera to pick up the poignant undertone in her words. If he was surprised that she'd taken his hands, or spoken with such warmth to him, Rex didn't show it. Maybe the twit could act after all.

Odette took her place on the set. They'd blocked the scene yesterday, so she knew her marks and was ready to go, as always. You didn't last forty years on a show without being the consummate professional, and she was determined that was what she'd be, right up until she walked out that door.

A couple of the stage technicians were still on the set, checking continuity and adding a couple of subtle placements, so they were a few minutes off getting started. Rex's make-up team swooped in for touch-ups and Odette was about to take a quiet minute to close her eyes and visualise the scene that was about to play out, when she felt a gentle nudge on her shoulder.

'I'll miss you, you know.' The Geordie accent was unmistakable, and Odette's smile was the first genuine one of the day. 'Tress, pet, I'll miss you too.'

The new set designer had only started here a few months ago, but she was one of the few people that Odette actually liked. She was always smiling, and she definitely passed the test of Odette's Untrustworthy Git Radar. She'd also learned Tress's backstory from Maisie in the canteen, and och, it was a heartbreak. It was like the saddest of *The Clydeside* storylines, but the difference was, the loss of Tress's husband and all the betrayals surrounding it, were very real.

'How's the wee fella doing?'

Tress's grin widened. 'He's doing great. It's his first birthday today.'

'And you're in here? Did you not want to take the day off?' Odette had never had children, so that was a genuine query rather than a judgement. What were the rules for small peoples' special days?

Tress shook her head. 'I didn't want to miss your last day. Besides, he has no idea what a birthday is yet, and he's with his aunties who are spoiling him to pieces.'

Odette could feel the warmth in Tress's words and it piqued something in her. Children had just never been part of her story, and there was no regret there because she'd had the career and the job of her dreams. But now that was over and what did she have left?

'Odette, we're ready to roll,' the director called over to her.

She leaned into Tress's shoulder. 'Let's grab a coffee one of these days. Or maybe something stronger? I'd like to meet that little one of yours.'

'I like your thinking,' Tress replied. 'I'm staying for your lunch, so I'll give you my number then?'

'Odette...' the director called again, so she gave Tress's hand a quick squeeze and went onto the set. It was Agnes McGlinchy's living room, an interior layout that matched the outside of the tenement building shot that signalled Agnes's home to the viewers. It was supposed to be in the evening, in winter, so the lights were low and the real fireplace was alight, flames licking the back of the chimney breast.

Odette sat in the chair in front of the fire, picked up Agnes's glasses from the side table and lifted her book. It was one of Agnes's trademark saga novels, set in the Glasgow shipyards of the thirties. Tress's attention to detail when it came to Agnes's home and life had been meticulous – Agnes had been working her way through this series of books for the last few months and now she was on the final instalment, just another layer to the final act.

The director hushed the set, Odette took a deep breath, closed her eyes, exhaled. This had to be perfect for many reasons. It was her swansong. A scene that would be replayed for years to come in the shows that covered landmark moments in TV. This was one of them. The demise of one of the longest-running soap characters in the country. She wasn't quite in the same bracket as Ken, Rita or Gail from *Coronation Street*, but she'd made the four-decade mark and that was something special, so this scene had to match it.

The producers had initially wanted to keep it under wraps, top-secret, but they'd gone for a ratings grab instead. For the last fortnight, there had been a media blitz of adverts proclaiming that Odette's last episode would be shown next month, in a special extended episode, and it was anticipated that they'd have the highest viewing figures in years. Strange how her goodbye was apparently something special, yet the new team of idiot producers and writers hadn't wanted to keep her around. Ageism. Sexism. Stupidity. It was all of the above.

The day she'd been let go, she'd gone into a meeting with the new production team to renegotiate her contract, just as she'd done every year. As always, Calvin was by her side. 'Head up, stomach in, a big fat pay rise we will win,' he'd chanted on the way down the corridor to the boardroom, making her laugh, as he always did when she was anxious. She really needed the money. She was still paying off credit card debts years after Mitchum had bled her dry and she needed to make the next few years count if she was ever going to be able to start enjoying her life again. Of course, Calvin knew the bones of her financial issues, but she'd kept the scale of it even from him, so he had no idea how much debt she had. Shame. Embarrassment. Humiliation. Secrecy. That pretty much summed up her situation.

As soon as she'd gone in, they'd got straight to it. There were apologies, platitudes, fake regret. Thanks for her lifelong commitment to the show. And then the announcement that they'd decided to write her out, that they were shifting the focus to the younger characters.

'You mean, cheaper actors,' she'd spat, ignoring Calvin's shooting glance of reproach, that said 'leave it to him', even though they'd both realised that his legendary negotiating skills weren't going to win here.

The show execs didn't spell it out, but what it all boiled down to was that after forty years of annual raises, she was too expensive. They could bring in two or three mid-level names for what they paid her and that was exactly what they planned to do. Calvin had tried everything from reasonable discussion to playing hardball and threatening to sue, but nothing worked. They'd made up their minds. Put her out to pasture. And there wasn't a damn thing she or Calvin could do about it. Her contract was up and so was her time on the show. Killed off. No return.

'At least this way, you're going out in a blaze of glory, my darling,' Calvin had consoled her, although, as always, he couldn't resist adding a teasing, 'I mean, I can think of worse ways to go than being up close and personal with Rex Marino.'

The thought caused her glance to wander now to her manager at the side of the set, and he returned her gaze with a smile of such affection she almost crumbled. Almost. But not yet. Right now, she had work to do.

'And... Action!' Carl, the director, bellowed.

The whole room immediately fell silent. This was a show with insane shooting schedules and deadlines, so where possible, they got the scenes in the first take. No room for error. When it came to discipline and preparation, this was the best training ground any actor could have.

Agnes was dozing, her book on her lap, her head tilted to one side on her red plaid armchair, when the door burst open. Her son, Hugh, roared, 'Ma!' and stormed across the room. Startled from her sleep, Agnes's head shot up, just as Hugh's snarling face crowed over her, spittle coming from his mouth as he shouted, 'What have you done, you stupid old...'

'Hugh!' Agnes blasted back, 'Don't you dare raise your voice to me! How was I to know? They tricked me...'

His eyes were blazing as he spat, 'You mean us! Us! That money should have been coming to me. And now you've lost it all.'

Fearful, but not one to back away from a fight, even with her own son, Agnes's temper began to fray, and her voice went low and cold. 'That was my money, not yours. And how dare you charge in here...'

She was cut off by the hand that went round her throat, and began to squeeze. Her eyes widened as she saw for the first time that her son was unhinged, dangerous.

'Hugh, son, don't...' she croaked.

Consumed by rage, he didn't even register her words. His other hand joined the first one and he began to choke her. She tried to fight back, but he was too strong, and her blows didn't even dent his grip on her.

His face was almost touching hers now. 'If there's nothing left, then all you're worth is the life insurance.'

Agnes was still struggling, but weakening, her voice now gone.

'I hope you've got no regrets, Ma,' Hugh growled. 'Because it's too late for you to fix them.' With that, and one final squeeze, Agnes McGlinchy, the cornerstone of *The Clydeside* for the last forty years, took her last breath, before, eyes still open, her head flopped to one side.

A pause. One second. Two seconds. Three seconds.

Carl yelled, 'Cut!' and the silence lingered another moment, before the whole set erupted in cheers and applause, a tribute to one of the most beautifully acted scenes that had ever been shot on *The Clydeside*. The director and his assistants were gathered around the monitor, re-running the tape, but they all knew there would be no need for a retake. It was perfect. And the sheer ferocity of the emotion could never be repeated.

Odette raised her head, stretched her neck from side to side, as Rex offered his hand, this time to help her out of her chair. The applause was still rolling as she stood up and they both took a bow. Odette realised that her throat felt like it was in a vice, not due to the authenticity of Rex's hands squeezing her neck, but because a wave of grief, of fear, of devastation had just risen from her breaking heart.

It was over. Just like her character Agnes McGlinchy, the very real Odette Devine had breathed her last breath. And Olive Docherty had no idea who she was supposed to be now. Somehow the emotion of the scene, the fatality, the end of her career, the recurring thought that her life falling apart was karma for what she'd done to become Agnes McGlinchy, all of those things collided like a car crash in her head and she couldn't muster the cool, collected diva she'd been until the last breath of her character.

Rex Marino released her hand and stood off to the side, joining in the applause, and allowing her to take a bow. Odette felt her eyes fill up, then her cheeks dampen, and she knew tears were falling, but she couldn't wipe them away for fear of revealing her shaking hands. After the third bow, she straightened up, and thankfully Calvin caught her darting gaze of panic and he immediately read the situation. For the first time ever, she needed to be out of the limelight, away from the eyes of the cast and crew. She was about to crumble, to fall apart, and Odette would rather meet Agnes McGlinchy's fate than do so in a public setting, with eyes and cameras fixed on her every move and reaction. He executed her retrieval perfectly.

'Odette, darling, you were magnificent,' he announced loudly, for the benefit of the crowd, as he approached her, arms wide, before enveloping her in a very luvvie, dramatic embrace. 'I'll get you out of here,' he whispered, out of earshot of the assembled spectators and the microphone of the documentary crew. His voice rose again. 'I'm sorry, I need to whisk you away. There's a very special phone caller waiting to congratulate you on your final scene. A very "*royal*" caller,' he threw in pointedly. 'We'll tell you all about it as soon as we get clearance from the palace,' he added jubilantly to the onlookers.

Odette somehow managed to smile, before he strategically manoeuvred her off set, the lens of the documentary camera following her the whole way.

At the door of her dressing room, Calvin put his hand up to stop them. 'I'm sorry, chaps, you'll have to give us a minute. The other side are insisting that the call is confidential.'

With that, he opened the door, practically shoved her inside, and followed her, immediately locking the door so that they wouldn't be interrupted. Odette barely made it to her seat, before she buckled over, eyes bulging, mouth wide, her face twisted as she convulsed into a silent scream.

Calvin gave her space, either sensitive to her pain, or just paralysed by the shock of this utterly uncharacteristic display of emotion. Not that it would have mattered. Odette couldn't hear, couldn't see, couldn't feel anything but the visceral, excruciating pain that was ripping through her. Her breaths were shallow rasps, her heart was beating out of her chest, every muscle in her body was trembling and she couldn't make it stop.

Eventually, Calvin, perhaps unable to bear watching her like this any longer, came to her side with a bottle of water, his arm going around her shoulders as if he were trying to squeeze her distress out of her. 'Darling, just breathe. Take a sip of water. And breathe. I know, it's awful, but you're strong. You're Odette fucking Devine.'

Something in his words permeated her pain and she caught her breath, then exhaled, inhaled, exhaled, forcing her lungs to slow back into a steady rhythm. After a minute or two, she felt her heart begin to calm, her shaking gradually subside, and her vocal cords were finally released from the vice-like grip of her grief.

'The line...' she panted. 'It was the line.'

How could she explain it to Calvin when she wasn't sure she understood what had happened herself? She'd read the line in the script a dozen times when she was preparing for the scene, and it had washed over her. Maybe it was because her mind had revisited the past earlier. Or it could have been the fact that his words came at one of the most devastating moments of her life. But even now, she could hear Rex's warning thunder in her ears. '*I hope you've got no regrets, Ma. Because it's too late for you to fix them.*'

Regrets.

Too late for Agnes. But not too late for Odette. Or more accurately, for Olive.

Olive Docherty had a huge regret, one that she'd suppressed until today, because it had been worth it to be a star. Tonight, the sun would set on that stardom and tomorrow morning, she'd wake up with no job, no applause, no spotlights, no money, no friends.

There would be nothing left. Except, perhaps, a chance to apologise and ask for forgiveness.

She'd wronged one person more than any other in her life.

The question was, after four decades, was it too late to make amends?

6

TRESS

Standing in the wings, watching the action, the emotional impact of seeing Odette film her last scene hit Tress like a hammer to the gut. It was testimony to the sublime acting of Odette and Rex, that for a moment there the set had faded into the background, all sense of pretence had diminished, and Tress was right there as a desperate elderly lady was brutally murdered by her evil son.

It had clearly shaken Odette too. Tress had spotted the pain in her beaming smile as she took her bow and her heart had hurt for her. Tress was heartbreakingly aware how it felt to come to the end of an era, of a way of life, and to stare at a brand-new future full of uncertainty, with a void where the thing you loved once was. Tress had adored every second of her marriage to Max. The sheer joy of waking up next to him every morning. The sexiness and warmth of going to bed with him every night. They'd often lamented the injustice of meeting so late in life, when they were both in their thirties, but that had been soothed by the unexpected wonder of falling pregnant at forty-one with Buddy, when she'd thought her chance to have a child had passed her by.

'You know I don't do that in real life, right?' The words snapped

Tress back to the present and she jumped. Something in her mind hadn't quite readjusted from fiction to reality, and the sound of Rex Marino's voice made the hair on the back of her neck bristle. He had a towel round his shoulders and his usually swept-back raven hair was falling over his forehead, dislodged by the violence and the physical effort of the scene. 'Go around murdering old ladies, I mean,' he went on, with that easy, sexy grin that she'd seen on adverts and billboards for years before she joined the show.

She covered up the momentary reaction with a chuckle. 'I hope not. I'm trying my best to avoid homicidal maniacs in real life. It's one of my general rules. No homicidal maniacs. No pathological liars. No serial killers.'

He leaned against the wall so that he was facing her, his teasing expression matching the levity in his words. 'How's that working out for you?'

'Haven't dated for a year,' she shot back, deadpan, making him laugh. And, oh dear swirling ovaries, she could see why the viewing public were obsessed with this man. He was the romcom Mr Right, the sexy action hero, the gallant officer in the civil war. Or, as Nancy often put it, one glance from those blue eyes could make a woman shudder in her slippers.

Tress had no idea why he gave her the time of day. None. Yet here he was, chatting to her as he'd taken to doing every day for the last few months. It had started just a few days after she'd landed the job, when she'd been sitting in the canteen, having a rare half-hour to herself. She'd still felt out of place, still wasn't one hundred per cent confident in her ability to switch from interior decorating to set design. She'd landed the job by sheer fluke, after working on the home of Lina Worth, the former producer of the show, before the new team had replaced her. They'd got into a conversation about the authenticity of the home environment, of Tress's talent for making a house reflect the character of the occupant, and Lina had asked her to help out with the design of the kitchen for a new arrival on the street of *The Clydeside*. Tress had done it as a favour, with no idea that it could result in a job, but she'd been both surprised and thrilled when it had. Even so, she knew she had a lot to learn, so she'd been alternating eating her tuna salad with doing research on her laptop, when he'd casually slid into the chair opposite her, and waited until she'd lifted her head before saying a word.

'I hope you don't mind. This seat was free,' he'd commented. 'Please carry on with your work and I'll just sit here quietly and wonder who you are.'

That had made her shoulders relax a little. 'I'm Tress Walker. New set designer.'

'Hello, Tress Walker.' He'd stretched his hand towards her. 'Pleased to meet you. I'm Rex Marino.'

'You do look vaguely familiar.' She couldn't help but make fun of him. Odette Devine and Rex Marino were the galactic stars of this universe, and their faces were everywhere: huge portraits in the corridors, photos on every set, articles in every newspaper and magazine, and they were at the top of the images that popped up when you googled the show.

That was the first day they'd spoken, and it had gone from a chance encounter to an almost daily habit. After a week or so, she'd opened up and told him the story of her husband's relatively recent death and he'd seemed genuinely moved. After that, when the sad stuff was out of the way, they'd built a friendship based on Rex being funny and lovely, and Tress making him laugh and mercilessly poking fun at him. She was fairly sure rumours were swirling on set, but she didn't pay any attention, mainly because she knew the truth. They were just friends. Or, at least, that's all it had been until yesterday...

The crowd that had formed to watch the final scene was dispersing, so Tress began walking to her office, with Rex falling into step beside her. 'Listen, about yesterday, I'm sorry if I over-stepped...'

Tress felt heat rising up her neck and knew there would be a very attractive red rash of embarrassment accompanying it. She was hopeless at this stuff. Out of practice. She kept right on walking forward, although her mind was spinning backwards to the day before.

They'd been leaving the studio at the same time last night, just like they'd done countless times before. When they were going down in the lift, they'd been chatting about... actually, Tress couldn't remember. It was just normal stuff. Probably about how their day was going. Maybe a bit about her preparations for Buddy's birthday breakfast. Everyday life stuff. Until, like a scene from a million TV shows and movies, he'd leaned over and pressed the STOP button, before turning to face her.

'Tress, if I don't do this now, I never will, because at least here, I know you can't run away. The thing is... I want to take you out. To go on a date. To kiss you. To see if maybe we could have something more than just friendship, because for me, there's definitely a whole lot more to this.'

Tress was fairly sure she'd slid right into an impersonation of a guppy fish, mouth dropped, nothing coming out.

'So, the question is, will you go out with me? Maybe dinner, next weekend? I was thinking that new restaurant in the West End. They've invited me to the opening next Saturday night and I'd like to take you.'

What? Tress's brain was exploding. He wanted to take her out. On a date. And not just any date. A very public one. To a fancy restaurant. Where there would no doubt be cameras. And press. And crowds of people gathered to see the VIPs arriving. It was about as far from Tress's idea of a lovely night as possible. She'd always preferred the background. It was one of the reasons that her marriage to Max had worked so well. Despite finding out that he'd been sleeping with Anya since before he even bumped into Tress for the first time, Tress would always believe that her husband did truly love her, and on a day-to-day basis they were genuinely happy. Tress knew that was because they'd balanced each other out. Max was the showman, the extrovert, the adrenaline junkie who lived a life of spontaneous excitement, whereas Tress was his anchor, the consistency in his otherwise unpredictable life.

With the lift still groaning in its suspended state, Tress had felt the need to check she was understanding this correctly. 'You want me to go out with you? On a date? Why?'

It was a genuine question. Rex Marino was a drop-dead gorgeous actor almost ten years younger than her and he quite literally had women falling at his feet. A lady had almost been run over by his buggy on the studio lot last week because she had sneaked past the guards and lain down on the road, desperate to get his attention. Tress knew that some of the most popular actresses and models in the country had slid into his DMs (he'd had to explain what that meant). Meanwhile, she was a forty-three-year-old single mother, with avalanching boobs, a whole trunk of baggage and she hadn't shaved her armpits since last summer. She couldn't quite fathom the attraction or the compatibility here.

'Because you've become my very favourite person to spend time with. And instead of having lunch in the canteen, I'd like to talk more to you in a room that doesn't smell of chips.'

'I don't... I haven't... I can't...' Tress hadn't been able to form a sentence.

'Look, just think about it. If this weekend doesn't work, then the offer will stand. Any time. You call the shots.'

He'd stared right into her eyes, and for a moment she'd thought he was going to lean down and kiss her. Panic had spurred her into action, and she'd pressed the lift button, blurting, 'I need to think about it. I mean, it's complicated. There's babysitters. And you know, kid things.'

He had stepped back, totally chilled, with that trademark, bloody gorgeous smile of his. 'No worries at all. Like I said, the offer will always stand, and I hope we can figure it out. I like you, Tress.'

Just then, the doors had pinged open, and she'd managed to mumble some combination of 'okay, thanks, right then, need to run,' as she'd bolted out the doors, across the studio reception and into the car park. As always, there was the usual crowd of fans waiting for the stars to leave the building, so she knew that he'd get caught up signing autographs and posing for selfies.

When she'd jumped in her car, she'd been one hundred per cent positive that she would never go out with him. By the time she got home there was a slight possibility. When she'd woken up this morning, it was fifty/fifty. While she was having breakfast, the odds had swung again, and right now, despite the fact that she'd just watched him bump off one of the icons of Scottish television, Tress was finding the prospect almost irresistible. She just had to find the courage to say yes.

'You didn't overstep,' she assured him, still walking, because somehow the motion helped her deal with the anxiety of the situation. At the end of the corridor, a couple of people alighted from the lift, allowing Tress and Rex to step right in. Her office was one floor up and she usually took the stairs, but today she was making an exception.

'I didn't? Okay, I like where you're going with that.' He was teasing her, but she didn't mind in the least. In fact... sod it. She punched the STOP button, just as he'd done yesterday, turned to face him, stepped forward, reached up on to her toes and kissed him, stopping only when she realised she was no longer breathing and could faint at any moment.

'I like you too. And I say yes to Saturday.'

'You do?'

He leaned down, kissed her again, and she could smell the coconut of his body lotion, taste coffee on his lips. Somewhere inside her, a rampage of feelings that had been locked in a vault a year ago burst free. Lust. Attraction. Sexiness. Excitement. And most of all... hope. Maybe she could do this again. Perhaps she could find the courage to open herself to someone new.

And Rex Marino would be a damn fine place to start.

'I do,' she answered, pressing the lift button so she could get moving again and out of here before her courage failed her and she changed her mind about going.

The lift doors opened, and she exited. She'd taken a few steps when she realised that instead of staying in the lift and returning back down to set, Rex was walking beside her. Ten metres. Twenty metres. She reached her office, and without saying a word, he followed her in and closed the door behind them.

7

NOAH

It was a relief when the clock on Noah's office wall struck 10.30 a.m., and he was forced to stop replaying what had happened downstairs over and over.

Anya.

It was her.

Walking towards him.

Looking almost the same as she had four months ago, when he'd taken her to Glasgow Airport and said goodbye, before she boarded a plane back to New York, to start a new life in the city she'd grown up in with her American dad and Scottish mum.

Another snapshot. They were twenty-one. Newly arrived in Scotland after deciding to study in her mother's homeland, she'd walked into the vaulted hall of Glasgow University, where tables had been set up by all the clubs and societies on campus, to welcome freshers and enlist new members to their groups. Noah and Max were manning a table promoting the university's basketball teams, and the minute this five foot ten goddess walked into the room, eyes like dark pools and cheekbones that belonged on a magazine cover, he'd fallen hopelessly in love at first sight. Or maybe lust. He was young and the lines were a little blurry. Max had asked her out first, and she'd refused him, choosing Noah's invitation for drinks instead, and that was it. Lost. Game over. He was hers.

Another image. She was walking towards him again, this time dressed in white, smiling at their friends and families that lined each side of the aisle. They'd lived together for a few years by that point, often with Max in the spare room for weeks or months at a time. Clichéd as it sounded, Noah's wedding day had been the happiest moment of his life. *For richer and poor. In sickness and in health. To the exclusion of all others. For as long as you both shall live.* Years later, he would discover that Anya had broken one of those vows, with the man he considered a brother.

The next picture in the album of their lives. The one that he still saw almost every day. The two of them, Max and Anya, in an overturned car, bloodied, battered, somewhere between life and death.

Then he was back to the start. The last scene. Saying goodbye. Until now.

'It's okay. I've got this,' he'd murmured to Keli, who had been standing beside him, rooted to the spot, going nowhere. Keli had only been twelve when Noah had first brought his new girlfriend home, but it had been love at first sight there too, and from that very second they'd grown as close as sisters, right up until the moment they'd all learned of Anya's betrayal. As far as Noah knew, the two women hadn't talked since. It was unspoken, but in the DNA of their family – if someone hurt one of them, they hurt them all. Ranks closed while they took care of whoever had been wronged or damaged.

In Noah's case, it had brought him and Keli even closer and redefined their relationship, no longer big brother and little sister, but now two adults who were friends and equals.

Downstairs, Keli had backed off as he requested, with a glare of warning over her shoulder to the woman who had decimated his heart.

'Noah, can we talk?' He'd recognised the anxiety in Anya's voice and the strain on her face, her wide eyes, the white knuckles as her hand clutched her bag strap. She was nervous. Uncomfortable.

'I have clinic in ten minutes, and I can't keep them waiting.'

A sad smile had appeared on her beautiful face. 'You never could. It was one of the things I loved about you,' she'd said softly.

Alarm bells, claxons and bloody great bullhorns had sounded off in his brain. What the hell was happening? What was this? What was she doing here? And why was his heart thudding like a fricking train?

He'd shrugged. 'Some things don't change, I guess.'

He'd spotted a flinch and realised that she might have taken that as a jab at her. It hadn't been meant with any kind of malice, and she should know that. Even in their worst moments, in the hospital after the accident when she had finally told him the truth, he had tried to act with some kind of compassion and decency. She'd made a horrible mistake, but he'd tried not to allow that error to rewrite the history of who she was and what they'd had together. She had reasons. Flaws. Issues. Just as he had. Only difference was, he hadn't shagged her best friend.

'How did you know I was here?' he'd asked, keeping his voice calm, reasonable. After almost two decades of medical training, keeping steady in a crisis came naturally to him, regardless of how he was feeling on the inside.

'I went to the house and you weren't there. Figured this was the next place to try. I remembered you often did an overspill clinic on a Friday. I hope it's okay? I know I should have called, but I wasn't sure you'd pick up.'

'I would have answered, Anya,' he'd told her. 'How long are you here for?'

'Until tomorrow. I just came for a couple of days... I had some things I needed to do. One of them is speak to you. Not here. Somewhere we can talk properly.'

His heart had begun thudding faster. What could they have to discuss? They'd said goodbye, drawn a line in the sand. Now it seemed that the tide was rushing back in, and he wanted to run, but what would be the point? Whatever it was, she was leaving tomorrow. He could give her the courtesy of a conversation.

In his mind, Noah had run through his plan for the day. Clinic. Then late lunch with Cheska. He wasn't going to cancel on her for Anya, especially when she was the one who had arranged this lunch today. No, the friend that had stood by him for the last year took precedence.

'I've got a late lunch meeting after clinic,' he'd told her, 'but I'm free after that. Around five o'clock. Does that work?'

She'd nodded, and he'd seen the expression of relief that crossed her face. Not that he was defending her, but he knew that it must have taken a lot of courage for her to come here. It couldn't be easy facing the worst thing you've ever done and the people you've hurt the most. But then, she'd always been courageous and strong. That was one of the many things he'd loved about her. And it was one of the things that had shocked him most when he'd found out the truth, that she hadn't been brave enough to tell him what she was doing. 'Five o'clock is good. Do you want me to come to the house?'

'No,' he'd blurted before he'd even thought it through. He still lived in the home they'd shared, and it had taken all this time for him to finally be there without thinking of her constantly. He didn't want her back in that space, creating more memories, more images that would play in his mind. 'How about Carlo's Café?' he'd suggested. It was the Italian place in the square just a few hundred metres away, and where he was meeting Cheska for lunch. She was due back on shift by 4 p.m., so he could just hang out there for an hour and wait for Anya, or pop back to the hospital and do some paperwork.

He'd known that today was going to be emotionally tough, but damn, this was turning out to be even more challenging than he'd expected.

'Yeah, I remember the place. Okay, I'll see you there.' She'd taken a couple of steps away, then paused. 'And, Noah, thank you. It really is good to see you again.' With that, she'd carried on out the door.

Noah had made his way over to the lift, and almost unconsciously found his way up to the paediatric ward on the third floor. Clinics were usually held in the outpatient department, but Noah had campaigned for them to be moved to his office on the ward, where previous patients were familiar with their surroundings and first time visitors could be distracted and comforted by the brightly painted walls and playrooms. It also helped that there was a brilliant team on the ward to keep the patients busy if he needed to talk to their parents alone.

At the nursing station, the charge nurse for the day, June, had raised her head when she'd heard his footsteps. 'I was about to send out a search party for you. You're not twenty minutes early and getting under our feet, so I figured you must have been taken hostage somewhere.' He'd known June since he was a trainee just out of university, and she was one of his favourite people. Her irreverence and relentless cheek just made him love her even more. She'd been down in ICU for a few years, then transferred up to Paediatrics about six months ago.

Noah had dropped his backpack on the counter top. 'Can you

book a call to HR into my schedule? I have a complaint about nurses being relentlessly sarcastic.'

'How about if I bribe you with an apple turnover?'

'Complaint dropped.'

'Excellent. Your records for today are on your desk. Three patients, and the first is—'

She'd filled him in on his cases, then he'd headed to his office to prepare it for the families that were on the way. And to let the conversation with Anya ruminate over and over in his mind.

Now, as the clock on his wall flicked to 10.30, he gladly and gratefully switched his brain to work mode, and he popped his head out of his door. 'Jean, is there any sign of Ol—'

'Dr Noah! I brought my new car to show you!' Ollie Lopez, aged six and three quarters, cut him off and answered his question, as he barrelled down the corridor holding a vehicle that looked suspiciously like... 'It's the Batmobile!' Ollie confirmed.

'That's awesome! I think it's the coolest car I've ever seen.' Noah held out his arm and fist-bumped his tiny patient, who, sticking to the theme, was dressed head to toe in a Batman suit. Behind him, Ollie's parents, Jason and Lisa, made eye contact as they approached, and Noah knew from the tight smiles and the searching gazes exactly what was going through their minds. He saw it every day.

Ollie Lopez was here today to get the results of his one-year scan after the removal of a brain tumour. The chemotherapy he'd endured afterwards had ravaged his little body, but he'd recovered incredibly well and if the scan was clear today, there were good odds that it wouldn't return. Right now, his parents were trying to see if they could read Noah's face for some indication of whether he was about to make this one of the best days of their lives or one of the most devastating.

Noah had already read the report, so he knew the best plan of action. 'Ollie, do you want to hang out here for a minute and show Nurse June your Batman moves?' He stretched down so that he could feign a whisper, 'And don't tell her I told you this, but she might have some chocolate buttons in her drawer.'

It was against hospital policy, which advocated no sugar or sweets for children, but Noah and the nursing staff on this ward didn't pay much attention to those rules. After everything these kids had been through, and as long as it was okay with the parents, they took the view that the joy on the little ones' faces was worth it.

Jason and Lisa's smiles tightened just a bit more, so he swept them into his office as quickly as possible. They hadn't even sat down, before he reassured them with a calm, succinct, 'It's good news, don't worry.'

He wasn't sure if the couple sat down or collapsed at the knees, but tears immediately sprang to Jason's eyes, and Lisa grasped at her husband's hand as she double-checked. 'Really? It's definitely okay?'

This was why he preferred not to have the child in the room, even when the results were good. The emotional reaction could be just as strong, and this gave the parents the space to seek all the reassurance they needed.

Noah nodded. 'It's definitely okay. The scan is clear, every test came back fine, no sign of any recurrence. He's doing great. Obviously there are no guarantees, but there's nothing to suggest it won't stay that way. If you ever notice anything that concerns you, call me any time and bring him in to see me. Otherwise, we'll scan him every year, just as a precaution, but I've no reason to think that the results will be different. So you can take Batman home and get on with having a great life.'

Both of them were smiling through their tears now, and Noah was thrilled for them. This was the best kind of moment in his job, and he never took it for granted.

'Another happy customer,' June murmured to him, as they watched the Lopez family head off down the corridor, two ecstatic parents and one happy Batman, clutching his chocolate buttons.

The next appointment was a check-up with three-year-old Ivy, who was making a full recovery from meningitis. He sometimes saw a different outcome, so this was another one to savour.

When her family left, June popped her head in the door. 'I just got word to say the Smiths have cancelled. Wee Demi has suspected chickenpox and they don't want to risk bringing it onto the ward, so that's you done for the day. You can resume your day off and count the hours until you're back in on Monday morning.'

'Every moment will seem like a lifetime,' he bantered back.

She leaned against the doorway, tilted her head and spoke with uncharacteristic sincerity. 'How are you doing today? And how's Tress? Can't be easy for either of you.'

June had been on shift on the day of the accident and had helped him through the nightmare of caring for his grievously injured wife, his fatally injured best mate, and the much-loved friend who had unexpectedly gone into labour and been rushed into the maternity wing. Later, just hours after Tress had given birth, they'd brought her and the baby over to the ICU to say goodbye to Max, and he'd died shortly afterwards. Not one of the medical staff who was working that night would ever forget it.

This wasn't the time or the place to get into specifics, but he appreciated June's thoughtfulness. 'Tress is doing great. Obviously, it's Buddy's birthday today, so we had a celebration this morning. There was singing and stuffed zoo animals, so he loved it. We're having his official party on Sunday, so we're making the most of the opportunities for cake.'

'Aw, bless him. You know, he's going to have a great life that wee one – despite the traumatic start. Anyway, tell Tress I send my best.'

'I will do.' He checked his watch. 'In fact, I might go drop in on her now, since we've finished early. I've got some time to spare.' *The Clydeside* studio was only a ten-minute walk away and she'd probably be about to go on her lunch break just now. Or, if not, she could maybe stop for a coffee. He thought about phoning, but he wanted to tell her in person that Anya had resurfaced. This affected Tress too. Anya had been her friend before they'd discovered she was also Max's mistress. It was a tangled web, and Tress was the only other person who truly got it and who felt the same pain. She deserved to know straight from him what was going on.

He got up, grabbed his bag and jacket, and June stepped back from the door to let him past. 'You know, Dr Clark...' she always switched to his formal name when she was in a professional setting or teasing him. No one else was around, so he guessed she was going for the latter. He wasn't wrong. 'I watched that programme that was on last night about Shania Twain. Do you know that...'

He didn't stick around to hear the rest.

8

KELI

Her shift had been relentlessly busy and Keli welcomed every second of the distraction. There were twenty-eight patients between the ten rooms on the ward and Keli had checked in on all of them, bringing herself up to speed before Dr McVitie was ready for his rounds, which then kept her busy for another hour. Dr McVitie was old-school, abrupt, sharp, but the nurses on the ward forgave his gruffness because he was a brilliant doctor who genuinely cared about his patients.

It was almost noon by the time she got a minute to pause and check her phone.

The first thing she did was text Noah.

Are you ok? What happened? If you need me, just holler.

She waited to see if the three dots appeared, showing he was replying, but nothing. Assuming Anya hadn't kidnapped him, he'd still be in clinic. She decided to wait a while and then text back, but just as she had that thought, a text dropped in.

All okay. Will explain later. Just heading to see Tress. Thanks for being my bodyguard. Nx

Relieved, and trying not to let curiosity compel her to phone him right now and demand full information, she fired off a quick reply.

Bodyguarding services available any time. Love you. Kx

She pressed send, then checked the rest of her notifications.

One missed called from her mum, immediately followed by a text.

Keli, this is your mother. If you don't send proof of life in the next hour, I'm arranging a search party.

There was a second text message straight after that one.

Also, don't forget to come for dinner. And make sure your brother comes too. You both need to eat.

She was a twenty-nine-year-old woman who'd been living on her own since she went to college at eighteen. Noah was almost forty, a medical professional with a pretty dedicated workout regime, yet their mum still thought they could keel over at any moment if they didn't have her home cooking at least twice a week.

Realising that her mum might just be serious, Keli quickly typed back.

I'm fine, Mum, and really sorry I've been MIA – it's been hectic. Will be there for dinner tonight. Love you xx

The reply was immediate.

Search party called off. Love you too.

Keli swallowed down the lump that had just formed in her throat. They were lucky to have their parents and she never forgot that. No matter what, her mum would stand by her and be support-ive, but the nerves under her skin still prickled at the thought of telling her she could be pregnant to a man who'd very obviously ended their relationship – even if he hadn't had the balls to tell her that to her face. Not because her mum would disapprove, but because she'd be highly likely to use her crack interrogation skills to make Keli tell her every detail about this guy, then storm his place of work and forcefully give him her opinion of his behaviour.

Keli knew she should probably do the same thing, but what was the point? He'd made his feelings clear by the fact that she hadn't heard a word from him for the last month. At first, she'd wondered if there was something wrong with his phone. Maybe her texts weren't getting through. She'd called him, but it went to voicemail every time. She had a vague idea of where he lived, although she'd never been there. Somehow, it had always seemed easier for them to hang out at her place. He'd told her he had family staying with him for a few months while their house was being renovated and that he'd invite her over as soon as they were gone. And yes, in hindsight she realised how shady that sounded, but he'd been so plausible, so utterly fucking believable, that she'd fallen for it all. And that, right there, was what she didn't want to admit to anyone. Her mum had brought her up to value her worth, to be strong and smart, yet she'd fallen for his bullshit and his charm when she should have known so much better.

Without thinking, her fingers crossed the screen to Instagram. That's how she knew that he was intentionally avoiding her. He'd blocked her on social media, and she'd had to resort to signing in under a new email address to see his posts. And there they still were. Almost every day. Him looking 'just out of bed sexy', drinking coffee in the morning. A late-evening walk with his dog along the river. His life was just carrying on as normal while hers was spinning like an emotional tumble dryer. Hurt. Sadness. Anger. Disgust. Disdain. And then finally acceptance, which was blown away in a heartbeat a few days ago when, after yet another bout of inexplicable nausea, she'd realised her period was late. Her first reaction was that it must just be stress. Anxiety. Utter fricking heartbreak that someone she'd thought had been so special had clearly been playing her all along. And besides, they'd taken precautions. Condoms. And they'd used them religiously. Okay, apart from that one time that it had burst, and they hadn't realised until...

'Are you okay?' Yvie leaned on the top of the desk and interrupted her thoughts.

'I'm fine – just texting my mother before she sends out a search party.'

'Wise move. Can you do me a favour please? Dr McVitie wants a rush on this swab for Mrs McDandy in bed 16 – fancy dropping it down to the lab? I'd go, but I don't trust myself not to detour to the café for a ginger slice and a bacon roll, and I'm on day two of my diet.'

'Eh, didn't you break the diet last night when you were drinking wine with a side of flaming hot Doritos?'

'Shit, you're right. Okay, well, I'm on day one of my diet and it's only noon – I can't break it yet, so if you wouldn't mind...' She dangled the clear bag containing the tube with the swab in front of Keli, who laughed as she took it.

'I'm on it. But, for the record, you don't need to diet.'

'Tell that to the jeans I'm wearing this weekend.' Keli was already on her feet and moving, when Yvie added with exaggerated innocence, 'The lab is also on the same floor as the chemist. Which sells all sorts of things. You know, like tests. Just saying. Oh, and the staff lift is out of action for the next half-hour, so you'll have to use the public one.'

Her friend got one out of ten for diplomacy, and ten out of ten for persistence.

After an interminable wait for the lift, Keli got in and was immediately faced with two women, both holding babies. It was almost certainly just a twisted coincidence, given that Paediatrics, her brother's mothership, was two floors above her, but it really felt like the universe fricking hated her today. One of the babies was sound asleep in its portable car seat, while the other one was fussing up a storm in its mum's arms. Keli had always been ambivalent on the subject of having children. She'd done rotations on Maternity and Paediatrics, and enjoyed them both, but the prospect of introducing tiny humans into her life had always been a fairly abstract notion, a vague 'one day, if I meet the right guy'. And hadn't she thought that had happened?

The doors opened on the ground floor and she let the two women go ahead of her into the huge hospital foyer. She followed them out, before doubling back and using her security pass to get through the nearby door that took her down one flight of stairs, into a warren of corridors that weren't accessible to the public. The staff canteen, the labs and a dozen other hospital services were located down there.

It took Keli five minutes to drop off the sample, plead for a swift return, and then get back up to the main foyer. Of course, the first thing her gaze landed on was the row of shops next to the front entrance: there was a Tesco express, a gift shop, a sandwich shop, a bakery and… the chemist. Right there. Calling to her.

She thought about ignoring it, but something about the babies in the lift, the mums, Yvie's nagging, her constant yo-yoing between fear and desperation to know propelled her forward and right into the shop. She had a quick scan to see if she recognised anyone before deciding the coast was clear and taking the box to the till. Stomach flipping, she paid using her phone, popped it in a bag, then marched right back over to the lift and got in, before she could change her mind.

This time, there was a bloke holding the hand of a wailing toddler. He met Keli's gaze, then grudgingly picked the little boy up. 'Sorry, son, but I've already told you no more sweets today. Now dry your eyes, so that you look nice for Mum.'

Keli read between the lines. They were going to see the boy's mum, outside of the normal visiting hours. That meant it was probably something serious and the nurses on the ward were making an exception. This wasn't a bloke being impatient with his crying child. It was just a dad, doing the best he could under what might just be awful circumstances. Keli gave him an understanding smile, then said goodbye when they reached her floor first.

Back on the ward, she nipped into the staffroom to ditch the package until her break, still not entirely sure that she had the courage to do the test just yet, but at least she had the tools if she was ready.

In her mind, she saw the strong but anxious face of the dad in the lift, and it gave her the kick she needed. She could do this. She could. As soon as she had a free five minutes, she was going to do the test and retake charge of her life, no matter what the result was.

She tossed the bag into her locker, closed it and then washed her hands, ready to get back on the ward. The hand towel had just been dropped into the waste bin beside the sink when her phone pinged again. No doubt her mother, with another request about dinner.

She pulled the phone out of her scrubs' pocket and checked the screen. Not her mum. A number she didn't recognise.

A flick of her thumb opened the message.

Hi. Sorry to do this, but I think you've been sleeping with my boyfriend. Can you call me back?

Keli froze, rooted to the spot, just as Yvie came through the door. Her recognition of the shock on Keli's face was instant. 'What's wrong? Oh God, did you do the test? Was it positive? It was. Okay, don't panic. I've got you. We'll figure this out. We can...'

'No.'

'No? It was negative? Then why aren't we celebrating?'

'I didn't do the test.'

Yvie's confusion was obvious. 'Then why do you look like that?'

It took Keli a moment for her brain to unfreeze long enough to send a message to her arm to hold out her phone. 'Because I just got this.'

Yvie came close, read the message... 'What?' she gasped. 'No! Yes! Oh shit! What are you going to do?'

Again, a pause for instructions to be relayed from her brain.

'I'm going to call her back.'

NOON – 2 P.M.

9

ODETTE

'Right, are you sure your emotional equilibrium has been restored and you're ready for this?'

The concern that was in every lasered pore of Calvin's face was touching, but even though Odette knew it came from a place of care, she was so embarrassed that she responded with a brusque, 'Of course I am. It was just the power of the scene that caused my little... interlude.'

They both knew that was a lie, but she was far too proud and too mortified to admit it, even to Calvin. Oh, the shame of it. Showing vulnerability and falling apart like that in front of the whole bloody cast. Calvin had assured her that he'd got her out in time, and that no one had clocked on to her having a genuine melt-down, and she was choosing to believe him because the alternative was too horrendous to contemplate.

All these young ones nowadays seemed to think it was a national bloody sport to show their feelings. She was barely social-media savvy (her choice, given that she refused to give all that nonsense a moment of her time), but she'd seen enough to know it was changed days from her generation of stoicism and inner resolve. All those posts declaring their woes and their worries. Attention-seeking, that's all it was. And as for the Tok-Tiks, or whatever they were called... piece of nonsense. Filming themselves eating their lunch or crying over whatever ridiculous thing that was going on in their life. What was the point? Genuinely, she was baffled. As for those... what were they called? Influencers. Yep, that was it. Well, she couldn't get her head around that at all. In her day, you only got famous if you were either a criminal, a politician or someone with a talent. Singing. Dancing. Acting. Writing. Not for putting up pictures of your arse hanging out of a bikini the size of two teabags and a pocket square in Marbella.

She was back in her chair in her dressing room, and after a quick session with the hair and make-up team, all traces of dowdy Agnes McGlinchy were gone, and in her place, Odette Devine sported a flawless visage and a perfect coiffure. If the glam squad had noticed her red-rimmed eyes and blotchy skin, they hadn't mentioned it and that suited Odette fine. The old adage of 'Never explain, never complain' was one that she thoroughly subscribed to. And she'd be sticking to that in this next session with the documentary team. Thankfully, there was only going to be time for a quick exchange before her official farewell lunch.

'Okay, let's get this over with,' she sighed, and Calvin responded by swinging the door open and beckoning to Elliot and his cameraman, who'd been in the corridor for the last forty-five minutes, patiently waiting for their next audience with the freshly dethroned queen.

Elliot opened the session with a compliment. 'That scene was incredible, Odette. The sheer force of your performance shows us why you're regarded as one of the greatest British actresses of your time.'

Odette wasn't buying what he was selling. Not that she disagreed with him, but she wasn't a wet-behind-the-ears novice who fell for flattery and let their guard down. It was the oldest trick in the book, and she was a thousand press junkets too experienced and savvy to let that work.

'Can you tell us how you feel now that the scene is over and Agnes McGlinchy has breathed her last breath?'

If she were one of those Tok-Tickers, she'd well up and start pouring out her feelings to anyone who would listen. Thankfully, she wasn't.

'I feel... satisfied. I think the scene was the perfect ending for one of the most iconic characters in soap history. Agnes will be up there with the likes of Dot Cotton, Pat Butcher, Peggy Mitchell, Hilda Ogden and Vera Duckworth. If there was a soap hall of fame, I'd like to think she'd get a star there.'

Elliot nodded, letting her give her full answer. All his questions would be edited out in the final documentary, and her answers would be interjected between clips to form a narrative. She just had to make sure that it was the story she wanted to tell. 'Great, Odette, thank you. Just a couple more and then we'll let you go. Your son, Hugh, has been played by Rex Marino for the last two years. Can you give me some comment on Rex and the rumours that he has hopes of transitioning to a movie career?'

She was tempted – so, so tempted – to announce to the world that he was an overrated arse whose ego was far greater than his talent, but again, she gave the politically prudent answer.

'I think he's a fine actor and I'm looking forward to watching where his career goes from here. The Glasgow streets to the Hollywood stars would be something, wouldn't it?'

He didn't have a snowball's chance in Satan's kitchen of making it on the other side of the Atlantic. Here he was a big fish in a small pond. Over there? He was just another good-looking guy with mediocre talent.

Calvin could sense that she was getting impatient, and smooth as ever, he stepped in. 'Elliot, I'm sorry to intervene, but Odette has lunch with the cast and crew shortly, so we'll have to wrap this up.'

Elliot nodded sagely. This man had the patience of a saint. If she could give advice to her younger self, it would be to forget the bad boys, the arrogant tossers, and go for this type of guy: attractive enough, level-headed, no desire to share her limelight or profit from it. A wave of angst made her jaw set and she quickly readjusted her smile, careful not to give them any unflattering shots that they could use if they tried to add some grit to the piece by showing her in a negative light or in more sombre moments.

'Okay,' Elliot agreed. 'Let's finish off with one final question.'

Odette flashed her well-rehearsed, strategically precise smile – just wide enough to show off her perfect veneers, but not too wide that it gave her crow's feet or emphasised her mouth-to-nose lines.

'I've read several different accounts of how you got the role on *The Clydeside*. I'd love to hear the true story straight from you.'

Odette's perfect veneers almost rattled.

This was it. She had two choices. She could stick to the same old rubbish she'd been spouting for decades, about how she'd been working in a café (a lie), and one day, Alf Cotter, the original director of a new Scottish soap called *The Clydeside,* had come in for a pie and beans (more lies). It was a low-budget project in the beginning (true, and that hadn't changed too much) and the show had only been commissioned for six episodes, so there were no flash restaurants for the executives yet, she would joke when she was retelling the story for the hundredth time. Anyway, in that fictionalised version, Alf sat down, opened his newspaper, and barely glanced up when a young Odette Devine came to his table to take his order. At least, at first. As soon as he heard her voice, he'd lifted his head, and when he saw her smile, he was captivated. After his pie, and three cups of tea, during which his eyes had barely left her, she'd marched over and demanded to know what he was staring at. She'd expected him to ask her out, but instead, he'd asked her if she'd ever thought about acting. Which, of course, she had. After all, she was only working in the café in her spare time, in between the modelling jobs that were getting more frequent every month (she'd never modelled a day in her life). He'd asked her to come back to his production office there and then, where she'd read in front of the director, and well, the rest was history.

That was the version she should give Elliot for this documentary, even though every word of it was nonsense.

Olive Docherty hadn't been working in a café at all. At twenty-eight years old, she'd been working as a school dinner lady, in some godforsaken village on the outskirts of Glasgow, a job she'd only got because the previous person in the role had been her Auntie Vi, who'd died the year before after her gin-soaked liver had packed in, leaving Odette without another living relative. Her mother had passed when she was twelve and she'd been brought up being told by her mum and Auntie Vi that Robert Redford was her real dad. She still couldn't watch *Love Story* without tearing up. She'd hated every single thing about that job in the school, except the banter between the rest of the women. Three of the canteen crew had been in their twenties, and the rest were in their forties and fifties, all of them women who drank, who smoked, who loved their families fiercely. They gossiped relentlessly, their language was choice and they used caustic humour to get them through every hard time, and to keep each other grounded when things were good. Every one of them had played a part in inspiring her portrayal of Agnes McGlinchy.

It had been one of her co-workers of a similar age who'd brought the newspaper in. She'd pointed out the advert for actresses for the new show, said she was going and suggested Odette and another of their work pals should tag along. What neither of the other women knew was that Odette had immediately recognised that it could be a way out of her hellish existence, of living day to day on her own, trying to eke out enough money to eat, for her bus fares, to put coins in the gas meter so she could stave off hypothermia and get a bath a couple of times a week. That was no life for anyone. She'd been desperate for comfort. Security. Fame and fortune would be a bonus. All she'd ever known was miserable poverty. The prospect of an acting job had been a fantasy way out of a world that she hated and she'd been fully prepared to fight for her chance. In the end, she'd won the battle, but she'd had to lie and cheat her way to victory.

Question was, should she come clean now, try to right the wrong, and absolve her conscience? Telling the documentary crew would get the story out, be the first step in trying to find a way to repent for what she'd done and maybe even balance the karma that was shredding her life to tatters right now.

For the second time in a couple of hours, she heard Rex's words echo in her mind.

'*I hope you've got no regrets, Ma. Because it's too late for you to fix them.*'

This was her chance. She just had to have enough integrity to take it.

10

TRESS

Holy crap. This was not how she'd expected today to pan out at all. There was taking baby steps towards opening your life and your heart to someone new, and there was shooting yourself out of a cannon into some hot-and-sweaty passion with a drop-dead-gorgeous man. And, by some crazy turn of fate, Tress appeared to be doing the latter.

Rex had followed her into her tiny cupboard slash office, and she'd automatically assumed that, like everyone else who stopped by, he was angling for a coffee and maybe even a biscuit on the side. She should have known better. The man's body hadn't seen carbs in a decade.

She'd turned, perched on the edge of her desk and expected him to flop into the armchair in the corner, just as he'd done the last few times he'd dropped by. But no. Instead, he'd taken a few steps forward, until the front of his thighs were almost touching her knees, then he'd reached over, lifted her chin, used the soft flesh of his thumb to gently caress her cheek. And... yep, right on cue, prickles of desire swept around her for the second time in his company. At least she thought that was what it was. It may have been prickles of absolute fear because she hadn't locked the door, or because this wasn't the type of thing that she thought acceptable in the workplace, or because she still wasn't confident in what the hell she was going to do with this specimen of physical perfection. And... stomach-flipping thought – if she ever actually found herself having sex with this man, the light would have to be off and she would run the risk of fainting from holding her stomach in for a prolonged period of time.

No such trifling matters had seemed to be concerning him in the least.

'For the second time this week, I find myself in the position of wanting really, really badly to kiss you.'

'Oh.' She was pretty sure she'd done one of those cartoon gulps that resembled a ping-pong ball being swallowed and travelling down her throat.

'And I was just wondering...' He'd moved closer, pressing against her knees now. 'If that...' Using his free hand, he'd nudged her thigh and, like some biblical parting of the denim-clad seas, she'd opened her legs so that he could step forward between them.

Now, her pulse was thudding, and she could feel a tiny rivulet of sweat running down inside the back of her white shirt, a sure sign that her temperature was reaching the diagnostic bracket for malaria. And she still couldn't decide if it was because she was loving it or some kind of human-contact terror had set in.

'Rex, I don't think...' The words drifted away as his lips came down to her upturned mouth and gently, so very softly, grazed her lips. Bugger. They hadn't seen lip balm since it got lost between the baby wipes and the nipple pads in the bottom of the oversized landfill site that she used as a handbag.

He pulled his face back, his hips still firmly pressed against her groin, a bulging reminder of what sexual attraction felt like. His hand began tracing a faint trail down her neck, across her collarbone, then down further until it reached her top button and she gasped. 'If you tell me to stop, I will,' he whispered, and she wondered if anyone ever did.

Then she heard a voice that was like a higher-pitch version of her own say something that sounded like, 'Stop. I need a minute.'

He carried on for a couple of seconds more, then did as she asked. 'You don't like it?' he asked, and if she didn't know better, she'd think he was channelling Richard Gere, circa *Pretty Woman*. Or maybe Jamie Dornan in *Fifty Shades of Grey*. If he pulled a cat o' nine tails out of his back pocket, she was calling security. Maybe.

'I like it. I just... Like I said before, it's been a while. And the last person who touched me was... well, it was my husband. I know I need to get past this, and I really want to... *really, really* want to right now. But it just kind of feels like it shouldn't be here, like this, when I'm absolutely terrified that Alf could barge in at any moment demanding that I redesign the household goods aisle of the corner shop.' She was babbling. She knew it. Yet she couldn't stop.

Her words made him laugh, but he didn't back off, didn't take his foot off the sexual chemistry gas. She was fricking doomed. 'I get it. I really do,' he told her softly, lifting her hand then kissing her palm, her thumb, her fingers, one by one. In the name of the holy erogenous zone, what was he doing? And why did it feel like she was in a Swedish sauna? 'I tell you what,' he went on. 'Why don't I just stand here and let you take the lead? You can do whatever you want. I won't touch, I won't push. It's all on you.'

Knickers would be flying at half the ladies' nights in the country if Rex Marino made that offer, and yet she felt like she'd been tasered and was only just getting back the use of her motor skills. It was a good offer. Maybe this way, she could enjoy it, without the pressure. Or maybe she should just stop this nonsense and offer to make him an erotic cappuccino instead.

Yet again, the voice in her head asked her what the hell was holding her up and the truth was, it felt awkward. It felt... dishonest. It almost felt like she was being unfaithful to Max. She wasn't prepared for the flash of rage that thought invoked. Screw Max. Not to speak ill of the dead, but he'd been unfaithful to her with Anya for their entire married life. Even when she was heavily pregnant and in danger of going into labour at any time, he had still sneaked off with his mistress for one last shag. She honoured him for the happiness their marriage gave her, and for the wonderful gift of Buddy, but she owed him nothing. Some internal determination to prove that point fired up something inside her. She would not back down from this. She deserved pleasure. She was worthy of love. For the last year, she had put her life to one side to bring up her child and she'd done a bloody good job of holding it all together. She was an independent, confident, cosmopolitan woman of the world. So she could damn well feel up Rex Marino when he was standing right in front of her and telling her to call the shots.

Deep breath in. Deep breath out. Come on, Tress, demanded her internal monologue.

Her thighs were still on either side of his hips, which she was sure were about a dozen inches smaller than hers. She reached up and stroked his face, just as he'd done to hers. That jawline was rock hard, then she felt her finger dip as it reached the dimple on his chin. Her gaze locked on his and stayed there while she reached up and ran her fingers through his jet black hair. All the while he stood stock-still, just as he'd promised.

Her fingertips came down and grazed across his lips, then this time she was the one who slid her fingers down his neck, then over his shoulders. He was wearing a black, skin-tight T-shirt and she had a sudden urge to feel what was underneath, so she ventured down across rock hard abs, then slipped her hands up under the hem, flinching as they reached skin. He didn't move a muscle. Not in his face. His jaw. Or in the six-pack that felt like rows of speed bumps under her touch.

Still under the cotton of his top, she moved further north, hitting pecs that belonged on a Calvin Klein model. The T-shirt wouldn't allow her to rise any further so she came back down again, slowly, with the softest touch, until he groaned, voice thick and sexy, 'Tress, you're killing me.'

'I think I'm killing myself too,' she admitted in a whisper, torn between wanting to stop and wanting to go further. She pushed both her hands into his hair this time, and pulled his face down towards her, stopping when their lips were just a centimetre apart. She held him there for a second, before pulling him closer, kissing him, letting her hands drop and go round his back, tracing a line down his spine, across his buttocks, which had clearly been carved from stone.

She was still kissing him, but the perfection of his body was having the opposite effect to the expected outcome. Her libido should have been cranking up to irresistible, but instead it was stuck at quandary. She wanted him to speak, to connect with her, to make her laugh, to dispel her fears.

He slid away from her kiss, and she felt the warm, provocative touch of his lips as they worked their way down her neck. His hands entered the game again, sliding up the denim on her thighs. 'Tress, I want to lock that door, and I want to clear this desk and make love to you right here. Tell me you want me to.'

Oh shit. Shit. Did she? From the waist down, she definitely did. From the neck up, she was in full-scale panic. She had a sudden premonition of what the seconds after they shagged on the desk would look like. When all the sweaty, grunty stuff had finished, he'd be on top of her and she'd be on top of the design for the set that would host next Wednesday's Scottish Slimmers meeting at the Clydeside community centre. He would push himself up and they'd stare at each other as acute embarrassment kicked in. Then there would be the toe-curling mortification that her bikini line hadn't seen a razor (or a bikini) in a year and was full-scale Leylandii underneath granny pants that had been washed with Buddy's red Power Ranger pyjamas and were now a subtle shade of ham. Not to mention she'd need to nip over to Farrah in costumes and ask her to iron this shirt.

And, in fact, she wasn't even sure that this desk would hold their weight, because she'd built it from flat-pack and she'd had a whole bag of screws left over at the end. If they went sprawling on the floor, she'd have to quit her job, take Buddy and emigrate to somewhere she'd never see Rex's face again. Did they have British channels in Alaska?

But all that aside, even if it was mind-blowingly fantastic, and the earth moved in a non-desk-calamity way, and she had the best sex of her life, every single time she walked into this office afterwards, she would be reminded that she had shagged Rex right here, and she wasn't sure that she could live with the face-flaming mortification of thinking about his penis while at work. It didn't feel intimate, or special, or right. And while she was a firm believer that there was a place for a lustful quickie, this wasn't it.

No. She didn't want this here. Not now. Not today.

She was about to tell him that when the situation and the options were taken out of her wandering hands.

She was vaguely aware of a distant knock on a door, then shockingly aware of the air in the room moving as the door swung open, then a startled voice saying, 'Sorry! I was looking for Tress. Apologies for interrupting.'

Tress's head snapped up, her chin coming close to leaving Rex needing rhinoplasty, which would have been almost as painful as her jumping off the desk and landing on his feet. Bollocks. Hopefully there were no dancing scenes planned for the next week or so.

Rex yelped and staggered backwards, giving her a clear view of the open doorway, in which stood...

'Noah? Erm, hi. I'm right here.' She peeked over Rex's shoulder. 'Give me two seconds and I'll just wrap up this meeting.'

11

NOAH

'So, on a scale of one to a million per cent awkward, where are we sitting?' Noah asked, laughing. He wasn't sure what had shocked him more today – Anya pitching up out of the blue, or walking in on Tress manhandling that actor from the show. Although, in fairness, he should probably have texted Tress to let her know he was stopping by, but he dropped in so regularly, he didn't think it was a big deal. Neither did Bob, the security guard at the front door, mostly because Tress had given him the authorisation to let Noah in any time, but also because Noah had taken out Bob's grandson's burst appendix and he'd made a full recovery.

Thankfully, Romeo had made a swift escape when Noah had interrupted them, so now, Noah was sitting on the old, battered armchair in the corner of Tress's office. She'd once told him it had been a staple of Agnes McGlinchy's living room, before she treated herself to a recliner when her storyline had her winning a thousand pounds on a lottery scratchcard.

Tress was in the chair behind her desk, head in her hands, her shoulders shaking with laughter. 'Oh, we're dinging the bell at the top of the awkward scale. And I know it didn't seem that way, but

I'm so glad you walked in. It was about to get highly contentious, because I was about to stage a retreat and ask for a rain check.'

'Uh-huh,' he teased her with a tone of cynicism. 'Had you told your hands that? Because from where I was standing, you were hanging on to his arse for dear life.'

'Noooooooooo,' Tress wailed, her head on the table now. 'And by that I mean, yes. You're right. What kind of mother am I? My son's first birthday and I'm at work, feeling up one of Scotland's Top Ten Hogmanay Hotties?'

That memory came back to Noah. A few weeks ago, between Christmas and New Year, Tress reading a newspaper and pointing out that number two on the Hogmanay Hottie list was in her show. Number one was Sam Heughan, but according to Tress, he got his kit off regularly in *Outlander*, so he had an advantage. Noah had just been confused and more than a bit surprised that they still ran features like that in 2023. That said, when he was a junior doctor, he'd been persuaded to do a calendar of 'Dishy Docs' to raise money for new play equipment for the hospital. Noah had been Dr June, and he had barely left the house from May until the first of July, for fear that someone would recognise the doctor in the blue scrub trousers, who had remembered his stethoscope but appeared to have misplaced his top.

'Somehow I don't think Buddy will be scarred for life. Nancy and Val are probably on their 2436th rendition of "Wheels on The Bus". So this is a thing?' His curiosity got the better of him. At least he thought it was curiosity. Maybe a bit of protectiveness too. Tress had been through so much in the last year, and he couldn't stand the thought of anyone else hurting her. Not that she was the type of person to make impulsive or dodgy choices. No. She was smart, and she took her time to make the right decisions – which made it all the more fucking infuriating that Max had turned out to be a cheating dick in the end. Max had fooled them both, the two people who'd loved him unreservedly – his best mate and his wife. Tress deserved so much better and Noah wasn't sure if this hottie was it.

Tress lifted her head. Shrugged. 'I have no idea. Yesterday, he kissed me in the lift and asked me out. I told him I'd think about it. And then today... that just happened. What am I doing, Noah? I'm a single mother...'

'Eh, as your best mate I'd like to add "gorgeous single mother". I'm just trying to be as suave as Mr Smooth Moves with the muscles.'

He had to duck when she picked a brush up off her desk and launched it at him. 'Don't take the piss!' she objected, but at least she was laughing. 'I'm in an emotional dilemma here and you're not helping.'

He held his hands up in surrender. 'Okay, okay. Right, I'm listening. I just can't believe you didn't tell me about this.'

'I know, I know. I was just... processing it. I mean, I've been totally closed off to any kind of entanglement for the last year, and then this happens. It just caught me off guard.'

'Yep, me too. I thought I was in the wrong room.' He was playing with her again, and she was still trying to act indignant.

'Stop! Did you not hear the bit about the emotional dilemma? Don't pick on the chick with the issues.'

'I'm sorry, you're right. Okay, give it to me – what's the dilemma?'

She reached up and grabbed two bottles of water from the shelf behind her, then tossed one to Noah, before going on, 'I just don't get the point of starting something with a man who is clearly at a completely different place in his life than me. That's an accident waiting to happen. And I don't get why he's interested. Don't get me wrong – I'm not fishing for compliments or doing myself down, but come on.'

'I know. He's a Hogmanay Hottie.'

'Can we stay on track here?' she demanded, with a touch of amused exasperation.

Noah cleared his throat, swapped his grin for his very best serious expression. 'Sorry. Couldn't help myself. Okay, then looking at this objectively...'

'Yes?'

He was almost afraid to say it. 'Could you not just use him for sex?'

Tress gave him her very best death stare. 'You're not helping, you know that? No. I couldn't. I'm way too fricking terrified for that. And besides, much as it felt great in some bits, it also felt... weird. Awkward. Self-conscious. It never felt that way with Max, not even in the beginning. I'm a lost cause. I am. I'm destined to grow old and haggard and never have sex again. They'll find me at eighty, prowling the corridors of the old folks' home, looking for a date for Saturday night karaoke.'

'Nah, I'll be there too. I'll take you to the karaoke as long as you'll do Dolly Parton and I can be Kenny Rogers. We'll sing "Islands In The Stream" until all the choruses about running water make us want to pee.'

It was an inside joke that had kept them going in the aftermath of the nuclear explosion that had detonated in both their lives. They'd never be able to face another relationship, but they'd have each other, and in decades to come, they'd pass the time racing their Zimmers in the garden. Somewhere along the line, for him, things had got better. A few months ago, when his decades-long friendship with Cheska became something more, he'd worried that Tress might resent him moving on, or feel sad that it was no longer just the two of them – plus Val and Nancy – against the world, but, of course, she hadn't minded in the least. She'd been happy for him. Told him he deserved it. Much as he wanted that for her too, he wasn't sure this hottie was the right one, but whatever Tress decided, he'd get right on board.

Tress's mobile began to ring and saved him from having to express that. Probably just as well. She checked the screen and then answered it, putting it on speaker. 'Hello?'

'Hello, ma love, it's me. Don't panic, your boy is well and nothing is on fire.' Nancy started every call with a variation of that announcement. 'I'm just checking in on you and letting you know that me and Val are taking Buddy, Oliver and Gerald to the petting zoo at the park.'

Tress and Noah looked at each other quizzically, before Tress replied, 'Nancy, who are Oliver and Gerald? Have you stolen two children? If so, you need to give them back.'

'Nope, Oliver the Octopus and Gerald the Giraffe. Anyway, two things. First of all, I just wanted to let you know where we'll be in case you need us. And secondly, I wanted to offer to stay and watch Buddy tonight. My Johnny is away on a golf weekend with Leo Clark...' Noah automatically smiled at the mention of his dad. '... and the rest of the lads from the club. It's a relief really. I adore the bones of him, but if I have to listen to one more story about a hole in one that almost happened, I'll be ditching him and getting on the Tinders.'

'Nancy, that's so lovely of you but—'

'No buts. Val and I thought maybe you and Noah could have dinner. Mark this day in some way.'

Noah heard the music in the background at Nancy's end and realised exactly what was going on here. 'Nancy Jenkins, I see your game here.'

'Noah, is that you?' she retorted, voice full of innocence. 'Och, well, how lovely is that – I got the both of you together. I'm sure you'll agree it's a smashing idea. So, anyway, don't come home. Go wild. Buddy will be in his bed by seven o'clock anyway, so you won't be missing much. Right, have to go, byee-eee.' Click.

'Did I just hear what I thought I heard?' he asked, laughing.

'Yep. Nancy Jenkins and Val Murray trying to play matchmakers while listening to "Man, I Feel Like A Woman".'

'I don't understand it.' Noah took a slug of his water, before going on, 'They love Cheska. Why are they trying to throw us together?'

'Maybe it's a test. Or just a daft notion. They adore Buddy so much that maybe they just want to ensure he'll always have consistency in his life, and they think us being together will make sure that happens.'

'He'll always have that, even if we're both with other people.'

'You and I know that,' Tress agreed, 'but those two are a bit more old fashioned. And you know what they're like when they get something into their heads. How did this become our lives? You being here will have them talking all afternoon, dying to know why we're together when I'm at work and you're... Actually, bugger, I'm sorry. I've been too preoccupied with my romantic turmoil to ask – why are you here? Is everything okay?'

There was a huge part of him that didn't want to tell her, but they'd promised each other there would never be any secrets and he wasn't going to break that now.

'Yeah, it's fine. Kind of,' he sighed, sitting back, re-experiencing that lurch of confusion that he'd felt this morning when he'd clapped eyes on his ex-wife. 'Actually, I've no idea if it's fine. I had a visitor when I got to work this morning. Anya was there.'

Tress jerked her head up so quickly his mind automatically ran through whiplash protocols. 'What the hell...? Why? What's she doing here?'

'I don't know. She asked to meet me, says she wants to talk.'

'And you agreed?' She looked surprised and Noah got it. Today of all days, this was the reminder that none of them needed. He watched every bone in Tress's body slump as she exhaled, and he felt a pang of guilt for making her feel this way.

'I agreed. I'm meeting her at five o'clock tonight to hear what she wants to say. I wasn't going to turn her away, Tress. We were married for almost twenty years. I'll always be civil to her.'

'I know,' she said softly. 'You're too bloody nice, Noah Clark. How did it feel when you saw her?'

Noah ran his hand over the top of his head, as he struggled to pinpoint the right answer. 'Shocking, mostly. Keli was with me and for a tense moment I thought she was going to go full-scale ninja warrior on her. That's the thing though, isn't it? It wasn't just us who took the body blows. Keli viewed Anya as another sister, and my mum and dad treated her like a daughter. Everyone in our world was affected by it and I don't know that there's any coming back from that for any of us.'

'Would you want there to be? With Anya and you, I mean?'

He'd be lying if he denied that the thought had ever crossed his mind. The truth was that he missed her. Missed the marriage they'd had and the lives they'd spent together. Until the end, their world had been simple. Straightforward. But some hurdles were just too huge to climb over.

'No. Cheska and I... we're good. I don't want anything to spoil that.' He checked his watch. 'Talking of which, I need to run. I'm meeting Cheska for lunch and I'm going to be late if I don't get a move on.'

'So you're meeting Cheska first, then Anya. Packed social schedule there, Mr Clark.' Tress was trying to keep it light-hearted, but Noah could see the tension across her brow.

'It is. I'll give you a call later...'

'Eh, I don't think so. Not later. Immediately. Within ten seconds of hearing what Anya wants, I demand to know. Now that I'm possibly, maybe, might be, dating a star, I'm going to develop diva tendencies and start snapping my fingers and shouting orders to everyone around me.'

Noah was already on his feet and a couple of strides took him over to her. He kissed the top of her head. 'Remind me to buy earplugs.' He got as far as the door, before something made him turn around. 'You know, Tress, that bloke would be lucky to have you. You deserve someone good. Someone right for you. Don't rule it out until he gives you a reason to.'

Outside, he picked up the pace so that he got to the restaurant on time for his late lunch. He was halfway there when his phone rang. Cheska. She must have been reading his mind. 'Just checking you're on the way, Noah. I've got an hour and a half and then I'm back to work.'

'I'm on my way now.'

'Great, because there's something I need to discuss with you. I'll see you soon.'

She disconnected and Noah stared at the phone, a prickle of uneasiness creeping up his spine as the restaurant came into view. She'd sounded sharp. A bit off.

Why did he get a sudden sense that she didn't want to discuss anything good?

12

KELI

Keli almost kissed Sima when she barrelled through the doors of the ward just before two o'clock, wailing, 'Sorry, sorry, sorry. Three fillings and a meltdown. That child will never see another ounce of sugar or a fizzy drink until the end of time. Keli, you're a star. Thank you so much for covering for me. Tell me everything I need to know, then you can get out of this godforsaken place.' Sima made no secret of the fact that while she was excellent at her job, twenty years after qualifying as a fresh-faced student, the shine had gone off it. She wasn't alone. Morale in most hospitals had tanked in recent years, between budget cuts, post-pandemic stress, overcrowding and the never-ending stretch of their job descriptions, it was a different role from the one most of them had signed up for.

Carla, the other charge nurse on duty, was at the desk and stepped in. 'On you go, Keli, and thanks for covering. Yvie, do you want to take your lunch just now and I'll bring Sima up to speed?'

'Good plan. Shall we retire to the staffroom for witty conversation and carbs?'

Keli realised that Yvie was talking to her and nodded, almost robotically. The last two hours, since she'd murmured, 'I'm going to call her back,' had been the longest of her life.

She'd thought about doing it right there and then, but her professionalism had kicked in, as had the knowledge that they were already short-staffed on the ward. This wasn't the time to let her personal life interfere with her work or with patient care. In fact, the chat and the motions of the job had kept her mind focused and helped her hold it together.

She'd almost cracked. Almost. She'd gone into Freda's room to do her stats, and Emily, the lady in the next bed, had returned from the day room and was trying to switch on the ward TV.

'One o'clock. Time for the rerun of last night's episode of *The Clydeside*,' Emily had told her as she stabbed at the remote control with shaking fingers.

Keli's anxiety, her stress, her whole whirlpool of emotions had ramped up a hundred per cent. Until just a few weeks ago, she'd watched every episode, but now the heartache, drama and duplicity struck way too close to home.

'Oh, I love that Odette Devine,' Freda had announced. 'I'll miss her when she goes. She always seems like such a lovely person.'

Vera and Janet in the beds opposite had both nodded.

Emily was still pressing the temperamental remote control with no success. 'I bloody hate these things. They never work. I'd be quicker papping it out the window and hoping it lands on the right button.'

Keli had taken the remote from her and had summoned every ounce of strength she possessed to keep her voice normal. 'I'll sort that out for you, Emily. It's probably the batteries again. And I'll take your blood pressure last,' she'd said kindly, 'because it'll be through the roof with all that jabbing.'

'Aye, my husband used to say the same thing,' Emily had quipped. 'He was reluctant to work and unreliable too.'

A gale of laughter had swept through the room and Keli shook her head. 'What are you like, Emily Montrose? I'll be reporting your complaints to your Ted when he comes up at visiting time,' she'd teased.

Emily had eyed her tartly. 'You go right ahead. He'll have forgotten by the time visiting ends. That man would forget his hat if his head wasn't cold.'

Somehow managing to smile, Keli had got the TV on to the right channel, relieved that the programme hadn't started yet, then attended to the charts of each patient, marking up their vitals.

By the time she'd finished with the ladies, and then repeated the tasks in the other rooms, Sima was charging through the door, Keli was relieved of her duties, and Yvie was steering her into the staffroom. Thankfully, it was empty, because Keli wasn't sure she could hold herself together for another second.

'Bugger, it's felt like a lifetime since that text,' Yvie groaned, flicking the kettle on. 'Okay, what do you need me to do? Do you want me to stay with you or leave you on your own to make the call and do the test to establish whether or not you're up the proverbial duff?'

'Stay. Please,' Keli shot back. It wasn't even up for deliberation.

'Oh, thank God you said that, because you'd have had to bring in a hostage negotiator to get me to leave. Right, what are we doing first, the test or are you going to phone her back?'

Keli pondered that for a moment, changing her mind a hundred times. There was no good option here. If the test was positive, she'd crumble and be unable to make the call. If she made the call first, the anxiety of knowing that she might be knocked up by another woman's boyfriend would kill her.

No good option, she thought again, so she was as well just getting to the quickest bad choice first.

'I'll call her back. It has to be a mistake. Doesn't it? A wrong number?'

Even as she was saying it, she could hear how desperate that sounded, especially when her gut was telling her something completely different.

Was there ever a sign that he could have another woman? Other than never letting her stay over at his place, nothing jumped out. At least... nothing that she'd caught on to.

Yvie came over to the table with two cups of tea and opened the biscuit tin. 'I'll start the diet again tomorrow.'

Keli's trembling hands opened her phone, checked the text again.

Hi. Sorry to do this, but I think you've been sleeping with my boyfriend. Can you call me back?

Yep, it still said the same thing. She hadn't imagined it.

She clicked on the text, got the number of the sender, pressed 'call', then put it on speaker and placed it in the middle of the table. It rang twice before it was answered. 'Hello?'

Keli froze. Gulped. Saw her wide-eyed shock and panic reflected right back at her from Yvie.

She tried to speak, but her vocal cords were stuck. She cleared her throat. Tried again. 'Hi, I got a text from this number earlier. This morning. A couple of hours ago.' She was rambling, so she pulled it back to the point. 'The text said something about me knowing your boyfriend. I think you must have the wrong number.'

A pause. The woman on the other end of the phone was probably embarrassed. She'd been upset, and must have keyed the wrong numbers.

'Is your name Keli?'

Her gasp was audible. Across from her, Yvie had her hand over her mouth and looked like she was about to combust.

Keli somehow managed a strangled, 'Yes.'

'Then I haven't got the wrong number.'

'I'm sorry, I don't understand...'

'My boyfriend,' the other woman interjected, 'has texts from you. Loads of them. And he probably deleted them from his phone, but they showed up on his iPad. The one that I'm staring at now.'

There was a roar inside Keli's skull. Nooooooooooooo. It couldn't be. It just couldn't.

'Oh my God, I had no idea,' she blurted, scrambling to make sense of this. Maybe this was a recent girlfriend. Or they'd split up and got back together. 'How long has he been your boyfriend?'

'Three years. And no, before you go all Ross and Rachel on me, we've never been on a break.'

That delivered an absolute whammy of a punch to her gut, and there was a pause that stretched until Keli forced her lungs to kick back in. Yet still she thought there had to be some mistake. It came to her that there was one way that she would know for sure.

'I'm sorry, but I still can't get my head around this. Are we definitely talking about the same guy. Is it... Ryan?' she asked, then held her breath.

The other woman had no such hesitation. 'Ryan...' she repeated slowly, then followed it up with an almost triumphant, 'Ryan Manning. So now you know we're on the same page. With the same guy.'

Keli responded to Yvie's questioning expression with a nod of her head. Ryan. Bastard. Manning.

She had no idea what to say next, but the other woman solved that problem, by going on, 'Look, I can hear from your voice that this is all coming as a complete shock to you.'

'It is. And I need to tell you I'm so sorry. If I'd known... Well, if I'd known I promise you this would never have happened.'

Keli wouldn't blame this woman if she didn't believe her. Not in the least. I mean, even to Keli it sounded ridiculous. How could she have gone out with someone for three months, fallen head over heels for him, given him her whole heart and not known he was already attached to someone else?

Her mind flew backwards. The night they'd met. It had been at a party, and they'd literally bumped into each other, then he'd insisted on refreshing her spilled glass of wine. They'd talked all night and she'd been so utterly captivated by him that she'd allowed him to take her home. They'd sat up talking until dawn, when he had to go to work, but not once did he seem uneasy, or act like there was somewhere else he should be.

Then there was Christmas. She'd done a double shift to let Sima have the day off with her kids, but he'd come round and picked her up when she'd finished at 11 p.m. On Hogmanay, they'd celebrated the turn of the New Year in her apartment, lying naked in front of the fire, watching his favourite old movie, *The Sting*, and eating a dinner that was cold because they'd been too lost in each other to eat it when the timer had buzzed and the oven had switched itself off.

They'd even spent two nights in a log cabin at Loch Lomond, not long before he'd disappeared off the face of the earth. That's what had been so confusing. That weekend, he'd told her he thought he could be falling in love with her, and she'd told him the same. They'd stayed in bed from the moment they arrived until they left, having food sent over from a nearby hotel. It was perfect. Yes, it was a whirlwind, but it felt completely real. He was the first man she'd ever said that to. And he was the first man who chose to walk away from her.

How could he have done all of that if he had a girlfriend? Apart from the emotional and physical betrayal, how could he possibly have explained his absences, especially on special days? This didn't make sense. There was still part of her that believed it had to be a mistake. Or a prank. Or some other kind of messed-up scam to get information from her.

Keli tuned back into the conversation, admitting, 'It's a complete shock. I still can't quite believe it.'

'And I'm guessing you're wondering if this is some kind of crazy set-up.' It was like she was reading her mind. The strange thing was, the woman at the other end didn't sound angry now. It was as though all the air had gone out of her ire, and she just sounded deflated. Confused. Crushed.

Keli recognised all those emotions because it was how she'd been feeling for the last month. 'Well, it's shocking and more than a little confusing. I have so many questions.'

'Me too. Look, can we meet up? I know that's going to sound incredibly random, but I just think we need to talk about this in person. I'm sorry I came on to the call so fired up, but I just thought you must have known and went out with him anyway. I'd really like us to have a conversation.'

Yvie was shaking her head furiously, mouthing, 'No. No. No way.'

'Y-yes.' Keli stammered. 'Okay.'

Yvie was now mimicking stabbing herself through the heart.

'Thing is, I know it's short notice, but are you around today? I'm free this afternoon. No. Sorry. I shouldn't have asked that. I can't expect you to drop everything...'

Yvie was gesturing wildly again. No. Don't do it.

'I can do that,' Keli agreed, much to Yvie's very obvious disgust.

Yvie grabbed a pen from the table and scrawled PUBLIC PLACE!!!!!! on her biscuit wrapper.

Keli was already going down that train of thought. 'How about the lobby of the St Kentigern hotel in an hour? Would that be okay?'

It was about a half-hour drive from the hospital, but it was on the way to the motorway that would take her to her mum's house in Weirbridge and she was headed there anyway, so it made sense. It was also somewhere very public, somewhere she felt safe, and somewhere there was a bar if she needed to ditch the car and drink an emergency glass of wine.

'That would work.'

'How will I recognise you?' Keli had waited her whole life to ask the classic movie line, but never imagined it would be in a situation like this.

'I'll recognise you. I'm looking at a picture of you right now. You're wearing a red dress.'

Keli knew exactly what picture it was. It had been at her mum's birthday dinner. The theme was scarlet. Ryan had said he couldn't make it – which had been disappointing as she'd really wanted him to meet her family. Up until then, they'd been in this little bubble of solitude, just the two of them, locked away from the world when they were together. He'd asked her to send a photo since he couldn't be there, so she'd had Noah snap a pic of her. She had been laughing at something her brother had said, happy, excited that she would be seeing Ryan later that night. This woman having that photo was even more proof that this definitely wasn't a prank. This was serious. It was a high risk situation. One that was almost certainly going to hurt. One that she should definitely avoid. And yet...

'Yes, that was me. I'll see you in an hour.'

2 P.M. – 4 P.M.

13

ODETTE

Odette had been trying to navigate the device for the last half-hour, with no success. Just when she was at the point of hurling it across the room, Calvin came back into her dressing room, arms wide. He stopped. Shocked.

'Are you using an iPad? Is it a blue moon? The dawning of the apocalypse? Are pigs flying?'

His surprise was understandable. The iPad had been provided by the studio and had sat in a holder on her desk for years. Odette knew most women her age were perfectly competent with technology, but it had never interested her in the slightest to learn. She barely even used her mobile phone. Why waste time figuring these things out when there was always someone else around to do it all for her?

As for the iPad, she had a basic knowledge of how to work it, thanks to Calvin's patient instruction, but the only time she ever used it was to put on a bit of Tony Bennett or Michael Bublé. Until twenty minutes ago, that was. That's when she'd given Elliot, the documentary director, the same old made-up story about how she'd got her first break, then watched him and the cameraman leave. As soon as the door closed behind them, she'd opened it and went on to the page that searched for stuff.

'No, I'm just trying to track someone down. Will you help me?'

'I will indeed, but not right now, because at this very second you're being summoned to feast on sausage rolls and tuna vol-au-vents,' he drawled, with a mock bow.

Odette sighed, checked her lippy and dragged her aching bones off the sofa. One more official function. This was it. A buffet lunch with the cast and crew. Then, tonight, she was having dinner with Calvin. As soon as it was over, her diary was empty. She was free. And that thought absolutely devastated her.

'Calvin, can I ask you something. Why are you always so damn happy with life?'

He thought about that for a second. 'Because I love my job, my Botox is on point, and I go home to my husband every night, who, for his sins, is stuck with me until death do us part.'

Odette nodded ruefully. 'I thought that about my last husband too. Number four. And number three before him. Admittedly, I realised on my honeymoon that my second marriage was a spontaneous mistake and the first one was a folly of youth.'

'Ever wonder what happened to them all?' Calvin asked, and he seemed genuinely intrigued. Odette had ensured that it had been written into the documentary contract that it would focus on her career, and not on the trials and tribulations of her personal life. It was there in black and white that they couldn't contact any of her ex-husbands. The last thing she needed were those skeletons coming out of that closet.

'First one, Jake, passed away when we were in our thirties. Motorbike accident. Second one has been living in Marbella for the last thirty years, thanks to a very generous divorce settlement. The third one, same story, but lives on a golf course in Florida and the last one... Still haunting me, like the arse that he is. Last I heard from Mitchum Royce was a letter to my lawyer, saying he was suing me for fraud, because it turned out the Elvis impersonator we used for our wedding in Las Vegas wasn't ordained. He's saying that I had prior knowledge of this and claims that he's emotionally traumatised and unable to form emotional connections due to my duplicity. Although that didn't seem to be an issue when he was buggering off with Tootsie from Tallahassee, the waitress he picked up on his next trip to Sin City. The truth is, he's pissed off because if the marriage wasn't legal, it means he can't take anything from me in a divorce.' She stopped before she revealed that there was nothing left to take, because he'd already spent it all, and left her with a mountain of debt. She still couldn't bear to admit, even to Calvin, that Mitchum had ruined her.

It was such a bloody cliché – the actress getting exploited by men who swore they loved her for herself, not for the stardom or the money. Odette told herself that if it happened to Marilyn Monroe, it could happen to the best of them.

Calvin's chin was on the ground. 'Noooo. So, hang on, did you know that it wasn't legal?'

'Of course not. If I had, I wouldn't have bothered with the prenup. He just keeps coming back, looking for ways to get a payday from the cash cow. That would be me.'

'Well, the cash cow is about to have her way with a satay stick, so such matters will have to wait.'

Odette paused. 'In case I don't tell you this enough, I know I'm a handful...'

'Caustic but true,' Calvin retorted.

'But I really appreciate every single thing you do for me. And I'm aware that this is our last day together too. I supposed I hadn't really thought about that.'

'Odette, you're not dying. You're just retiring. I'll still be in the office if you need me, and I'll still handle any enquiries we get for work for you.'

'Urgh, the bloody optimism is almost as annoying as the relentless happiness. There should be a law against it.' They both knew that there had been zero enquiries, zero offers, zero interest. She was done. Washed up. Over. But right now there was still one more part to play. If it was an Oscar category, it would be 'Sacked Actress in a Graceful and Dignified Exit'. 'Right, let's go show those bastards what they'll be missing.'

She touched up her own lippy in the mirror, using her trademark Dior Rouge scarlet lipstick. Agnes McGlinchy would have been outraged at the extravagance.

Calvin held the door open for her, and for the second time today, Odette pulled herself up to her full five foot two inches, shoulders back, chin out, and wafted on down the corridor. After her emotional response earlier, she was determined to show that she was a paragon of calm composure, class and elegance, even though inside, she was still screaming at the injustice of being pushed out to pasture. For forty years, she'd called the shots and enjoyed the acclaim. This was the first time in her professional career that she was being rejected. She didn't need a therapist to tell her that she was going to have a visceral reaction to that. She just hadn't expected it to be in public.

As soon as she walked into the canteen, the room erupted in applause and Odette began to work the crowd, steering clear of the buffet that had probably had sticky fingers all over it. Out of the corner of her eye, she saw the documentary camera following her every move, so she made sure she gave them her best side and never dropped her face. They weren't getting any loose chins on this chick.

There were only two genuine goodbyes in the room. The first was to the team of women who ran the canteen. After her tenure as a school dinner lady, she'd always had an affinity with the women, some of whom had been there as long as her. The second was to Tress, who, as promised, slipped a piece of paper into her hand with her telephone number on it. The younger woman had been standing chatting to Rex Marino, but she took a step to the side to speak to Odette.

'Please do keep in touch, Odette. I'll miss you. And it would be lovely to have a proper chat when we're not surrounded by all these ears,' she joked.

Odette, not usually one for public displays of affection, gave her a hug, then cursed herself when the entanglement of arms somehow got caught in her hair and shifted her wig. She swiftly readjusted it and prayed the camera hadn't caught it.

A quick glance to the side told her that Elliot was gesturing to the cameraman to pan the room, so hopefully she was in the clear.

The sound of a spoon clanging on a glass rang out and a hush fell as the show director, Carl Newman, stepped up onto a makeshift stage at the front of the room. 'Ladies and gentlemen, if I could have your attention, please.'

Of course, everyone obliged. Carl was one of the new hires that the studio had made to shake the show up and bring in a new generation to its dwindling viewing figures, so, of course, everyone was concerned that they'd be next on the chopping block and therefore treated him like he was the second coming of Jesus.

Carl cleared his throat, and then held his hand out in Odette's direction. 'Odette, if I could ask you to join me on the stage, please?'

All she wanted to do was tell him to foxtrot right off, but she couldn't drop the congeniality act, because she refused to look petty. Instead, she glided gracefully to the front of the room, and elegantly stepped up, ignoring the hand he was offering her for balance, an internal monologue running in her mind. *I'd rather fall flat on my face than take your hand, you two-faced little shit.*

'Odette, it really has been magnificent to have worked with you over the last few months...'

Right up until you fired me.

'And I know that I speak for everyone in this room, when I say that your talent and your presence will be greatly missed by us all.'

You won't give me a second thought from the minute I walk out of that door.

'Hear, Hear!' Rex Marino cheered loudly.

Her internal voice now lashed out at her co-star. *And you should stop trying to attract attention to yourself, you flash arse. I see right through you.*

Carl was speaking again. 'So, on behalf of the cast, the crew and the studio, we wanted to honour you with this award...' With that, he handed over a glass ornament, carved in the shape of *The Clydeside* logo, with the words on the front...

Odette Devine,
a shining star on *The Clydeside* from 1983–2023.
With love and thanks from all at the show, and your millions of fans.

Forty years, and all I get is a crappy ornament.

But, of course, she showed her gratitude to the watching crowd with a beaming smile and a bow, which took more acting skill than she'd had to muster for her farewell scene this morning.

'All we ask now, is that you enjoy every second of your retirement...'

I was sacked...

'And spend wonderful days with your family...'

I have no one. Not a single family member on this earth.

'And your friends.'

None of those either. Sacrificed them all for my career. In fact, the last time I had genuine friends, was...

'And enjoy the memories of a stellar career and four spectacular decades of achievement here at *The Clydeside*.'

That was it. 1983. The last time I had genuine friends. How was that a life well lived?

Another rumble of applause, with cheers and hoots of congratulation filled the room and Odette felt the same crushing tightness in her chest that she'd had this morning, right before she'd crumbled into a sobbing mess.

'Speech! Speech!' someone in the crowd yelled out.

Odette inhaled, exhaled, used every exercise she'd ever been taught to calm her nerves and her racing heart.

Somehow, by some miracle, she managed to find her voice. 'I'd just like to say thank you. For forty years. For Agnes McGlinchy. And for the wonderful members of the cast and crew who have shown me so much kindness over the years.'

Except the ones who've been truly fucking horrible to me. I hope karma serves up the same kind of misery that it's doled out to me.

That thought was so powerful, like a kick to the side of the head. Karma. That's why her life had been a complete shit show. It was why she had no one left. Why she was going to finish her days in lonely misery.

She couldn't get another word out, so instead, she held up the pathetic glass award and smiled, like a football player holding up a trophy after a winning game.

Karma had screwed her. And the regrets that had been on her mind all day, were the reason that the Gods of Karma were decimating her life.

Once again, Calvin helped her from the stage, and guided her out of the canteen and back to her dressing room. If anyone tried to say a personal goodbye, she didn't see them, too focused on staring straight ahead, holding it together until she could get out of here and find some kind of way to deal with the prospect of the empty, barren life that was in front of her. If this was what karma had done to her, it was time to start fighting back. And she was ready to start doing that.

Since this morning, an idea had been forming in her mind, but she didn't think she'd have the strength or courage to see it through. Now she knew that she had to. If she had any hope of putting her life right, she had to make amends for what she'd done forty years ago.

As soon as she got back into the dressing room for the final time, Calvin blew out all the stresses of his day. 'Right, my lovely, let's get the hell out of here. We've got the studio limo for one more night, so let's ride home in style, get dolled up, then head out for a feast tonight. It's on the company credit card so you can eat caviar off your thumbs if you like.'

The mention of the limo brought up another problem that Odette was going to have to contend with. She'd never learned to drive, so she didn't have a car. How was she going to get around now? The cost of taxis was horrendous and the thought of going on a bus made her shudder. More karma. And besides, her over-60 bus pass was still in a drawer in the kitchen, because she preferred to remain in denial that she was old enough to be eligible for it.

'Indeed, let's go,' she replied, picking up the bag that was packed and sitting by the door. As almost an afterthought, she snatched up her dressing room iPad. Strictly speaking, she supposed it could be called theft, but she was going to choose to call it a parting gift. She handed it over to Calvin. 'Can you take this, because on the way I need you to do me a favour.'

If he questioned the liberation of the iPad from the room, he didn't bring it up. 'Anything for you,' he told her, with dramatic exaggeration.

'Good. Because remember I said I need you to help me find someone I used to know? Well, no time like the present. Her name is Nancy Jenkins.'

14

TRESS

Tress was actually a little taken aback as to how sad she was that Odette was leaving the show. There had been speculation that she had been pushed, as opposed to jumping ship, but Tress didn't know that for sure. She'd only been with the studio for six months, so she wasn't on the inside track with production or network decisions yet. She hoped the rumour wasn't true. Just as she hoped the rumours that Odette could be a demanding diva weren't true either. Tress had always found her to be perfectly pleasant and she'd enjoyed getting to know her, so she was going to take the stories with a pinch of gossipy salt.

Gossip, she'd realised, was rife in this studio. That's why she'd only spoken to Rex for two minutes at Odette's lunch, and even then, there were people around them, so it was purely professional. Although, her face had been burning the whole time, so she'd been relieved when Odette had come over and interrupted them so she could say goodbye.

After Odette left, the assembled crowd split into two groups – those who had imbibed a few glasses of wine and who were looking like they wanted to make a boozy afternoon of it, and the others who were intent on getting back to work. Tress was in the latter group.

She'd quietly slipped out of the canteen and headed for her office, deciding to take the stairs, because, well… strange things seemed to be happening to her in lifts these days.

She'd just pushed through the fire door and out onto the landing when she realised someone was coming through behind her. 'Hey!'

There was no need to turn around to see who it was, but she did anyway.

'Look, I just wanted to say sorry. About earlier. And I really hope that wasn't some secret boyfriend, because if it was, then I'll expect him to be waiting outside to kick my arse later.'

'Not my boyfriend. That was my friend, Noah.'

'Ah, the best friend you told me about – the one that people are constantly suggesting you should hook up with.'

Tress grinned. 'Something like that.'

Rex leaned back against the banister, arms crossed, that gorgeous laconic smile on his face. 'Well, I thoroughly recommend that you definitely do not get together. Not under any circumstances. In fact, I recommend that you consider a new relationship with someone far more exciting.'

Okay, they were flirting. She could do this. Somewhere in the basement of her dating game memories, there was a handbook she'd last read many years ago.

'Oh really? And do you have any suggestions as to who that should be?'

He nodded thoughtfully. 'One or two.'

Tress's turn to cultivate a thoughtful response now. 'Okay, well, if you send me their dating profiles and headshots, I'll take a look.'

That made him laugh, and at the same time he reached over and gave the waistband of her trousers a playful tug towards him.

She didn't resist. When they were toe to toe, he leaned down and kissed her. For a glorious second, there was a rush of heat around her body, until she remembered where they were and quickly broke away and stepped back.

'I'm sorry. I can't. Not here. If anyone saw us, it would be...' It took her a few seconds to find the words. 'It would be a nightmare for me. It would put me right in the centre of attention, and that's somewhere I make it my life mission to avoid.'

'You're right,' he said and, to her relief, didn't make another move forwards. 'Although, I will point out that no one uses the stairs in this place.'

She felt herself begin to relax, now that they were just two colleagues having a chat in a stairwell.

'So, I have a problem...' he continued, and she could sense from his tone that he was playing with her.

'Really? What's that?'

'Well, despite having hordes of fans waiting outside for me every day, and even though I get at least a dozen naked pictures sent to me on a weekly basis, it would appear that I'm not all that special after all. You see, I asked this woman out... She's gorgeous, you'd like her...' The twinkle in his eye was making her blush. 'And she took ages to finally agree that she'd go on a date with me next Saturday night. But now, I find myself unable to stop thinking about her, so I'm thinking that perhaps I'd like to take her out tonight as well. What do you think? Any chance she'd say yes?'

The prickles of anxiety that had been coming and going all day came bristling right back. Tonight? No. She couldn't. It was Buddy's birthday today. It was also the anniversary of a piece of her heart being broken off forever. Tonight, she wanted pyjamas, she wanted wine, she wanted snacks, she wanted back-to-back episodes of *Property Brothers*, and she wanted to indulge in alternating between feeling grateful for her son, feeling furious with his father, and being heartbroken that he was gone. Oh, and she planned to have a good cry at least once. That was a whole load of emotional pendulum swings there, and she felt that she had every right to allow herself to sit in her feelings, given that she'd spent a year trying to mask them.

But then...

Her thoughts flicked to the phone call earlier, with Nancy offering to spend the night babysitting Buddy, and saying that he'd be in bed by seven o'clock anyway. That part was definitely true.

She then heard Val and Nancy's voices, giving her a stern lecture about living her life, seizing moments and getting back on the relationship horse. This wasn't the particular stallion they had in mind, but at least it was a trot in the right direction.

Tress made a quick calculation. If she left work now, she could go home and work there for a few hours, just as she usually did on a Friday. That way, when Val and Nancy brought Buddy back from the petting zoo, she could spend some time with her son and give him his dinner. Then, when he went to bed, she could park the idea of wine, home-makeover shows and a huge bucket of self-pity, and instead, say yes to the handsome, successful man who was standing in front of her right now, asking her to go out with him. The same one she'd snogged the face off earlier in the day. And maybe this time, it wouldn't feel so fricking awkward and she'd actually relax enough to enjoy it. Sod it, she might even shave her legs in case she got lucky, because, after all, she didn't owe anyone any kind of self-restraint. Hadn't her husband been off with his mistress on the day he died? Well, she damn well deserved to allow herself to rejoin the human race and have a bit of fun too.

'Did I also mention that the woman I asked out takes a really long time to make a decision and when she's thinking really hard about something, she gets the cutest little lines on her forehead?'

And, sod it again, she was damn well getting Botox.

'Okay.'

'Okay?'

'Yes. The old hag with the wrinkles on her forehead will go out with you. Tonight. But tell me where I've to be and then run before I change my mind because I'm finding this all mildly terrifying.'

'Yasssss!' He punched the air. 'And you don't have to be anywhere, because I'll come and collect you.'

'No,' she blurted, and his expression made it clear he didn't understand the objection. Or maybe he just wasn't used to that word. Tress had a feeling he didn't hear it often.

'No?'

She desperately backpedalled on the outburst. 'I mean, I live out in Weirbridge. It's miles away. I wouldn't ask you to come out there to pick me up.'

'I live in the West End, and it'll take me twenty minutes from there. Honestly, it's fine. At least that way I know you'll show, and I won't be left staring into the bottom of a beer bottle like Nobby No Mates.'

Tress pondered that. It did make sense. It would make life easier. And if Nancy found out that Rex Marino was taking her out tonight and she didn't get to see him, she'd be apoplectic and may never speak to her again.

'Okay. Pebble Cottage. River Lane. Weirbridge. And can you make it 8 p.m., because I'll need that time to put my son down, grab a shower, and schedule in at least three panics because I haven't dressed up to go out at night for the last year.'

'Done.' Wow, the dimple in his chin was so sexy when he smiled. 'And you can wear anything you like. Joggers. Pyjamas. Bin bag.'

'Don't joke. At least one of those was on my previous plans for tonight.'

He leaned over, kissed her on the lips, just a warm, gorgeous, brief, touch.

'See you later?' he murmured.

'You will. Now run.'

Laughing, he turned, bolted through the door, and left her to travel one flight of stairs to her office. There, she packed up her stuff, changing her mind with every item she put in her bag. Laptop. *I'm going to cancel.* Pen. *No, I'm not.* Mobile phone. *I can't do this.* Notepad. *Don't be bloody ridiculous, of course you can.* It was a relief when she grabbed her jacket and made her way out to the car, because at least she was forced to pay attention to the world.

At the front entrance, Bob, the security guard, gave her a nod as he opened the door for her. 'Bye Tress. Great to see Dr Noah today. Lifesaver, that man.'

'He sure is, Bob. Have a good weekend. Love to Mrs Bob and the family.'

'I'll be sure to tell Mrs Bob you said that.' She could still hear him chuckling when she crossed the road to the car park.

For a moment, she couldn't remember where she'd put the car, because this morning had been a bit of a blur, but a press of the key fob set off a beep that told her where it was.

The traffic was just starting to get busy, but she still made it back to Weirbridge in the usual half-hour. As Tress drove into the village, she spotted an empty space right outside the general store. It felt like a sign, so she pulled in and hopped out of the car, deciding to pick up some flowers for Nancy and Val. Not that a couple of bouquets could even begin to repay them for all they'd done for her and Buddy over the last year, but she took any excuse to show them that she cared and that she was grateful for them.

On the left of the flower section, there was a pyramid of Budweiser cases, so she picked up one of those for Noah too. He'd mentioned that he was popping over to his mum's for dinner tonight, but she could leave them at his house for when he got home. And yes, maybe she was just pre-empting the guilt of texting him to say that she was going out on a date on the most significant day of their year. The thing was, she knew he wouldn't mind. All she and Noah wanted for each other was happiness. No pressure. No rules. No expectations. Just unconditional love and mutual support.

Back in the car, she whipped round to his house, only a couple of streets away from her own, jumped out, grabbed the case of beer and was halfway up his path when she realised that someone was sitting on the bench by his front door.

Not just someone.

Tress's body took charge and shut down. She stopped dead. Her legs refused to move. Her eyes narrowed on the woman in front of her.

Her former friend.

Noah's ex-wife.

The woman her husband was sleeping with for the entire duration of their marriage.

After the longest of pauses, the words that came out sounded nothing like her own voice.

'What are you doing here, Anya?'

15

NOAH

Keli had called just as Noah was running to the restaurant. He'd answered with a breathless, 'Hey, you.'

'Are you okay? Are you being chased? Or running a marathon?' she'd asked.

'How did you know?' He'd still been panting as he got the words out. 'Margot Robbie and Cameron Diaz are chasing me up the street, demanding I become their personal physician. It's hellish being this popular.'

'I wouldn't know. I've made it my life mission to try to be unpopular. Saves a fortune on stamps and birthday cards. Why are you breathing like that? What's going on? Don't answer that if it's something inappropriate for your sister to hear.'

'Definitely nothing inappropriate. I'm just rushing to meet Cheska for lunch and I'm late. I popped in to see Tress at the studio and got held up.'

'You've no idea how happy I am that it's nothing to do with Anya. What did she want? And whatever it was, I hope you refused.'

Noah would have sighed but he was too busy just trying to breathe. 'She wants to meet later. Says she needs to talk to me.'

'And I hope you said no?'

'I said yes.'

'Argh, you are too fricking nice.'

'I believe I've heard that already today. Look, whatever it is she needs to say, I'll listen, then I'll leave.'

'You promise? Please tell me you're still coming to Mum's tonight for dinner. Takes the pressure off me when the golden child is there.' It was a never-ending source of teasing that Noah was their mum's favourite. Of course, it wasn't true. Gilda treated all her children with equal amounts of love, care, affection and dictatorial tendencies.

'I'll definitely be there. I said I'd meet Anya at five o'clock, though, so it'll be after that.'

'If you don't show up, I'm rounding up a posse to come find you,' Keli had warned.

'You do that. What are you up to now? Are you on the way to Mum's already?'

'Yeah, but I'm stopping off to meet a...' Pause. 'Friend first.'

'A male friend? Keli Clark, are you finally going to stop being secretive about your love life and bring someone home to meet Mum? I beg you to do it. Take the heat off me.'

'Nope, it's the penalty for being the golden child. Good and bad, it's all about you.'

He was laughing when he'd replied, 'Happy to pass that title over to anyone who'll have it. Look, I have to go. That's me at the restaurant. Love you, sis.'

'I love you too. Say hi to Cheska for me. And Noah, when you see Anya, don't be too easy on her. Remember what she did to you.'

'Like I could ever forget.'

Cheska had already been at the table when he'd rushed into

the restaurant and as he'd crossed the room, he'd watched her stirring her coffee and thought how she'd barely changed in the twenty years he'd known her.

They'd first met at university, where they were both studying medicine and living in the same halls of residence. In their first year, they'd hung out in the same crowd, and she had recently reminded him that they'd once had a drunken snog after way too many shots at the student union. Then, of course, at the start of his second year, Anya had walked into the freshers' week reception, stopped to talk to him and that was it. He was locked in, and even the very cute aspiring doctor, with auburn hair, deep green eyes, a ferocious brain and the highest marks in the class couldn't make him stray. But they'd stayed in touch, just as friends, and he'd given her the heads-up about ten years ago that his hospital was looking for a new A&E doctor. Of course, she'd got the job, because she was brilliant.

Working in the same building had made their friendship even easier. A couple of years ago, he'd supported her when she'd gone through a divorce from her husband of a decade, and over the last twelve months she'd done the same for him and more. If stepping up to help a friend was an Olympic sport, she'd have been a medal winner. A few months ago, they'd finally graduated from friends to something more. This morning, talking to Nancy and Val, he'd referred to her as his girlfriend, but that had just been in jest. The reality was that they were just two friends who spent the night together when it suited them. That was all he was ready for, and it gave Cheska the freedom she needed to focus on her work.

He'd occasionally wondered what his life would have been like if he'd got together with Cheska back at Uni. They'd have graduated together, worked a million hours each, barely seen one another for all the years that they were frazzled, overworked junior doctors, and then he'd have felt nothing but pride as he watched her climb through the ranks to be the youngest chief of A&E in Glasgow Central's history. Not that it was a surprise. In the hospital, she was a powerhouse of organisation and decisiveness, and when those skills were combined with her razor-sharp medical brain, there was no one more impressive.

Out of work, though, she was a completely different person. Kind. Fun. Generous. The type of woman who had volunteered to come on holiday when Val and Don, Nancy and Johnny, Tress, Buddy and Noah were all going off to Cyprus for their first group trip. For the last few years, as well as her own job, Cheska had been working on a research project around dementia and Alzheimer's, so she'd offered to come along with them and help Val take care of her husband. That was probably the moment that he'd realised they had a shot at making this work. Although, they were both quite content to just go with the flow and see where they ended up.

'Hey, gorgeous,' he greeted her, and she flinched with the surprise of someone who had just been interrupted when they were deep in thought. He leaned down to kiss her, and she automatically turned her face up to meet his. She still had the auburn hair, and the pretty green eyes, and now she also had the most endearing frown when she was mulling something over. Today, the frown was there, so she clearly had something on her mind. He thought back to her comment earlier about wanting to talk to him about something, but before he could ask, the owner, Carlo, came over to greet him. 'Dr Noah! Good to see you. Your lovely sister tells me you're working too hard and that's why you haven't been in for weeks.'

Keli frequented this place weekly, because her friend, Yvie, was engaged to Carlo. If Noah was ever having a secret meeting, this wasn't the place to do it.

'Yep, she's probably right. How are you doing, my friend. All good?'

'Too much work, not enough sleep, and I'm getting older every day,' Carlo answered with his stock reply, as he put the menu down in front of Noah. It wouldn't be needed – he already knew it off by heart.

'The usual?' Carlo checked. 'An Americano and a still water?'

'You read my mind, Carlo.'

'One of my many gifts.' With that, he bustled off to the next table, arms wide, greeting the diners like long-lost friends.

Preliminaries over, Noah was about to ask Cheska if all was well, when she got in there first.

'How's today been? Are you okay? How's Tress?'

Leaning forward, elbows on the table, he took one of her hands, feeling a sudden need for human touch.

The truth? Today had rattled him. He'd been dreading it for weeks, and now that it was here, he couldn't wait for it to be over. All anniversaries were difficult after the loss of a partner, especially the first ones. The first birthdays. The first Christmas. The first holiday. But Noah had lost not just his wife, but his lifelong best mate too. Not that he'd ever say it aloud, but he still wasn't sure who he missed more.

The biggest struggle of all after the accident was, however, that he'd also lost all faith in his judgement. How had he not seen any of it coming? How could he not have known that the two people he was closest to on this earth were capable of the lies, the subterfuge, the betrayal. The surprise visit from Anya this morning had just brought back that feeling of ambush.

'It's been... unexpected,' he answered honestly. 'It started out well when I stopped in to have a birthday breakfast with Buddy, but then when I got to work, I had a visitor.'

Cheska took a sip of her coffee. 'A good visitor? Or the kind of visitor that makes you want to pretend you're not on duty?'

'Anya,' he said simply, answering her question in the most direct way possible.

Cheska almost spluttered her coffee out. 'Noooooo.' She sat back, puffed out her cheeks and the frown reappeared between her brows. 'Christ, she's got some balls. What did she want?'

Noah shrugged. 'I've got no idea. She just said she wants to talk.'

'And you refused, because you're a normal human being who has instinctive emotional responses that make him avoid people or things that can cause him pain?' She was staring at him, waiting for confirmation. When she didn't get it, she visibly deflated. There was a thick overtone of resignation in her voice now. 'No, you didn't. You agreed to talk to her because you're way too decent to turn her away.' Noah couldn't read if that was a compliment or an insult.

'I'm seeing her at five o'clock. And please don't give me a lecture about being too nice because Tress and Keli beat you to it. I just... She was my wife, Cheska,' he repeated the same mitigation he'd thrown out earlier to Tress.

The irony of this situation was that the one person who used to balance him out, tell him to buck up when he was being too soft, or stand right next to him in times of conflict, was Max. Bastard.

Noah braced himself for Cheska to try to talk him out of it or give him a dozen reasons why he shouldn't do it, but the objections didn't come. 'I know there's no point arguing,' she said, almost wearily. 'You'll do it anyway.'

There was an uncomfortable silence that lasted a bit too long and he wasn't sure how to tackle it. Cheska was usually so easy to talk to, and there had been barely a cross word between them since they'd been together, so this was way out of his wheelhouse.

Cheska broke the agitated silence first. She took a deep breath, as if resetting the conversation. 'You didn't tell me how Tress was. Today can't be easy for her.'

One of Carlo's waiters arrived with Noah's drinks and, in all honesty, he was glad of the interruption. He wasn't sure how to describe how Tress was today. That scene in her office earlier had been the second surprise of the day. 'She's... bearing up.'

The waiter interjected with, 'Do you need more time with the menu or are we good to go?'

'Are you ready to order?' Noah asked Cheska, almost a hundred per cent positive that she would go with the Caesar salad, no cheese, no anchovies.

'Caesar salad, no cheese, no anchovies, please,' she said, handing the menu back to the gent with the notepad.

Noah did the same. 'I'll have the chicken tagliatelle please.'

The waiter nodded and retreated back to the kitchen, forcing Noah's attention back to the conversation. Where were they? Tress.

He told Cheska all about the birthday breakfast, about how Tress was determined not to spend the day wallowing in memories and regret. The waiter brought their meals, just as he was saying how he was blown away by her strength and resilience and her determination to carve out a happy life for Buddy.

'And I think she's having a pretty unexpected day too,' he remarked.

Cheska raised an eyebrow of curiosity.

'I went by the studio to tell her about Anya's reappearance and she was in her office, lip locked with that actor from the show. Rex.'

A whole series of emotions crossed her face and he wasn't sure he was keeping up with them. 'Wow,' she blurted. 'And how was that? Awkward?'

Noah's fork paused mid-air, as he realised that he wasn't quite sure what to say.

'Erm, yeah, a bit. Just strange really. Haven't seen her with anyone since... well, Max. But I'm happy for her. I'm glad she's met someone.'

Cheska leaned forward on the table. 'Really, Noah?'

That surprised him. 'Of course. I want her to be happy.'

Okay, this was going left and he wasn't quite sure why. Cheska was acting strange. Sceptical. Agitated. It was so unlike her. Their time together was usually nothing but chilled-out togetherness with some laughs thrown in. What was he missing?

Their conversation from earlier came back to him again and he immediately pivoted. 'Shit, sorry – I've just rambled about everything that's been going on with me today and I haven't even asked what you wanted to talk about. Is something wrong? Are you okay? What's happening?'

Before she replied, she picked up a piece of bread from the basket in the middle of the table, broke a piece off. That's when he realised she was trying to figure out what to say. Oh, shit. This wasn't good.

'I've been offered a new job.'

'What? That's amazing! You really should have led with that,' he told her, a mixture of relief and genuine happiness for her. 'You didn't say you'd applied for anything. Keeping secrets, Dr Ayton?' he teased her. It took him a second to spot that she wasn't laughing. Didn't seem thrilled about her news. Wasn't exactly celebrating.

'I guess I was. Noah, the job is in Seattle. It's a research post with a non-profit that's looking at potential correlations between the early identification of Alzheimer's and presentations in A&E. Could have been designed for me.'

Fork down, he sat back, appetite gone. Seattle? Hang on. What was happening here? What did this actually mean? This wasn't making sense to him. 'Wait... Are you going to take it?'

'I am. I'm just sorry I had to tell you about this today, but I handed my notice in at the hospital this morning and I didn't want you to hear about it before I told you.'

Wow. All the jubilation from a few seconds ago had just been sucked out of the room.

'And you didn't want to talk to me about it before you took the job either? Even just as a friend?'

As she shook her head, he saw that her eyes had filled with tears. He'd never seen that before. Cheska had spent most of her career working in A&E and she'd long ago mastered the ability to hide her emotions in difficult situations. 'No. I didn't. Because I didn't want you to change my mind.'

'But what about us? You're walking away from you and me?'

What the fuck was happening in his life? And why today? Next year he was going to stay home on February 9th and just let the world turn without him.

'I am,' she said, words oozing sadness. 'Because I don't really think we have an "us". Noah, I love you. And when we got together, I thought maybe...' The words caught in her throat, so she paused, before repeating herself, then going on, 'I thought maybe this was it. The forever. All that hearts and happy ever after stuff. And I knew you'd need time, but, Noah, nothing is going to change. The way we are is the way we are always going to be.'

'That's not true...' he began to object.

She reached over and put her hands over his. 'It is. And that's okay. I'll always be the person after Anya, the one who came along when your life had been crushed by someone else. I'll always be the friend that became someone more. And I'll always be second to the other priorities in your life, to Tress, to Buddy...'

That irritated him. 'Wait a minute, Cheska, I never said you were second to anyone...'

'You didn't have to. Noah, we never talk about the future. We never discuss what we are to each other. You never talk about where we go from here. And you never say that you couldn't live without me.'

The force of that stunned him. 'But that doesn't mean I don't love you, because I do.'

'I know you do. The thing is, Noah, shallow as it sounds... I want to be the priority.'

'But wait, you always said that your work was your priority. So doesn't that go both ways?'

She nodded. 'Yes. You're right. But I think an element of that was a defence mechanism, because you weren't ready to go all in. I would have changed that for you if you'd asked, but you didn't.'

'How was I supposed to know that?' He felt blindsided. Completely confused.

Cheska shrugged. 'I guess I wanted you to fight for me. I want to come first with the man I love. And if I can't have that with you, then I'd rather walk away now because it hurts too much to keep waiting and hoping.'

The thing that stung the most was that he couldn't argue with anything she was saying. Or give her guarantees.

'Cheska, give us more time. Bear with me...'

'No. I can't, Noah.' Tears were streaming down her cheeks now. 'I want more for myself. I'm sorry.' Lunch abandoned, she lifted the strap of her bag off the back of the chair and brought it round to her lap. 'I'm going to go.'

'Wait, so that's it? There must be something we can do. Talk to me. Tell me what I can do right now to make this work.'

There was a flash of something in her eyes, as if she were daring him.

'There's only one thing that will fix this, Noah. Come to America with me. Choose me. Do you think you could do that?'

16

KELI

Keli had almost changed her mind and turned her car around at least ten times on the journey. As soon as she'd got into her little Mini, out of habit, and mostly to distract herself, she'd called Noah, to find out what had happened with Anya this morning. Noah had answered straight away, but his breathing had been laboured as he'd given her the update. Yet calling him had helped. Despite every single part of her life being in the toilet, Keli couldn't help but feel better when she spoke to him. The way he'd taken care of Tress in the last year hadn't surprised her one bit. He'd always been the one who'd looked out for everyone else and the whole golden child tag was just their way of teasing him for being far too bloody perfect. Tall. Handsome. Doctor. Funny. Caring. And all-round good guy. If Keli didn't love him so much, she'd get a complex.

If ever there was someone who surprised her with their actions, it was her former sister-in-law. Keli had adored Anya. Looked up to her. Wanted to be just like her. Yet, the whole time, Anya was lying to them and cheating on her brother with his best mate. Keli had no idea how Noah could even give that woman the time of day now, but it did prove the point that had been going back and forth in Keli's mind since she'd got that text earlier: if the sister-in-law who'd always seemed like the most decent of people could tell the most horrific lies, then so could the bloke who had swept her off her feet and then vanished off the face of the earth.

What. A. Mess. For all of them.

Although, it was ironic that she'd promised to round up a posse to track Noah down if he didn't show at Mum's tonight, given that she was the one who was on her way to meet a complete stranger. This could be a kidnap plot that would have her tied up in the back of a transit van within the hour. And yes, she'd binge-watched too many episodes of *Special Victims Unit* over the last month.

But still... What was she thinking? Seriously. Meeting this random woman had to be – as Yvie said – the most batshit crazy idea ever. This could be a complete set-up. It could be a highly slick, devious scam. Or maybe... another sickening wave of nausea... maybe it was a journalist, fishing for a story, or one of those catfish documentaries. That thought had caused sweat to pop out of every pore and she'd put her window down, even though it was bloody freezing outside.

Keli had hung up just as she was coming round to the parking spaces in the street in front of the St Kentigern. A grand building, overlooking a beautiful garden square, it was one of the most stunning hotels in the city, a triumph of Victorian architecture.

She checked the clock. A few minutes after two. Today had already felt like it had lasted a lifetime and it was only mid-afternoon.

She spotted someone pulling out of a space right in front of the door, and slid straight in after them. It was the first lucky thing that had happened to her all day.

As promised, she fired off a quick text to Yvie.

About to go into hotel. If I show up on some dodgy Insta Live in the next hour, let me know.

The reply came straight back.

The ladies from Ward 4 are ready to storm the building with me. Walking sticks at the ready. Be safe. Call me as soon as you're done.

Butterflies performing somersaults in her stomach, Keli got out of the car, and marched to the door of the hotel before she changed her mind.

The doorman opened it and greeted her with a cheery 'Good afternoon,' which she reciprocated, although nothing felt good about right now. Not a thing.

She wasn't sure what to do next. Sit in the lobby? Wait at the door? Go to the ladies' and check if she looked as terrified as she felt inside?

'Keli?'

The voice from behind her made her spin, and the sight that she saw there was not at all what she'd expected. Somehow, based on nothing but her imagination, she'd thought this woman would be glam and brash, perfect make-up and wearing a trendy, over-the-top outfit. But no. She was stunning, for sure. Tall, about the same height as Keli, around five foot ten. Brown eyes. But that was where the similarities ended. This woman had long caramel hair, parted in the middle and falling in natural waves. No make-up and she certainly didn't need it because her face was all cheekbones and full lips. With her willowy frame, black jeans and polo neck, under a grey suede jacket, she could be a model, out on a casting call, for a shoot that was searching for a naturally gorgeous girl next door.

'Hi, I'm Laurie. It was me who called you.'

'Erm, hi.' There was a hesitation as they both stared each other, before Keli broke it. 'I'm not sure what to say, or how this should go, but do you want to go into the bar, and get some coffee? Or something stronger, if you want.'

Laurie nodded. 'Sure.' This was so bizarre. They were talking as if they were meeting for a work chat. Or they were pen pals getting together. Or strangers going on a date.

In the bar, Laurie asked for a glass of Pinot Noir, but Keli stuck to herbal tea. Despite the fleeting thought that she might need wine earlier, she wasn't taking any chances. If she were pregnant, she didn't need the guilt of knowing she got pissed at lunchtime. And getting drunk with the girlfriend of the baby's father was the stuff of really bad reality TV shows.

'Look, I'm just going to start,' Laurie began. 'Because you must be wondering if this is all a big joke. Or some kind of mistake. I brought pictures to show you so that you'd believe me.'

Keli didn't need them. She could see by the devastation on Laurie's face, the defeat in her voice, that either this was real or she deserved an Oscar. Laurie flicked through a dozen images on her phone, each one making Keli wince. They were clearly a couple.

'I just want to say again that I'm sorry. I had no idea.'

'I believe you,' Laurie answered, pulling the glass of wine that the barman had just poured towards her. 'I could tell when I spoke to you earlier, to be honest. You sounded as shocked as I feel.'

Keli nodded, lifting her tea. 'You said you'd been with him for three years?'

'Yes, but we kept it completely private. I didn't want my career to be defined by being his girlfriend and he... well, I thought he was just respecting my wishes. Now I realise it suited him because he could play the single man.'

'I'm sorry. I know I've said that before and I might say it a few more times. I really am.' Keli knew the apologies should be coming from him, but that didn't change the fact that her heart hurt for this woman, who'd just found out her partner of three years was a duplicitous tosser.

'I get that. Honestly. I'm not blaming you here. I just can't believe that I didn't see who he was before now, but I was just too wrapped up in him, right from the start.' There was an almost wistful melancholy in her words. 'We met on a photo shoot in London. The moment I met him, I fell crazy hard for him and that's not me. I don't normally do shit like that.'

'I don't either,' Keli empathised. 'He just had this... weird effect. I can't explain it. It was nothing to do with how he looked or who he was. It was more of a way...'

'That he made you feel,' Laurie finished the sentence for her. 'He love bombs. Goes in hard and fast. Makes you feel amazing. Like he can't get enough of you. Like you're the most special person in the world. I feel so pathetic saying that. And I can't believe that he kept me reeled in for three years.'

'No, no, but you're right,' Keli agreed, leaning into Laurie and the conversation. This was in no way how she'd expected this to go. She thought there would be conflict. Animosity. Instead, it was like two kindred spirits that had watched the same movie and were comparing notes.

It turned out that her first impression had been pretty much correct. Laurie was a model, mostly catalogue and internet fashion work. 'Don't be impressed,' she managed a bashful smile when she said that. 'It sounds glam, but it really isn't. I'm not Kate Moss, swanning around for *Vogue*. I spend most of my days freezing my bits off posing in bikinis in winter for start-up fashion brands who don't have the cash for big names. Ryan didn't mind, though. He preferred that I was relatively anonymous. That I wasn't in the spotlight.'

They talked on, feeding off each other, throwing out comments or observations that the other one immediately caught on to and recognised. In some ways, it was horrific. In others, it was a comfort.

They established more facts. 'I worked out where and when you met him from the texts...' Laurie told her.

'At a party at his work.'

Laurie nodded. 'At first, I thought you were in the same business as him, but then I saw texts where you mentioned that you worked shifts...'

'I'm a nurse,' Keli answered the unasked question. 'Over at Glasgow Central. Our schedules didn't always line up very well, but he didn't seem to mind. I guess that's because it left him plenty of time to carry on with his real life.'

'I hate that he did this to you. I'm sorry.'

'I'm sorry he did this to you too. Jesus, what a dick,' Keli blurted, and Laurie murmured a rueful, 'Amen.'

'One thing I don't understand,' Keli went on, 'is how you didn't wonder where he was. I spent Christmas evening with him...'

'I'd gone to London to visit my family. He had work commitments, so he couldn't come. And personal commitments too, I realise now.' There was an unmistakable hint of bitterness as she said that.

'And New Year?' Keli went on. Her tea was cold now, but she was too engrossed in the conversation to order another.

'I flew to Prague on the morning of New Year's Eve for a job there. Evening wear, against the backdrop of the New Year fireworks. Never been so cold in my life. I was crazy busy all through October, November and December, travelling constantly. The start of January too. But I've pretty much been home the last month or so, because I only had a few local jobs. In fact, I was supposed to leave this morning to fly to London, but it was cancelled at the last minute, right before I checked in at Glasgow Airport. I went back to the flat, and that's when I saw his iPad. He'd left it lying on the kitchen counter – I guess he thought the coast was clear.'

Keli could feel her stomach sink and her temper rise. Laurie had been away most of the period from October to December. That was when Keli had been spending time with him. She was just a stop gap for a bored guy. 'Do you think… Do you think he's done this before? Were there other messages?'

Strangely, given the circumstances, it was Laurie who now threw Keli a sympathetic glance. 'I'm sorry, but there are. Only you for the last few months, but there were a couple of others earlier last year. I contacted all of you, but you were the only one who got back to me. I know that makes me sound crazy…'

'It really doesn't,' Keli said honestly, the butterflies in her stomach now replaced with the heavy weight of a depressing reality.

'But even though I was gutted and didn't want any of it to be real, I had to know the truth.'

This was all beginning to make hugely depressing sense. When his girlfriend was out of town, he shagged around. 'Is it strange that in some ways, I'm glad you called?' Keli told her. 'The last month has been excruciating, not knowing why he was ghosting me, not understanding what had gone wrong. At least now I know. Although I fricking hate the answer.'

Laurie sat up straight, tipped her head back. 'Aaaargh, how did this happen? How did we let this guy do this to us?' Her gaze returned to Keli. 'I mean, we're smart women. Decent people. How does this make sense?'

'I know it's pointing out the obvious, but I guess he's a really good liar...' Keli said with a sigh. 'Who is great at putting on a convincing act.' Something in that popped a bubble of rage inside her, and she felt it begin to rise to the surface. What a bastard. What an absolute arse. 'I suppose the good thing is that we know now. The question is, what are we going to do about it?'

4 P.M. – 6 P.M.

17

ODETTE

It was already dark outside, when Odette and Calvin climbed into the back of the car that had brought her to and from the studio every day for years. Back in the nineties, after only a few years on the show, she'd already started to garner star power and she'd used it well – getting a car and driver written into her contract. For the last two decades, the car had been driven by the same man, Harry, a chap of few words that she had a genuine affection for, one that was reciprocated in his typically understated way. A kind smile. A nod of the head. A reassuring conversation. And never, as far as she knew, a negative or badly spoken word about her in twenty years.

'Home please, Harry,' she said as she climbed into the vehicle, going along with Calvin's plan to rest for a couple of hours, then change into something fabulous for their dinner later.

Calvin clambered in next to her, put his leather briefcase on the seat between them, then did something on the iPad and his phone that Odette didn't understand. He explained as being some kind of... what was the word? Hot dot. No, hot spot. That was it. He then started furiously clicking away on the iPad, while firing off questions to her.

What was the person's name? Nancy Jenkins. Age? A couple of years younger than Odette, so maybe sixty-seven or sixty-eight now. Last known location? Weirbridge. A village on the outskirts of Glasgow, over to the west.

'And are you going to tell me why you want to find her?' he asked, obviously curious.

'Absolutely not.'

Calvin emitted a roaring chuckle. 'You know, I wouldn't need bloody Botox if you were easier to deal with, Odette Devine. Wrinkles. That's what you give me. But you're never dull, so you're forgiven.'

'Thank you,' she replied, genuinely, thinking again how much she'd miss him.

'Right, leave it with me and I'll get searching. Oh, I feel like Davina McCall and Nicky Campbell on *Long Lost Family*.' With that, the tapping got quicker, as he gave the small screen one hundred per cent of his attention.

Odette turned to stare out into the rush-hour traffic trudging home in the early-evening darkness. No wonder the population of this country was statistically low on Vitamin D. Not to minimise what she knew were genuine concerns, but a bit of global warming wouldn't go amiss around here. She'd had her electric blanket on every night since last September and her electricity bills were wiping her out.

Odette closed her eyes and sent up a silent prayer that Calvin would find Nancy. To the almost hypnotic sound of his perfectly buffed nails typing on the screen, she let her mind drift back to the time that had been floating in and out of her head all day.

The winter of 1982 had been a brutal one, and Olive Docherty, as she was known then, had already gone through two pairs of tukka boots and it was only bloody November. The slush on the ground played havoc with the suede ones, and the pleather ones had sprung a leak the first time she'd worn them in the rain. It was the trek from the bus stop to school that did it – every bloody morning and every bloody night. And, of course, in Scotland the mornings didn't get light until eight o'clock, and it was dark again by 3.30 p.m., so she hadn't seen a big orange ball in the sky for months. Even blasting Irene Cara's 'Fame' on her Walkman for the last three minutes of the walk hadn't cheered her up.

'Has someone died or is it just yer face that's in mourning?' her pal, Nancy, greeted her as she walked in the door. The chat with the rest of the dinner ladies was the only thing that kept her going in here. Olive, Nancy Jenkins and Fiona Jones were the three young ones on the team, and then there were eight older women who could knock out enough caramel cake and scoop enough mashed potatoes to feed an invading army.

The irony of Nancy's comment was that Olive had only got the job because it had been her Aunt Vi's before her, right up until one bottle of gin too many had shut down her liver for good. She'd died the year before, and Olive would never have admitted it to a soul, but there had been a tiny shred of relief. Vi's fondness for the booze had reached chronic levels in her last couple of years and Olive's whole life had been dedicated to looking after her, finding them money to eat, cleaning up vomit, forcing Vi into showers, and sobering her up just enough that she managed to hold down the one stable thing in her life – her job as a dinner lady at the Weirbridge Primary School canteen. The other women in the school kitchen, especially the supervisor, Maggie, and sisters, Cora and Gracie, had been Vi's friends. They had no money, no room in their homes, and no time to spare from their own families, so they'd taken care of Vi's niece, Olive, in the only way they knew how – they'd given Olive the job that her aunt had held down until the day she'd dropped.

And Olive hated every second of it.

She'd somehow managed to go from a grim, shit, lonely childhood, to being a teenage nursemaid to an aunt who valued booze over anything else, to inheriting a job she couldn't stand. She hated the trudge there every morning. She hated the crappy wages. And she hated the overwhelming stench of cabbage that permeated every corner and crevice.

The only thing she loved was the relationships with the other women. The banter. The support. The sarcasm and the relentless nosiness into every area of her business. That said, Olive knew she didn't have the tolerance to spend much longer stirring custard and serving up mince pies and jam sponges to snotty primary school kids.

'Only thing that's dead around here is your split ends and ma love life,' Olive shot back, making Nancy howl with laughter. One-liners and amusing insults were like rites of passage around here and they were traded back and forth all day long, cutting but with an edge of endearment. If merciless teasing and disparaging remarks were coming your way, it was because they knew you could handle it. And Olive could dish them out like the rest of them.

Fiona Jones joined them in the staff changing room, just as Nancy pulled a newspaper out of her bag. Olive barely paid attention at first, too busy trying to prise her sodden boots off her soaking socks.

'Right, ladies, I just want you to know that I'll be leaving you soon,' Nancy chirped.

Olive's head snapped up and she felt a thud of dread in her chest. No. Nancy was the one that kept her sane in here. Her closest pal. The one whose laughter made the endless days bearable.

'...Because I'm going to be a star.' She threw the paper down on the table and they all huddled around it as Nancy pointed to a quarter-page advert and then read it aloud. 'Actresses wanted. Aged twenty to thirty. New Scottish drama series. No experience required. We are looking for that needle in a haystack, a fresh face that will bring authenticity to the screen in the new weekly drama, *The Clydeside*. Come along to the open casting on Saturday...' Beaming, Nancy threw her hands up in the air, in typically dramatic style. 'I think we should all go. Come on, it'll be a giggle. We get paid on Friday, so let's go into town, have a wander around the shops, maybe even splash out on a bit of lunch and then go along and see what this is all about.'

Fiona picked up the paper, read it again. 'I'm definitely coming. I was Calamity Jane in the school play and my teacher said I had talent.'

'Is that the teacher you bumped into last year in Benidorm, the one who asked you out and turned out to be a complete lech?' Nancy asked, teasing her.

'Aye,' Fiona responded tartly, 'but that doesn't mean he can't recognise talent when he sees it. Said my stuff with the whip on Calamity Jane was the best stunt work he'd ever seen.'

Nancy and Olive were shrieking with laughter now. Fiona was never slow to tell anyone that she was only working as a dinner lady until her big break came along. She'd also been to every modelling agency in the city, and there was a rumour she'd applied to be a page three girl in *The Sun*. If she got her baps out in a newspaper, the gossips in the village would combust.

Olive took the paper off her. Saturday. What else did she have on? Nothing. That was all that was in front of her. A whole lifetime of nothing. 'I'll come too, Nancy,' she declared, trying to act casual. 'I had a date lined up, but I'll cancel.' She didn't. 'It's with a bloke from that nightclub I go to that's been asking me out for months, so he'll ask again anyway.' There was no bloke. And she didn't have the friends to go dancing with, or the money to get in. Her aunt had left debts in at least three local shops, where she'd been getting her booze on tick, and every time Olive went in, they added a fiver to her shopping bill to go towards it.

She had nothing to lose. And, if nothing else, it gave her a day out and some company. She didn't have to actually do the audition. Although, hadn't she been acting all her life? Pretending to be okay when her mum died, when really her heart was broken but she didn't want anyone to think that she was looking for attention – the worst crime in her mother's book. 'Don't you dare make a show of yourself,' her mum used to hiss, whenever there was anyone else around. Then, later, she'd put on a fine performance as the dutiful niece, when she picked a wasted Vi up off the floor for the umpteenth time and dragged her to her bed, cleared up her mess and then, next morning, acted like nothing had happened.

Yep, she'd been acting for years. Could doing it in public really be any different?

Turns out, it was. After a morning wandering along Glasgow's Buchanan Street, perusing the shop windows, and a burger in the Wimpy near Central Station, Olive, Fiona and Nancy had headed to the auditions. The advert had given the address – a nightclub just a couple of streets away. When they arrived, there was a line around the block of young women, some of them looking normal, just like them, and some of them so done up they looked like they'd just come off a stage with Bananarama.

'There's no way we're going to get to the front of this line,' Nancy had announced. 'Why don't we forget this, and just go down to that trendy bar on West Nile Street for a Taboo and Coke? My Peter says that's where all the football players go. You never know – you two might get lucky.'

Nancy had been married to 'her Peter' for years, and Olive was sick of hearing how perfect he was. Although, the thought of meeting a football player was one she liked. Just imagine. All that money. They would take care of her and she wouldn't have to boil another rotten pot of cabbage for the rest of her life. Nice clothes. Nice car. Unlimited credit cards and as much cash as she could spend.

'No way I'm leaving now,' Fiona declared stubbornly. She never changed her mind about anything, that one. 'This could be the day that changes our lives. School play Calamity Jane one day, TV actress the next.'

Nancy and Olive giggled at her optimism.

'Aye okay, Doris Day, we'll humour you. But I tell you, don't fall out with me if this bloke takes one look at me and gives me the part,' Nancy teased.

But, of course, that wasn't what happened, because, a few weeks later, Olive made sure that it was her name in lights, by doing something she'd never have believed she was capable of. She'd...

'Found her! Well, slap my thigh and call me Agatha Christie,' Calvin hollered, shocking Odette straight back into the present, to a comfy leather seat that was stuck in a traffic jam on a Glasgow motorway.

Odette's heart began to beat faster. 'You did? Are you sure?'

Calvin held the iPad across the seats so that she could see the information on the screen. The first thing was an obituary, saying that Peter Jenkins had passed away, and was survived by his wife, Nancy. The second was a photograph from the *Weirbridge Gazette*, of a school reunion the year before, and along the bottom were the names of the people in the photo – one of them was Nancy Jenkins.

Calvin used his fingers to zoom in and make the face larger and... Odette couldn't conceal her gasp. She was much older now, obviously, but there was the unmistakable smiling face that she'd stood next to in the audition queue that day. Nancy Jenkins.

'That's her. But how do I find her? Do you think she still lives in Weirbridge?'

'I know she does,' Calvin beamed proudly. 'Because look!'

He opened another tab, and there was a tiny advert from the *Weirbridge Gazette*.

Garage sale. Saturday 27 October 2018. Yellow Cottage, River Lane, Weirbridge. Please note that Nancy Jenkins will donate all proceeds to Macmillan Cancer Support in memory of her late husband, Peter.

'That's her. That's definitely her.'

'Great. Are you going to tell me why you're looking for her? Old friend? Are you bearing a grudge? Hang on, is she a long-lost sister, because if so, I'm calling Elliot and we're getting the documentary team in on this.'

'Old friend.'

'Ah well,' Calvin replied, showing obvious disappointment that it wasn't a long-lost sister. 'You could pop out and see her next week. Give you something to look forward to.'

Odette thought about that and immediately dismissed it. No. Who knew what could happen between now and next week? The sooner she went, the sooner she'd begin to fix her karma. Besides, next week she wouldn't have a car and a driver, so she was as well making the most of it on her last day.

'Harry, can you turn the car around. I want to go to River Lane in Weirbridge.'

'Now?' Calvin exclaimed. 'But... but... it's almost six o'clock and I've got dinner reservations for us at eight. I'm not cancelling, Odette. It's been arranged for ages, our final professional goodbye, and I've got some lovely treats planned for you.'

Odette was touched. The poor soul looked so panicked.

'Then we'll go straight there afterwards. A bit of lippy and some perfume and I'll be fine. Harry, head for Weirbridge please. I need to call on an old friend.'

Or at least, she used to be a friend. Odette was fairly sure there'd be no warm welcome waiting for her now.

18

TRESS

Tress had only seen Anya once after the accident that had killed Max and it was from a distance, at the airport, when Anya had left the country. All she'd felt then was relief.

But here she was again. And the woman who was staring back at her now looked so very different from the one that had left here four months ago.

The Anya who had been her friend for many years was tall and athletic, with corn row braids in her hair that fell down past her shoulder blades. She had captivating, deep brown eyes and the most glowing, gorgeous skin. Her outfits, whether business suits for the office or even casual at the weekend, were always the kind of colourful or monochromatic chic that a thousand articles in *Cosmopolitan* couldn't teach. One glance at her and anyone would say that she was stunning, classy, incredibly cool.

The lady sitting on the bench in Noah's front porch was someone different altogether. This Anya still had the small scars on her cheek, left by her face hitting the glass of the windscreen that had shattered on impact. Her hair was shorter now, shoulder length, just a basic bob style that didn't catch the eye. Her clothes were unremarkable too. Black jeans. Black jumper. A dark grey coat and boots. It was as if her whole appearance was designed to be anonymous. Invisible. To divert attention.

But the biggest change was that the mile-wide smile and the fiery eyes that had been her trademark were gone. It was as though she had lost her sparkle, been abandoned by her love of life.

Despite everything that had happened, Tress felt a pang of sympathy for her. Anya had lost everything – her home, her career, her friends, the two men she had loved, Max and Noah. And yes, what she'd done was awful. Unforgivable. But that didn't mean that on a human level Tress didn't have some compassion for her.

The question people asked most was 'How could they?' How could Max and Anya have an affair that lasted so long, despite both being married to people they professed to adore? Yet, Tress truly still believed that her husband had loved her, and that Anya had loved Noah.

After the accident, Anya had explained the affair to Noah, repeating the analogy that she and Max seemed to have lived by. They'd equated it to skydiving. For Max, Tress was his ground. His safety. His happiness. For Anya, Noah was the same. But every now and then, they wanted the excitement of the jump, the thrill of the fall. That's what Max and Anya were to each other. They'd never fallen in love. They just loved the adrenaline rush and the danger of the secret affair. It had been going on before Tress even met Max, and the bitter irony was that both Max and Anya had agreed to end it, because Tress was about to give birth. On the day of the crash, they were meeting for the last time. One final night together to give them their own private closure on their affair. Instead, they got the most horrific ending, one that cost Anya her marriage and friendships and cost Max his life.

Now this woman had to see the scars of her choices on her face every day.

'Hello, Tress.' If Anya was surprised that Tress was here, she didn't show it.

Tress stopped at the entrance to the porch, leaned against the wood balustrade. 'Noah said you were back.'

A brief, knowing smile crossed Anya's lips. 'Of course, he did.' There was no bitterness there, only something that sounded more like resignation.

'Meaning?' Tress asked archly, a hint of challenge in her tone. Confrontation didn't come easy to Tress. She preferred to walk away from an uncomfortable situation or from people she didn't want to spend time with, but if people mistook her calmness or kindness for weakness, they were mistaken. Thankfully, Anya didn't. She immediately backed down.

'I'm sorry. I didn't mean anything by that. I just... I take it you live here now?'

Ah. That made sense. Anya had put two and two together and ended up with Shania Twain.

'No, of course not. I live in my own house with Bu—' She stopped. Somehow, it felt right to give her boy his proper name in this situation, so she went with his official moniker. 'With my son, Noah.'

Anya's smile oozed sadness as she made a connection. 'Today is his birthday.'

'It is.' Tress was giving her nothing. She had no desire to chat or to make small talk, so she walked on past Anya, let herself in with her key, placed Noah's case of beer on his kitchen worktop, then came back out and locked the door. Anya was still there.

'I just needed to come here. To sit for a while.' Anya offered an explanation that wasn't requested.

'Does Noah know you're here?'

'No. I'm just about to go meet him. I asked him to see me today.'

'I know.' Tress was struggling to get the words out. She had nothing to say to this woman.

If Anya had an opinion on Tress's knowledge of her itinerary, she didn't share it. Instead, she sighed, spoke quietly. 'Feels strange being here. Like it was another life.'

'It was.' If anyone had told Tress this meeting would happen today, she'd have expected that she'd be anxious, angry, maybe bitter, but strangely she felt nothing. The actions of this woman and Max had caused her so much pain, so many tears, and now it was as if some strength, deep in her core, refused to give Anya the power to cause her another second of hurt.

'So, you and Noah. Are you... are you...?' Anya couldn't bring herself to say the words, but Tress knew what she was asking, and she wasn't going to give her the satisfaction of an answer.

She barely glanced at her, as she stepped down the stairs off the porch. 'Me and Noah are none of your business.'

'I'm sorry, Tress. For everything. I know that nothing I can say will ever be enough.'

Again, Tress kept an even, calm keel. 'It won't,' she answered succinctly, before starting to walk away.

She'd taken two steps before Anya added, louder, 'Is there anything I can do, or say...'

Tress spun around. Her calmness in the face of adversity was beginning to crack, but somehow that made her voice lower, her words rapid, like the dull sound of bullets coming out of the silencer on a gun. 'You had sex with my husband for the entire time we were married. You betrayed our friendship. You broke my best friend's heart. You are the reason that my son will never know his father, and yes, I know that Max Walker is every bit as much to blame, maybe more, but that doesn't mean I will ever fucking forgive you. Know that. And know that if you hurt Noah again, you'll just be adding to the things that you'll have to answer for in hell. Leave, Anya. This isn't your home now.'

Tress didn't even wait for a reaction, she just turned and walked back down the drive, jumped into her car and drove away. She was fine... for about thirty seconds. Then, as soon as she was out of Anya's sight, she pulled over, buckled forward, her hands shaking, her heart racing, her throat closed by the rush of adrenaline that her fight-or-flight instinct had sent coursing through her. In the early days, after the accident, when she wasn't too exhausted from taking care of Buddy, too grief-stricken from mourning her husband, too furious about what he'd done to her, too utterly despondent to lift her head from the pillow... Yep, in those days she'd thought so many times about what she'd say to Anya if she ever met her face to face, and how she'd feel afterwards. Now that it had happened, there were too many emotions ricocheting around her head to know the answer to that question.

Leaning back against the headrest, Tress closed her eyes, concentrated on her breathing, talked herself down, until the shaking stopped, then she drove the two streets home.

As soon as she walked in the door, she heard the shrieks of hilarity coming from the kitchen, and realised Nancy and Val were back with Buddy.

Another deep breath. Then another. Then she slapped a smile on her face, and walked down the hall and into the kitchen, scooping her gorgeous son up from his play mat on the floor, where he was hugging one of Ollie the Octopus's arms. Or was it tentacles?

She kissed him again and again, on the cheeks, the chin, the forehead, making him crease into intoxicatingly adorable giggles.

Tress felt her heart soften, her grin widen, and her blood pressure drop back down to normal. This kid could fix anything.

Val and Nancy were sitting at the kitchen table, mugs of tea in hand, biscuit barrel open in front of them. Both of them immediately greeted her with sunny smiles.

'Hello there, lovely,' Nancy chirped. 'What are you doing home? Just as well we weren't in here with two male strippers, Val. In saying that, I once went to see Thunder From Down Under and I don't think I've been right since.'

'Those fellas can give a woman high expectations,' Val whistled, shaking her head, before giving Tress her full attention. 'Are you okay, pet? How has your day been?'

Tress didn't even know where to begin to answer that one. Still carrying Buddy, she slipped onto the end of the kitchen bench and propped him on the table right in front of her, holding him while he attempted to eat her hair as his afternoon snack.

'Eventful,' was the best she could come up with to describe the dramas since she'd left the house that morning. 'I've two things to tell you. First, if it's still okay with you, Nancy, I'd like to take you up on that offer to look after Buddy tonight because I've been invited out.'

'Invited out? As in by Noah, and as in sweeping you off somewhere lovely?'

Tress was the one chuckling now. These two never gave up. 'As in, no, that's never going to happen, and as in, I'm actually going out with someone from work. Rex Marino. The actor on *The Clydeside*.'

'You are not! Oh my word, that's a fine-looking man,' Nancy exclaimed. 'When is he picking you up, where are you going, and do I have to grill him about his intentions?'

Tress laughed, making Buddy giggle too. 'About eight, we're going to dinner in town, and I think his intentions are to eat, drink and avoid really nosy ladies who love a bit of excitement.'

'They're going to put that on my gravestone. "Here lies Nancy. Really nosy but she loved a bit of excitement,"' she cackled. 'But I'm not wrong about that man. What I could have done with him before my knees gave up.'

Val wasn't as enthusiastic when she interjected with, 'I mean, back in the day, my Don would have wiped the floor with him, but he'll do, I suppose. Although, I've seen him being interviewed on *Lorraine* in the mornings, and is it just me or does he sometimes come off as if he's a bit too fond of himself?'

That was the biggest crime in the West of Scotland psyche. You could be all kinds of awful, but people drew the line at anyone who felt themselves to be something special.

Tress shook her head, then rebounded back quickly when she realised Buddy now had a firm grip on a large clump of her hair. She began gently trying to release his fingers. 'No, he's not, really. That's all just part of the show. He's very nice in real life, I promise.'

Val tried to hide her disappointment, while remaining supportive. 'Well, you've got great judgement, lass, so I'm sure you're right.'

Tress couldn't help raise an eyebrow at that. 'Val, did you meet my husband?'

The older woman flushed. 'Good point. Except for him. You might want to get me and Nancy to vet this one.'

Tress knew that neither Nancy nor Val actually watched the show. It had never struck her to ask them why, but now wasn't the time, not when she had other crucial information to impart.

'Okay, and the second thing I have to tell you...'

They both had mugs in mid-air, so Tress waited until they'd been put back down on the table before going on, 'I just met Anya. She's sitting on the bench on Noah's front porch.'

Nancy didn't even blink. This was the type of woman who offered to bury the bodies of anyone who hurt her friends. And Val would be right next to her with a shovel.

This was one of those situations. These two women had an almost maternal bond with Noah. They adored him, and more importantly, they were beyond proud of how the four of them had banded together and got through the most unimaginable destruction and loss. They were family.

Nancy didn't even hesitate. 'Tress, the birthday boy is all yours for now. Right, Val, get your coat. Let's go and see what that one thinks she's doing here.'

19

NOAH

'That's the face of a man who is not having a good day. Anything I can help with, my friend?' Carlo asked, as he brought over the bill.

'Not unless you want to pull up a chair and open a bottle of Scotch,' Noah replied, meaning every bit of the sentiment, even if it was delivered as a flippant comment.

Carlo chuckled as he cleared the table of Cheska's unfinished meal. 'Ah, Scotch only helps until you fall down,' he said. 'But pasta…' With that, he patted his generous belly and made his way, fully laden, back to the kitchen.

Noah had been sitting on his own, nursing a mug of black coffee since Cheska had walked out the door of the restaurant. Her words were still ricocheting around the inside of his skull. *There's only one thing that will fix this, Noah. Come to America with me. Choose me. Do you think you could do that?*

They both knew the answer before he'd said the words. 'I can't.'

'You won't,' she'd corrected him. 'You absolutely could. You're a paediatric consultant, one of the best there is, and you know you could walk into a dozen really good jobs there. Any college would kill to have you on their teaching staff. And you'd be in demand as a practising surgeon too. Didn't you get headhunted for a job in Philadelphia last year?'

'Yes.' There was no getting out of that one because she knew it was true. One of his former mentors was now head of surgery at a prestigious hospital there and had reached out to him only a few months after the accident. Noah had refused then. Just as he was refusing now.

'Then the correct answer isn't that you can't,' she'd repeated his reply. 'It's that you won't. You won't choose me.'

'It's not that simple, Ches. I just can't leave Tress and Buddy,' he'd said. 'We're a family. I can't just walk away.'

'Don't you think Tress would want you to be happy, though? She would never stop you being with the person you loved.'

'I know that...' he'd replied, truthfully, then stopped, unwilling to take that thought to the obvious conclusion.

'But you don't love me enough to leave them,' Cheska had cut in, too perceptive and too straightforward as always.

He hadn't said anything. There were no words he could have uttered that would fix this.

'You know, the sad thing is that if you said you would come with me, that you would leave them, I would probably think less of you, because that's who you are. You're the guy that takes care of people. Who doesn't let them down.'

There had been no malice in her words at all, just sadness. He knew that Cheska loved Tress and Buddy too, had seen what they'd been through for the last twelve months, and she was truly a good person so she wouldn't want to pile on any more pain. A good person in a bad situation. One who had got to her feet then to leave.

'Be happy, Noah Clark. You deserve it.'

With that, she'd walked out of the restaurant, and she hadn't so much as glanced back.

Now Noah was nursing a coffee, a sore head and a whole heap of questions. And his ex-wife would be here in an hour. Today just kept getting better and better.

Carlo returned with the card machine and Noah settled up. 'Can you keep this table for me for later? I just need to go get some fresh air, but I'm meeting someone here at five.'

'Ah! You're taking my suggestion about pasta,' Carlo teased him.

Noah didn't want to burst his bubble by letting him know that there would be no long, hearty dinner with his next guest. Whatever Anya had to say to him, he hoped it was short, sharp and didn't add in any way to the shit show that was already playing out this afternoon.

'I am, Carlo,' he laughed, rising from the table. 'You'll have to roll me out of here tonight.'

Outside, it was already getting dark, and the cold was biting. A typical February afternoon in Glasgow. Today, he was glad of it as he began walking, unsure at first of where he was going. He'd thought he might nip back to the hospital, but he wasn't in the mood for putting on a happy demeanour and chatting to his colleagues or – the thought made him groan – for any questions from anyone who'd heard that Cheska had resigned. She was right to tell him as soon as she'd done it because nothing stayed secret in that place. He loved where he worked, but, like all big hospitals, it ran on gossip and speculation.

He decided to bypass the human element and just go straight to the car park, get his car, and bring it back to the restaurant car park. That way, after the meeting with Anya was over, he could just jump in his Jeep and head off to his mum's house. Yep, good plan. He crossed the road and kept walking in that direction.

At one point, he took his phone out of his pocket to call Tress but stopped himself. She was at work. He'd already dropped in on her and she was doing just fine. Better than fine, actually.

Tress and Rex. Everything about that had taken him by surprise. Something had been sitting in the periphery of his mind since he'd seen them together this afternoon, and it suddenly came to him what it was. Rex reminded him of Max. The same swagger. The same presence. The same aura of unquenchable confidence. Not that he knew him well. In fact, they had never even had a conversation. But Tress had taken him along to a big party at the studio for the show's fortieth anniversary a few months before and they'd been briefly introduced. In fact, they'd taken his mum and Keli along with them too, because his mum was a huge fan of the show, and Rex had done the whole kissing his mum's hand and being way too smooth. At the time, Noah had put it down to being just part of the guy's job, but now, it was grating with him. The last thing Tress needed was another bloke who'd be careless with her heart.

He'd been so deep in thought he hadn't realised that he'd reached his Jeep. He climbed in and, thanks to the inevitable traffic jam leaving the hospital, it took almost as long to drive back to Carlo's restaurant as it had taken to walk from there.

It was five minutes to five when Noah sat back down at the table, and he'd barely had time to slide his jacket off when he glanced up and saw Anya being guided to the table. If Carlo was curious as to why he was meeting with two beautiful women in one day, he was way too discreet to ask. Instead, he provided a welcome distraction from the discomfort by taking their orders. Another coffee for Noah. A white wine for Anya.

'Thanks for meeting me,' she said, as soon as Carlo left them.

'Anya, I wouldn't ignore you or refuse to speak to you. Come on. You know that.' She did. In the couple of months after the accident, despite the fury, the rage, the pain that day had ingrained on his soul, he'd let Anya stay at the house and he'd taken care of her while her injuries were healing. For a split second, he'd wondered if they could repair the damage, somehow make it work again, but they had both quickly realised that their marriage had died in that car accident too. Flatlined. No hope of resuscitation.

'I know,' she said, almost apologetically. 'Listen, before we start, I just want to tell you that I met Tress earlier.'

Noah didn't understand. 'You met Tress? Where? When? I spoke to her earlier and she didn't say she was going to see you.'

'Not even an hour ago. And it wasn't planned. Please don't be freaked out, but I went over to our house.' It was no longer 'our house'. He'd bought her out of the mortgage when they'd divorced. It was his house. Just like it was his life. No longer a shared existence. 'I just wanted to see it again. Nostalgia, I guess. I'm trying to work through a lot of the stuff that's happened, work out how I messed up so badly.'

Again, he resisted the urge to say, 'Because you had sex with my mate for years.' No point. Nothing to be gained.

'Anyway,' she went on. 'Tress came by – I think she was putting a case of beer in the house for you...' That made him smile. It was the kind of thing she would do today. She was thoughtful like that. 'And she saw me, so we spoke.'

He nodded thoughtfully. 'How did that go?'

The trio of Noah, Max and Anya that had existed since university had naturally expanded when Max had met Tress and the four of them had been a collective for the next six years until the accident. They had spent almost every weekend together. Went on holiday two or three times a year as a group. Had dinner a couple of times a week. They were a family, just doing life together. After the accident, Noah and Tress had questioned whether any of that was real, or whether their foursome was just a convenient way for Max and Anya to meet. The crazy thing was, they both agreed that it wasn't. Sex between Max and Anya had been an extra perk for the two of them. They were both strong-minded, determined, and they never let anything stand in the way of what they desired from life, so if they'd wanted to leave their partners, they would have done it. He and Tress both believed that their partners had loved them – they just loved the excitement of the affair on the side too.

'About as well as expected,' Anya answered his question. 'She wasn't up for a long chat, but she was civil. I had the chance to apologise to her, and that was one of the reasons I'm here, so I'm grateful I had the opportunity to do that, and I just hope it was received in the way I meant it. Truly.'

It didn't surprise him that Tress hadn't engaged to any extent, or got into any kind of heated situation. Like him, Tress didn't do drama or lash out with her emotions. It wasn't her style. He'd seen her sink to the depths of sadness immediately after the accident and yet she'd still held it together, just put one foot in front of the other until she'd found a way back to a better place. It actually irritated him that Anya may have upset her yet again, today of all days. He decided to drop in on her later and make sure she was okay.

'I can't speak for her, but I do know that she has somehow managed to move on with her life and leave the pain of it all in the past most of the time.'

'Yeah, I get that. She also pretty much told me that if I mess with you, she'll hunt me down.'

He was taking a sip of his coffee, but that still made the edges of his mouth turn up. This still felt so strange, though. For two decades, Anya had been the closest person in his life. He'd told her everything. Had her back just as she'd had his. And now they were strangers, making what felt like small talk.

'How about Nancy and Val? Do they still have me on the Neighbourhood Watch hit list too? I think they must have, because just as I was driving away in the taxi, I saw them pull up at the house. I ducked down so they wouldn't see me. Self-preservation.'

He knew it was probably for the best that she hadn't encountered them. He couldn't confirm or deny that they'd floated the idea of banning Anya from within a hundred yards of their street. He might have found a way perhaps not to forgive, but at least to live with what Anya had done, and still treat her with basic human respect. Tress might have found the strength to honour the role that Max had played in her life and to keep his memory alive for Buddy. But Nancy and Val? Forgiveness wasn't an option. Not ever.

'I think rumours of a hit list are unfounded, but I wouldn't go inviting them for a cosy dinner any time soon. I think you'd be eating on your own.'

Anya nodded thoughtfully. 'I deserve that.'

He didn't disagree.

'And Cheska? Are you two together then?'

Ouch. 'It's complicated. I guess the answer to that is no.' Shit, he was saying that aloud for the first time and he didn't like the way it sounded, so he left it there.

He let the silence sit for a moment, before he decided he'd had enough. So far, it had been very one-sided, with her asking all the questions, but that was because he was waiting for her to get to the point. He had no interest in finding out how she was, what she'd been doing, where she'd been since she left. He only cared about two things: what was she doing here and what did she need to say? Time to rip the Band-Aid off. Between Cheska and now Anya, he'd had enough of the stuff that pierced the heart today. He just wanted to be out of here.

Carlo steered past with a top-up for his coffee, but Anya declined another wine. She'd barely touched the one in front of her.

'Anya, why are you here? What do you want from me?'

'Straight to the point. Okay. I need... I just need closure. After I went back home, I got into therapy, started doing the work to find a way to get past what happened, and to get to the root of why I behaved the way I did.'

'That's good. You had a major trauma. Therapy helps.'

The way this day was going, he didn't rule out booking a few sessions for himself. The need to rant and vent and expel the exasperation of the last few hours was getting more urgent by the minute.

'It did. It took me a while to be able to look in the mirror again. Not because of the scars, but because I didn't want to see the woman who'd done those things, who'd caused the carnage to all our lives.'

He understood that. He wouldn't have been able to live with himself either. But then, he wouldn't have been able to lie and cheat in the first place. It was the fundamental difference between them.

He listened as she went on, talking about her therapist, her journey, her realisation that she'd sabotaged her life because she was scared to commit to having a family, and that now she knew what she wanted, she had figured out her issues and got her life back together. He wasn't sure a many years long affair with his best mate could be brushed off as just a bit of self-sabotage, but he let it go. He just wanted to get to the point and get this over as soon as possible.

'And where am I in this? Do you need me to tell you that you're forgiven? That we can close that chapter? Because if that's what you need to hear, I can do that.'

It wouldn't be strictly true, but she didn't deserve to pay for her mistakes for the rest of her life. He was happy to release some of that guilt for her.

She shook her head, tears falling down her face now. 'That's not it. I guess... I guess I came here because I wanted to tell you that I love you. Despite what I did, that hasn't changed. I have always loved you since the moment we met, and the last few months, the time away from you, has convinced me, that I don't ever want to love anyone else.' Noah heard a sob catch in her throat, before she spoke again. 'So what I want to ask you is if you can find a way to separate the mistakes I made from the person that you know I am, from the woman you were married to? And if you could do that, is there any way that you would consider giving us another chance?'

20

KELI

Keli had to wait as the barman brought a fresh tea, and this time a coffee for Laurie, before they could address the question she'd just asked.

'I suppose the good thing is that we know now. The question is, what are we going to do about it?'

'Right now, I want to go slash his tyres, but I realise that's not helpful,' Laurie conceded. 'I just don't get it. How can someone do this to the person they're supposed to love?'

Keli had no words of comfort. 'I've no idea. My brother's wife did the same thing to him. An affair with his best mate for years. My only answer is that some people are just crap. That's all I've got.'

A voice in Keli's head chose to remind her right then that she'd somehow chosen to fall for one of those crap people. And that right now, in the bag that was sitting on the bar next to her, was a pregnancy test that would tell her whether or not there was a possibility that she could be connected to that crap person for the rest of her life. Only her anger was stopping her from dissolving into tears and searching for a dark corner to cry in.

'Shit, your poor brother. Is he okay? I hope he cut both of them right out of his life. That's unforgivable.'

'It's a long story,' Keli replied. She'd thought Noah had said a permanent goodbye to Anya, but with her showing up this morning, that might have changed. 'His friend is no longer in the picture,' she didn't feel this was the time, the place, or the conversation to deliver all the bombshell facts. 'But his wife is now his ex. It was awful for a long time, but he's a really good guy, so I just keep believing something great will work out for him.'

'I kinda wish I'd met your brother instead of the one I picked.' Laurie was obviously joking, but maybe there was something in that. Maybe if they all came out of this in one piece, and if Noah ever broke up with Cheska... Keli stopped herself. Focus. One problem at a time. And her anger was making her bravery rise.

'Look, I know you need to talk to Ryan and you have a three-year relationship at stake here, but...' She stopped, too unsure to continue.

Laurie was waiting for the rest. 'But what?'

Fuck it. Boundaries had already been broken here, and she had nothing to lose, so it was time to just go for it. 'Is it crazy that I want us to confront him together? That I want to march right round to wherever the hell he is right now, you and me, and see what he has to say?' There must be something in this tea. Bravery pills. Or some other concoction that was making her act completely out of character.

Laurie bit her bottom lip as she pondered that for a heartbeat, before replying, 'No.'

Oh well. Worth a try. Keli could feel the first stirrings of deflation, which were rapidly banished when Laurie continued.

'No, it's not crazy. To be honest, I'd appreciate the support and I've got a feeling that the only tiny hint of joy I'm going to get in this whole fricking mess is seeing his face when he knows that he's been caught. Besides… it's the only way that he won't be able to fob me off with some bullshit story or another pack of lies.'

That thought energised Keli. She sat up, leaned in. 'Do you know where he is right now?'

Laurie checked her watch. 'Probably still at work or at the gym. He rarely gets home before now. That's no use, though. Too many people. I want to embarrass him, not us.'

Keli didn't disagree. The last place she wanted to face him was at his day job. No. This had to be done on their terms, not where he controlled the narrative.

Laurie pulled her phone out of her handbag. 'One way to find out for sure. He still thinks I'm in London, so he'll have no reason to lie.'

Holding the handset between them so that they could both see the screen, she typed…

Hey babe, how's your day? Still at work? Missing you xx

She pressed send and Keli's butterflies made a grand reappearance as they waited for a reply, both of them staring at the phone. But nothing.

This was insane. Madness.

Laurie's shoulders sagged. 'He might be in the middle of something. Or maybe driving. Shit, my hands are shaking.'

The thought struck Keli that if she'd met Laurie in any other way, the two of them would probably hit it off and become friends.

Ping. They had synchronised sharp intakes of breath, as the reply flashed up on Laurie's screen.

Hey beautiful…

Another wave of nausea almost took Keli down. Until the whole ghosting thing, that's how he'd always answered her too. This was him. The guy she'd thought that she was falling in love with. And okay, it had been fast, and brief, and she could see now that there were a dozen red flags, but that didn't make this hurt any less.

She read the rest of the text.

I miss you so much too. Hate it when you're not here. Also horny, so there's that ;)

Oh fuck, a wink emoji. Seriously? What a tit. Had he ever sent a message like that to her, and she'd been so wrapped up in him that she hadn't realised how corny he was? Seeing this guy through a different lens was shaking her to her core.

Laurie's fingers were suspended over the screen. 'Oh shit, I'm sorry but if we want to find anything out, I'm going to have to play along and reply as if nothing is wrong. Is that going to freak you out?'

What did it say about this woman that they were in this situation, and she was still being considerate of Keli's feelings? Yep, they would definitely be friends.

'It'll absolutely freak me out...' She saw Laurie's face fall. 'But we're already in too deep, so let's just go for it. Screw him.'

A smile that she now knew had graced the websites of Pretty Little Thing, ASOS and Boohoo flitted across Laurie's face as she typed the reply.

Me too, baby. Wish I was there right now so I could do something about that. Xx

Laurie pressed send with a murmur of, 'Urgh, I want to vomit.'

'Me too,' Keli replied, and it wasn't just a throwaway comment. She really, physically did want to throw up.

A one-word answer came back.

Facetime? ;)

And what the hell was it with the wink emojis?
'Oh shit,' Laurie said again, before typing...

Sorry, babe. Too many people here...

Keli piped in, 'Ask him where he'll be after work.'
Laurie tucked a lock of her hair behind her ear, thought for a second, before her thumbs got to work again.

But what about later? Are you going straight home after work?

Another long pause. Damn, this was excruciating.
Ping.

Yeah, but quick turnaround. Going straight back out. Have a work dinner.

Oh cool. Where is it?

Ping.

Not sure. Need to check. Wish you were coming with me though.

Laurie lowered the phone, clearly pensive. 'I feel if I ask him any more questions, he'll get suspicious, because I don't normally check on where he's going. I didn't think I had to. Now all I can think about is that his work dinner is probably a date with his next target.'

Keli thought about all the times he'd said he couldn't make things, or that he was working late, or showed up at her place at midnight, because he'd been at a 'work function'. She'd never asked questions then either, always just too damn pleased that he was there. What a fool. She immediately retracted that thought. No. She wasn't to blame here. She didn't think that Laurie was a fool, so why was she making that judgement on herself? Nope, neither of them was in any way at fault here of anything more than just loving and trusting someone. The blame was all on him for being a faithless prick.

'What would you normally say right now? Just type that,' Keli suggested.

Was it getting hot in here or was it just her? As she glanced to the side, she realised that while they'd been transfixed on the phone, the bar had begun to fill up with people dropping in for a Friday night, after-work drink. Normal people. Folk who weren't sitting with their unfaithful former boyfriend's current girlfriend manufacturing texts to him so that they could in some way plan to ambush him and call him out on his lies. Again, what had happened to her life?

Okay, text me when you get home tonight, baby. I'll be waiting. Might be naked. Love you xx

Keli felt the need for a long shower. The last fifteen minutes had confirmed that voyeurism wasn't her thing.

'Are you okay?' Keli asked. 'I'm sorry. This must be so fricking difficult for you.'

'And you,' Laurie countered.

'Yeah, but at least I'm not having to whisper sweet nothings to him. Laurie, I don't know how we ever got into this, and I realise

I've only known you for a hot minute, but we are way too good for this vile excuse for a human.'

Laurie's laughter made a couple of good-looking, suited guys standing further along the bar turn and look appreciatively at her. If they knew what was going on, they'd probably turn right back round and stare at their shoes.

'So what do we do now?'

It was a rhetorical question, but Laurie, giving off model-perfect pensive, spoke up. 'The thing is, we could do something like post a pic on social media – even *his* social media.' She held up his iPad to reinforce the point that she had access to his apps on it. 'But I really want to see his face when he finds out we've connected. I know that when all this sinks in I'm going to be devastated that he's wasted three years of my life, that he's turned out to be a liar and a cheat and basically pond life, but right now I'm running on adrenaline and revenge and I want to see him squirm.'

'No arguments here,' Keli agreed, feeling exactly the same way. They were only going to get one opportunity to confront him, and she needed it to be soon.

Laurie exhaled with purpose. 'Okay, let's make a plan. Are you free later? Because I'm thinking I could buzz him again in a couple of hours, and try to establish where he is. I'll keep an eye on his Instagram too because he usually can't resist posting posed shots on there. You know, he never posted a single picture of us together in three years. Said he wanted to guard our privacy and I went along with it because I wanted to be known for myself, not my boyfriend. I'm seeing his reasoning in a whole different way now.'

Keli was having the same thoughts. Not a single picture in three months. This made so much sense now. 'Me too. Look, I'm just heading to my mum's house for dinner, but I can definitely meet anywhere, any time, later. Just text me and I'll be there. What are you going to do in the meantime, though?'

Laurie shrugged. 'Well, I can't go home, because I'm supposed to be away on a job all weekend and he doesn't know yet that it was cancelled. Also, I don't want to see him if he goes back to our flat to change. And I don't feel like going to a friend's house, because I really don't want to have to explain all this yet. So I think my best move is to check in here...' She had a mischievous smile as she gestured to their five-star surroundings. 'And then tomorrow, or maybe the next day, when I check out, I'll charge it all to his credit card.'

'Oh, I definitely approve of that plan,' Keli concurred.

They both slid off their bar stools and almost instinctively, Keli reached over to hug her new accomplice. It should feel absolutely wrong and weird, but strangely it didn't at all. She'd heard the phrase, 'Women supporting women' many times. That was exactly what this felt like.

'Text me. I can be anywhere in the city in half an hour. And, Laurie, I know I said this before, but I'm so sorry.'

Laurie returned the embrace. 'Not your fault. Let's just make sure that we put it right. For both of us.'

They crossed the foyer, then hugged again before Laurie headed to reception, and Keli went blinking out into the early evening darkness.

In the car, she fired off a quick text to Yvie.

Safe. On way to Mum's. So much to tell you so will call when you get off shift. Thanks for being a pal today. xx

She tossed the phone onto the passenger seat and switched on the engine.

Half an hour later, Keli realised that the whole journey to her mum's house in Weirbridge had passed in a blur.

When she opened the door, the delicious smell of her mum's

home cooking set off another wave of nausea, on top of the stress, on top of the anxiety, on top of the absolute fricking terror of what might be about to happen to her life.

Enough of putting this off. She needed to do the test so that she knew one way or another. And she needed support from one of the people in the world who would stand by her and have her back no matter what.

'Hello, lovely,' her mother greeted her, as always, with the warmest of smiles and with open arms.

'Mum, before you say another word, I've got a few things I need to tell you. And there's something I need to do.'

6 P.M. – 8 P.M.

21

ODETTE

Odette hadn't had butterflies like this since the time she did a skit for the Royal Variety show in front of the Queen. In it, she had played a Cruella de Vil-type character that was rounding up the nation's corgis and keeping them all on her private island, where she called herself Queen Agnes. She'd been assured that the real Queen Elizabeth had found it hilarious, but she still thought it might be one of the reasons that she'd never received so much as an OBE for services to acting. Dame Maggie Smith. Dame Judi Dench. And here she was, just plain Odette Devine. Or, to be factually correct, Olive bloody Docherty.

They'd managed to turn the car around and now they were heading in a completely different direction, out to the west of the city, then to Weirbridge, in the suburbs. Even under normal circumstances, it would take half an hour, maybe forty minutes, but God knows how long it would take in traffic. The motorway was still gridlocked, so they were moving like a funeral car on the way to a crematorium. It felt like time was passing even slower because Calvin was still moaning beside her.

'We'd better not be late for dinner, Odette Devine, because our relationship of a million years deserves to be celebrated and I will not have you bailing on me. God, I need a weekend at the spa after this. I deserve a medal – A BLOODY MEDAL – for working with you all these years.'

She put her hand over his. 'I'll leave you my jewellery collection in my will,' she said, teasing him, but already aware of the reaction it would elicit.

He immediately pivoted, purring, 'Okay, you're forgiven. And those diamonds had better be real.'

It was an exchange that they'd replicated a thousand times over the years, but it never failed to make them laugh. She'd miss this. Who would she talk to, who would she joke with, who would give her the time of day after midnight tonight, when Odette Devine became the Cinderella that was too old for the ball? And what would Calvin think when he discovered that the diamonds were big fat fakes, because she'd sold the real stones after husband number four had run up debts of over £200K at casinos?

Odette pushed the thought away. She'd be dead by then. Too late to do anything about it. But not too late to fix the situation that was destroying her karma now.

Her mind returned to the recollection that had been unfolding before Calvin had interrupted her to tell her that he'd located Nancy. Another flip of the stomach at the thought of her name, and the memory that came with it.

On that audition day four decades ago, they'd stood in that queue for hours, and it was almost 4 p.m. by the time they were in the group that was finally ushered through the door by a very serious girl with a clipboard. The venue was a nightclub, but it was in the middle of the day, so it wasn't open to the public yet. 'Oooh, this place stinks,' Nancy said, wrinkling her nose.

'I was in here last weekend and dancing in my bare feet,' Fiona wailed. 'I don't even want to think about the kind of diseases I could have picked up.'

It didn't help that their feet stuck to the carpet as they walked. Olive made a mental note that if the acting and the school dinner gig didn't pan out, she could come pitch her services here as a cleaner.

'Does my hair look okay?' Fiona again.

Looking back, Odette had to admit that the three of them had scrubbed up pretty well. Gone were the school dinner lady uniforms and hairnets, and in their place were three women in their late twenties who'd worn their best looks. Nancy was in tight jeans and a white flouncy shirt with a frilly collar. Olive had taken out a credit account at Wrygges and used it to buy pale blue cord ski pants, new cream tukka boots and a pink denim jacket. Admittedly, though, Fiona was the most striking of the three. She was wearing black tight leather trousers (fake, but you couldn't tell the difference), along with a black polo-neck jumper and a white furry jacket. She'd scraped her blonde hair up into a ponytail and she'd nipped into the toilets in Central Station to touch up her make-up while Olive and Nancy were in WHSmith buying a few packets of Tudor pickled onion crisps and a couple of Wham bars in case they got hungry.

Clipboard girl was bossing them again. 'Right, if you could all take a seat, please, and I'll give you all these forms to fill out. Alf Cotter, the director who will be auditioning you all today, will be calling the people he selects on Monday morning at 10 a.m. So please put down the telephone number you can be reached on at that time.'

For Olive, that had been a no-brainer. Her phone had been cut off after Aunt Vi's funeral because she hadn't had the money to pay the bill. She planned to get it reconnected at some point, but what was the rush? No one ever called her anyway.

They'd filled out the forms and then waited another hour or so, until they were summoned through to the small function suite in groups of five. It smelled just as bad as the main club, but the small, wily-looking gent in a black jumper and Fedora, waving chain smoker's fingers in a chair next to the stage didn't seem to notice. He introduced himself as Alf Cotter, then had them all say their names, ages and what they did as a job.

Olive went first. 'Olive Docherty. I'm twenty-eight. And I work as a school dinner lady.'

'Of course you do, love,' Alf had sneered. 'And I'm the bloke that directed *Jaws*.'

Olive didn't understand, and she could see the same look of confusion on Nancy and Fiona's faces too. 'No, really. I am. The three of us work together in Weirbridge Primary School. We're all dinner ladies.'

Alf sat back, took a cigarette out of his packet and lit it, before exhaling, an incredulous and slightly suspicious grin on his stubbly face. 'So, you're not just saying this because you've heard that one of the parts we're auditioning is Agnes McGlinchy, a school dinner lady from the East End of Glasgow? Thirty years old, one kid, another on the way, and a husband who can't keep his willy in his trousers?'

Olive felt herself flush, but she wasn't going to give him the satisfaction of embarrassing her. 'No. We're really dinner ladies. If you want to see the burns on our arms from the pie oven, we can show you,' she challenged him.

'Un-fucking-believable,' he crowed. 'Right, you on the left, you can go – Agnes isn't a ginger. And you on the right, that mole isn't going to work on my screen.'

They watched as the two strangers who'd come in with them in their group of five were dismissed, and Olive knew she should be outraged that he'd spoken to them in such a nasty, condescending way, but the truth was, she was pleased. That was two less people to compete against.

'Right, you three dinner ladies... You already know the job inside out, so let's see if any of you can act your way out of a paper bag. I don't need you to be polished. God knows, I've had every trained actress in Glasgow in here today and no one has nailed Agnes yet.'

Nancy went first, reading from the sheet of paper that Alf gave her. The scene called for Agnes to be having a furious argument with the headmistress of the school, bickering about a complaint that had been made about her. Agnes went on to threaten to tell every teacher and parent that she knew the headmistress was having a heated affair with one of the janitors.

Alf read the part of the headmistress, and Nancy threw her whole heart into it, leaving Olive open-mouthed and astonished at how great she was. Who knew she could act?

When the scene finished, Alf nodded thoughtfully. 'Not bad. Not bad at all. Right, Blondie, you're up next,' he gestured to Fiona.

As Fiona made her way to the middle of the room, Nancy joined Olive at the back. 'Bloody hell, Nancy, you were flipping fab. How did you do that?'

Nancy leaned in, spoke under her breath. 'Just imagined I was having a barney with Georgina Walker. She was the bint that I caught sucking the face off my boyfriend when we were at our leavers dance, years ago. Oh, it felt good to get that off my chest.' She gestured to their other friend. 'Fiona's giving it her best shot too, though. She looks like she's about to knock that bloke's head off.'

Olive turned her attention forward and saw that Nancy wasn't kidding. Fiona had taken a step towards Alf, and was using her whole body to gesticulate and rage as they argued. Everyone was full of surprises today. She'd truly thought this was going to be a waste of time, and that they'd all just have a bit of a giggle, but the other two were definitely giving it their all. She continued to watch Fiona, trying to pick up any pointers that she could use. Okay. Inhibitions gone. Try to look up as much as possible, even though you're trying to read the words on the sheet of paper. Act with her body as well as saying the words. She could do that.

When Fiona was done, Alf gave another considered nod, then thanked her for coming. 'Next!' he shouted to her.

Olive's hands were shaking and her knees felt like they could give way at any second, but she didn't give a hint of that. This was all those times the schoolteachers had asked her if everything was okay at home and she'd slapped on a smile and told them of course it was, despite the fact that she'd eaten nothing but beans on blue-mouldy toast for weeks. It was every time she'd answered the door to the landlord and told him her aunt was out, but that she would be coming to give him the late rent tomorrow. It was every time she'd pretended not to care that other girls had normal houses, with normal mums and normal problems.

Alf checked his sheet. 'Ready, Olive?'

Yep, this was going to be every single time she'd had to fake how she'd felt about anything in her life.

He gave her the opening line, and she went for it. Every word was delivered with vehemence, with commitment and with a level of bitterness that came straight from her gut and was aimed at every single bastard that had ever wronged her or treated her like dirt. It was aimed at the mum who'd left her. At the aunt who'd loved her gin more than she'd loved Olive. At the whole world for giving her the shit life that she had now.

She spat out the words until there were no more left on the page, and she realised that she was done, that she was back in the room, that Alf was staring at her and that her face was starting to beam with embarrassment.

'I don't know what goes on in your dinner hall, ladies, but I wouldn't want to complain to any of you three about the lumps in my custard.'

He thought he was being funny, but Olive was too shaken to feel amused.

She slunk back over to Nancy and Fiona.

'If we ever disagree on anything, remind me not to bother arguing,' Nancy whispered to her with a wink.

Fiona was too busy fixing her hair to comment, but Olive could see by her pursed lips that she knew Olive had given the best performance.

'Right, lassies, well done. Like they should have told you outside, I'll be phoning the person I've selected for the part on Monday morning.'

The three of them murmured their thanks, then calmly made their way outside, until the fresh air of the street hit them, and they dissolved into shrieks of laughter. 'Well, that Goldie Hawn will be shitting herself now that she's got competition,' Nancy announced as soon as she could speak, setting them all off again. 'Let's go for a drink, girls. I fancy a wee Malibu and pineapple before I get too famous and only drink champagne.'

Odette's car juddered over a speed bump, making the memory fast-forward to the Monday morning, when her younger self had nipped back to the dinner hall staffroom for a plaster after shredding her finger on a cheese grater. She was right next to the phone on the wall when it rang, so she'd snatched it up immediately.

'Hello...'

'Aye, erm, yes, hello. This is Alf Cotter. Can I speak to...'

'Odette!' Calvin barked at her, making her head turn sharply. 'Jesus, I thought you'd gone into some weird hypnotic trance there. You were miles away. Anyway, we're here. Yellow Cottage. That's it there. Shall I be Davina and come with you?'

'No,' she mumbled, staring at the house. It was a picture-perfect little bungalow that had flower boxes under the windows, a cherry tree in the front garden and she could see a light on in one of the front rooms. So this was Nancy's home. And now she had two choices. Go knock on the door. Or stay in the car and tell Harry to turn around and forget this crazy, half-baked notion to apologise for something that had happened four decades ago.

Odette Devine remembered what happened next on that phone call and felt a wave of self-loathing. This was the time to make it right. With a shaking hand, she reached over and opened the car door.

22

TRESS

Tress was wondering where the majority of the spaghetti bolognaise had gone – into Buddy's mouth or down the front of her T-shirt.

'Little guy, you have your daddy's appetite and your mamma's aim,' she told him, loving the cheesy grin that was the standard response to everything she said, unless he was cold, warm, tired or hungry. Even then, he didn't fuss much. For a baby who had been born in such stressful, horrendous circumstances, coming into this world in the same hospital in which his dad would succumb to his fatal injuries just a few hours later, he had the most lovely, laid-back, sunny nature. Tress put that down to his inherent personality, and to the joyful world they'd created for him, even though he was only one and all he cared about was cuddles and giggling as she sang him songs. Tonight, they'd got through at least ten choruses of 'The Wheels On The Bus' while she'd fed him his favourite pasta, then a dozen more renditions of 'Old McDonald Had A Farm' over his other favourite, the high-brow delicacy that was apple puree pudding.

Even in her darkest days, the need to care for this little person had forced her to get up, to shower and to function through the day. Those were the days that she missed her mum most. Julie had passed away when Tress was just a teenager, and there wasn't a day that Tress didn't think about her. Maybe that's why one of the things she'd relentlessly pondered over many sleepless nights after Buddy was born was the question of how to broach the subject of his father with him. What should she tell him? And when?

In the end, after speaking to Val and Nancy, to Noah, and to a child psychologist on Noah's ward, she'd decided that she'd talk to Buddy about Max right from the start, so that he'd know who his dad was and how much he was loved. When he was old enough to understand, she would tell him the story of how his father had passed away, but she would never reveal who Max was with or why. Buddy didn't need to know that. She'd much rather he always regarded his dad as a decent, loving man, taken far too soon.

Talking of decent men... she picked up her mobile and called Noah, but it went straight to voicemail.

'Hey, Noah, it's me. Just checking in with you to see how your day is going and how your chat with Anya went. Maybe you're still having it.' That thought gave her goosebumps of fear. 'Anyway, everything is fine here. Don't worry about calling me back, because I know you're going to your mum's for dinner. Oh, and that advice you gave me earlier? I took it. I'm going out with Rex tonight. Only mildly terrified. Actually, that's a lie. Definitely majorly terrified. I'll buzz you later, but if you need me, just call. Love you.'

She hung up, deflated. She'd wanted to tell him about her own encounter with Anya, to find out how his conversation went with her, and to check in with him, to hear his voice and know that he was okay.

Another ripple of anxiety pulled at her gut. What if he took Anya back? There. That was it. The question that she'd been trying to avoid all day. What. If. He. Took. Her. Back? She tried to shrug off the notion. To reunite with Anya, he'd have to end his relationship with Cheska and Tress didn't see him doing that. Although, it did surprise her that Noah and Cheska were still keeping things so casual. Not that it was any of her business, so she kept out of it. All she knew was that Cheska was great, Noah was a catch, and she hoped they'd work it out, almost as much as she hoped that he would say goodbye to Anya for the second time and that she would stay away.

Assuming, that was, that Nancy was being honest when she said that Anya was no longer on Noah's porch when she got there. However, she'd returned twenty minutes later, minus Val, whom she said had gone home to relieve the carer who came in to look after her husband, Don, one day a week, so Tress had no corroborating evidence the ladies didn't encounter Noah's ex-wife. Anya could, right now, be tied up in the boot of Nancy's car, praying for a SWAT team.

'What's that smile on your face for?' Nancy asked, as she came back into the kitchen after running a hoover round the rest of the house. Tress had tried to stop her, but it was hopeless – Nancy would tell anyone who would listen that hoovering was her favourite way of getting her daily steps in.

Tress would never stop being grateful for this saint of a woman who was now waiting for an answer.

'I was thinking there's a good chance Anya is in your boot.'

Nancy put her hands up. 'You'll never find her. I've watched every episode ever made of *Silent Witness* at least twice. I know how to hide the evidence.'

Tress played along. 'Excellent, because Buddy doesn't need to be visiting his aunties in jail.' After scooping Buddy out of his highchair, she perched him on her hip, and grabbed the bottle she'd made up for him earlier. 'Come on, little man, let's go soak the spaghetti off.' She kissed the tip of his spaghetti-blotched nose, before adding to Nancy, 'I'm just going to give him his bath, and then I'll put him down. Wee soul is rubbing his eyes already. You and Val definitely tired him out today. Are you sure you don't mind staying with him tonight? I can easily cancel.'

Nancy was already washing down Buddy's highchair. The woman was a cleaning machine. 'Oh no, don't you dare try to squirm out of this one, Tress Walker. You're going out on this date whether you like it or not and don't be trying to use me to get out of it.'

Tress was equal parts amused and anxious. 'I've almost texted him at least a dozen times. Is this what it feels like, Nancy? Getting back out there?'

Nancy stopped cleaning to think through her answer. 'I don't know, love, I really don't. After my Peter died... well, I didn't think I'd ever want to be with anyone again. And then Johnny came along...' Johnny had been a friend of Nancy's husband, Peter, when they were teenagers, and she'd met him again at a Weirbridge High School reunion the year before. 'And something just felt so completely right. I don't understand it and I can't explain it. I think there's just something that happens when your heart is in charge.' Tress got lost for a moment, letting the profound wisdom and loveliness of Nancy's words sink in, until she added, 'Or it might have been vodka that was in charge. The fruit punch at that school reunion nearly blasted ma heels off.'

'Greeting card companies should know about you,' Tress laughed, shaking her head and thinking about the sweet part of Nancy's words as she went off to track down Buddy's pyjamas. Did her heart tell her that Rex felt right? No idea. But it did tell her that one date wasn't going to kill her, so she was as well giving it a try, since Nancy was determined to stay here and binge-watch a few more repeats of *Silent Witness*.

* * *

An hour later, Buddy was bathed, jammies on, in his cot and she'd read him five pages of *House Beautiful* magazine. It was the closest she came to multitasking, because she'd realised that she could read anything at all to him and he had no idea what she was saying. She just made sure she voiced the new trends for window dressings and wallpaper in a soft, sing-song voice and he went to sleep happy, while she was left with gorgeous new ideas for bedroom curtains.

Should she really be going out tonight? Most people facing the anniversary of the loss of a loved one would have been mourning today, maybe visiting a grave or a garden of remembrance. Tress had done neither of those things. In fact, after his cremation, she'd allowed Max's parents to take his ashes back to their home in Cyprus so that they'd always have him with them. He was an imperfect husband, but to them, he was their only son and it had felt right to give him to them. She wanted no physical place of rest here that would make her feel guilty for not visiting. There was a happy picture of Max in Buddy's room, but no room for starting painful annual mourning traditions, especially not on her son's birthday.

As soon as his breathing told her he'd nodded off, Tress leaned down and kissed his forehead, then stroked the side of his cheek. 'Goodnight, little one. And happy birthday,' she whispered. 'Just so you know, I'm going to make sure you have a wonderful life, because I love you with my whole heart.'

He murmured and then exhaled, his perfect little rosebud lips turning up at the edges. Probably gas, but she was going to tell herself that it was because he understood every word.

She could hear Nancy singing a bit of Shania downstairs when she went into her room for a quick shower. When she got out,

Shania had transitioned into a power ballad by Celine. Apparently, Nancy's heart would go on. Tress wasn't so sure about her own.

Okay. Deep breath. What was the dress code? What did someone wear for their first date in years? And, even worse, what did someone wear when they were going out with Rex Marino, sexy TV actor, almost ten years younger than her, and touted by some Scottish newspapers to be the next James Bond?

She threw open her wardrobe doors and saw a sea of black. It was pretty much all she wore even before she was a widow in mourning.

Three hangers came out, three went back in. One out. One back in. Three pairs of jeans were tried and discarded until finally she abandoned all notions of trying to be trendy and went for classic instead.

A black crepe oversized tuxedo jacket, slimline trousers in the same fabric, a silver silk V-neck body suit underneath, high stiletto boots and finished off with the Valentino bag Noah had bought her for Christmas. She thought about compression knickers but changed her mind. She was anxious enough without adding a ten-minute wrangle with spandex before she could pee. She pulled her hair up into a ponytail, leaving some tendrils down to frame her face. A bit of make-up, a squirt of Chanel No 5 and she was ready.

In the living room, Nancy cheered when she saw her. 'Well, hello!' she exclaimed, taking in the suit and the hair and the heels. 'You look gorgeous, pet. You really do. It's lovely to see you all dressed up.' Nancy choked on the last word, and Tress immediately felt tears spring to her bottom lids.

'Don't you dare make me cry, Nancy Jenkins.'

Nancy was fanning her face by this point. 'I'm sorry, sweetheart, but there have been times over this last year that we were worried you'd never remember how it felt to get a bit of lippy on and go enjoy yourself. Another month and me and Val were going to take you to singles night at the bingo. Apparently, there's at least three men under fifty there.'

Tress swallowed the lump in her throat and managed to regain her composure. 'Well, if I'd known that I'd have got dolled up and dragged you there months ago.'

'There's still time if this one doesn't work out. I've heard one of the blokes still has his own teeth. Anyway, stand there a minute so I can take a photo. I told Val I'd send her a pic of you in your glad rags. And also, you know, it's good to have in case we need to give it to the police to help identify you. I really need to stop watching *Silent Witness*.'

Nancy picked up her phone and snapped away, and Tress indulged her by making faces at the camera. When she was done, Nancy pinged a few more buttons, then tossed her phone on the couch, and changed the subject. 'Did you manage to get a hold of Noah? I can't stop thinking about him with that Anya one. Honestly, that lassie has got some nerve on her.'

'I've tried, but it just keeps going to voicemail. I'll try again in a wee while.' Tress was cut off by the sound of an incoming text. 'That might be him now...' She glanced at the screen. 'No, it's Rex. He's outside.'

Nancy crossed the living room like a stunt woman half her age to get to the window for a good look. 'In the name of the flash git, has he brought two cars? There's a sports car outside and a big fancy black limo thing further down the street next to my house.'

Tress peered out. She could see Rex's red Ferrari, and then the limo just on the other side of Nancy's house. The streetlights above it were out, so it was impossible to see inside. 'No, I think he's in the sports car. The McKelvies on the other side of you must have posh visitors.'

'I'll be round at her window first thing tomorrow morning to get the gossip. If Hilda McKelvie has won the Postcode Lottery, I want to be first in the queue. Right, pet,' she gave Tress a hug. 'Have a brilliant time. And if you want to make it a sleepover, you go ahead. I've got my nightie and my slippers in my bag and Val is coming back round in a wee while to keep me company.'

Tress returned the hug, shaking her head. The last thing she had on her mind tonight was staying over with Rex Marino. The very thought of spending the night naked next to anyone scared her to death. Terrified her.

And she was going to ignore the little voice in her mind, saying that maybe that was the best reason to do it.

23

NOAH

'No.' His one-word answer was calm but unequivocable.

'But, Noah...?' Eyes pleading, she leaned forward, put her hand on his and he very calmly but quickly pulled it back.

He cut her off. 'Anya, I'm sorry,' he said as gently as he possibly could. This was the same voice he used when delivering awful news to patients. Calm. Lay out the facts. Have compassion, but don't give false hope. 'It's no. It'll always be no. There's no world in which that will change.'

She sat back in her chair, and he could see by the way she exhaled just how much it had taken for her to come here and say that.

However, there was a bigger part of him that questioned her timing. It made sense that she'd come back to Scotland on the anniversary of the accident. There was something significant in that. One year. A turn around the sun. Closing the door. Moving on. But to come to him with this? Why would she even consider it a good idea to do that? Today had just as much significance for him. How could she possibly think he'd be open to picking that scab on today of all days?

Or perhaps that was the point. Maybe she thought he'd be vulnerable today.

Or maybe that hadn't even crossed her mind, because, just like 365 days ago, when she had headed to a country hotel with Tress's husband for a last weekend of secret sex, maybe she was only thinking about herself.

Well, no. Not today.

In fact, not any day.

'Noah, please... I'm not saying move back in together. I just mean start slow... see where it goes. We had almost twenty incredible years together. Surely that must mean something?'

'It didn't to you.'

She flinched like she'd been slapped and he felt a tug of regret, then pushed it to one side. No false hope.

'I deserved that. But Noah, I can't live with the guilt. It eats me up. Every. Single. Day. It's the first feeling I get every morning, and the last feeling I get at night, and I can't stand it. The guilt. The regret. The desperation to make it right, to have you back, to show you that I love you.'

'No.'

'Noah, I explained earlier, there were reasons that I did what I did...'

'Anya, stop!' His words were so sharp, they cut right through her argument. He took twenty pounds out of his wallet and placed it on the table for their drinks. 'I'm going to go now because there's nothing else to say. We'll only start going over everything, re-litigating it all and doling out blame, and I think even your therapist would tell you that's unhealthy. I wish the best for you, Anya, I truly do...' He saw tears spring to her eyes when he said that. It was always the same. It wasn't heartache that was the most upsetting thing to deal with. It was the kindness and sympathy that people showed when you were at your worst. That's what broke down the walls that people put up to protect them from pain. 'I hope you find what you're looking for and get the life you want to live.' His tone was still calm, firm, quiet. 'But it won't be with me. I'm sorry.'

He wasn't sorry for his response, but sorry because she'd come all this way and it had been a wasted trip.

On the way to the door, he gestured goodbye to a surprised Carlo, then just kept right on walking. If this were a romcom, he'd realise the error of his ways and rush to the airport five minutes before her flight took off to tell her he'd changed his mind and he loved her and they'd all live happily ever after. This wasn't that. This was goodbye. Anya had pride and she had dignity, and most of all, she knew him well enough to believe that he wouldn't change his mind. Something deep in his gut told him that this was probably the last time he'd ever see her or speak to her. And that was fine. He was good with that. If there was anyone he'd rush to at midnight, and beg to stay, it would be Cheska. Could he honestly let her go? She was someone very special to him, and he was letting her walk away.

Jesus, what a day. He had absolutely no idea what he wanted any more, but he just knew that there was somewhere else he needed to be right now.

He left the restaurant, got into his Jeep and began to drive.

It took half an hour to get through the rush-hour traffic, but he didn't mind the drive. Gave him a chance to think, to try to process everything that had happened to him today, although there were two things that kept coming to the surface again and again. The first was Cheska's ultimatum. What a blindsiding moment that had been and he still hadn't even begun to process it. And the second thing? Tress's potential relationship with Rex. He couldn't let her get hurt again, but she, of course, had to make her own choices. He just had to be there in case this guy was another asshole who didn't keep his promises.

His car seemed to know where it was going, because he'd paid barely a thought to pointing it in the right direction and yet now it was pulling into the street he'd intended to come to.

He picked up his phone to take it with him and realised it was out of charge. He had no idea how long it had been that way. Last time he'd looked at it was when he was going into the restaurant to meet Anya, and, as always, he'd switched it to silent so any calls wouldn't piss off the other diners. His mind might have been slightly too occupied to check it when he left the building.

He put it in the glove compartment and jumped out of the car, making sure the Jeep was locked so none of the little toerags in the village could make off with his phone, his backpack or his laptop.

Crossing the pavement, he wasn't surprised that the gate was locked. It had always been controlled by the local councillor who probably figured that nothing good ever happened in a park after dark.

He remembered telling Tress about this place when she was in labour, a year ago right now. At that moment, she couldn't understand why Max hadn't responded to her calls and texts telling him the baby was on the way and she was in the delivery suite. She'd had no idea it was because he was in the next building, his life ebbing out of him. Noah hadn't told her because he didn't want to risk her or the baby's health, didn't want to rob her of the joy of giving birth to her first child. Instead, he'd held her hand, told her anecdotes from the past.

He climbed over the gate, found his favourite bench, let his mind stray back to that night again, as he'd desperately tried to keep Tress's spirits up. He'd told her how he and Max used to sneak into this park when they were kids, living in houses they could see from the gate he'd just jumped over. This had been their favourite hangout all through their childhood and teenage years and they were rarely out of it, so it was the place where he still felt closest to the past, to Max, to the life they'd all had before the crash.

'My mum just treated Max like one of us,' he'd told Tress that night. 'She once pulled us all the way up the street by the backs of our jumpers because we got caught sneaking out of the house when he was sleeping over at ours.'

Tress had laughed, her fingers winding around Noah's hand, ready to squeeze the life out of it when the next contraction came. 'What age were you?'

Noah had shrugged. 'Maybe eight? Nine?'

'And where were you going? I presume it was at night-time?'

'Yep, pitch-black. We were going to climb the fence into the park and play footie because we reckoned it would be brilliant to have the pitch all to ourselves.'

'No, no, no,' she'd chided him, playfully. 'Let me see if I can correct you there. I bet it was Max who had the idea to do that, and you knew you wouldn't be able to talk him out of it, so you went along with him, even though you were aware that there were very definite flaws in the plan.'

'I'm not even going to ask how you know that.'

'Because he hasn't changed a bit,' she'd said, her smile a curious mixture of happy and sad. 'It's one of the things about him that's always scared me and thrilled me in equal measure. He's fearless. Exhilarating. And I've never met anyone who loves life more or who's so obsessed with living it to the fullest. But sometimes I worry he'll go too far...'

Noah still hadn't had the heart to tell her that 'sometimes' had already happened. His best friend their whole lives. His brother.

The pain of the memory momentarily brought him back to the present, to the bench in the park, and he put his head back, stared up at the sky, felt the warm salty water of his tears run down his cheeks. He'd said goodbye to Max later, full of shock and rage over what he'd found out that day, and the devastation that their selfish bastard actions had wreaked on all their lives.

Anya had been in surgery, where they were trying to save her life. Max was in a coma that would end with his death only a few hours later. Shocked, dazed, still wearing shoes that were stained with his wife's blood, Noah had sat beside his bed, stared at the battered face of his best friend, and he spoke his truth.

'You've hurt Tress, Max. She is the most incredible thing that ever happened to you, and this will break her heart. I think it already has. Because you know where she is? Could you hear what I told you earlier? Or did you get her message and that's why you were speeding in that car? Panicking that you'd been caught out?

'Let me tell you anyway – she's over in the maternity wing of this hospital and I had to lie to her all day and tell her you were coming back to her. And you know what? She believed every word because she loves you more than life and she thinks you are the best fucking guy on the planet. I think we both know now that isn't true.'

Noah had sobbed, struggled to get the words out, his heart breaking.

'And the only reason I left her to come and see you now is because she's not in labour any more. Because, yeah, that was the other consequence of this, Max. You missed the birth of your baby.

'You've got a boy, Max, and man, he's the most beautiful thing I've ever seen. You missed him. Tress had to bring him into this world without you and I need to tell you she was amazing. You don't deserve her, you really don't. And you don't deserve him either.'

He'd put his hand on top of Max's, just as he'd done with Tress so many times that night.

'So here's what I have to say to you, buddy. All my life you've been my best mate, and I have loved you every day of it. I wouldn't go back and change a single thing about our lives until now, because we made each other better. I know that. I'd have done anything for you, and I know you felt the same. We both proved it a million times. I don't know how this is going to end, but if it's not good, then I need you to know that I love you still. Because to lose that would make me look back and regret so much and I don't want to do that.'

Noah's tears had fallen, dropping on to Max's face, and he'd gently wiped them away. 'But here's the thing... And if you were awake now, I know you'd call me a sanctimonious prick, but I don't give a crap because you need to hear about the rest of the consequences.

'Tress would never lie, so if he asks, then your son will know that you weren't there on the day he was born. And the truth always comes out. That kid is going to grow up and one day he'll learn that his father wasn't there because he was screwing his best friend's wife. Tress, or me, is going to have to explain just how someone could do something so fucking terrible. Your kid is going to have to think about that, and find a way to deal with it. We all will.'

Tonight, freezing his arse off on an old wooden park bench in the middle of the night, Noah knew he wouldn't take those words back. But he also knew now that they would never tell Buddy the truth. The little one would never know what his father had done, because Noah and Tress had agreed to protect his father's memory. Even in death, they were still protecting the man who'd betrayed them all.

Back then, he'd held Max's hand, stroked his hair, and the final words he'd spoken to his best friend summed up exactly why this had happened.

'All because you made the choice to take something that wasn't yours.'

Now, a year later, everything had changed.

His girlfriend wanted to leave him. His ex-wife wanted to come back.

And him?

Revisiting that night, and then everything that had happened today, had put a different thought in his head. One he'd been denying for a long time. One that scared him to death.

Noah Clark had just realised what he wanted to keep and what he was prepared to lose.

24

KELI

The white test stick was sitting in front of them both and Keli wasn't sure if she or her mum was more terrified as they watched the little squares on it, waiting for it to predict her future.

As soon as she'd walked in the door and told her mother she had something she needed to talk to her about, her mum had acted exactly as she always did when it came to her kids – she'd switched off the cooker, taken Keli's hand and led her to the kitchen table. It had always been that way, whether she was nine or twenty-nine. Their mum was no pushover, and she could dole out the rollockings when they were out of line, but they always knew, no matter what, that they came first. Keli could only hope she would be the same when she had kids. She just prayed that wouldn't be any time soon.

'Okay, tell me, honey. And don't look so terrified, because unless you're dying, we'll fix it or deal with it or find a way to help.' Then she'd paused, before blurting, 'You're not dying, are you? Can we get that out of the way first?'

Despite the absolute nightmare that she appeared to be living through, she had laughed. 'No, Ma, I'm not dying. Although, there's a good chance you might want to kill me or someone else when I've finished telling you this story.'

Her mum's eyebrows had knitted in consternation, yet even with that expression, she still looked beautiful. Gilda Clark had inherited her own Ghanaian mother's incredible cheekbones, piercing brown eyes and, even well into her sixties, there was barely a wrinkle on her gorgeous face. 'Well, your dad just left for a golfing weekend with his buddies, and none of your siblings, except Noah, are coming over and he won't be here until later, so you've got plenty of time. Take a deep breath and start from the beginning.'

Keli had done exactly as she was told. She'd taken her mother back to the night she'd met Ryan, and how they'd got together. Her mum's eyebrows had gone from knitted together to raised in surprise at that point, but she'd said nothing, just listened, even though Keli knew she'd be issuing death threats on the inside.

She'd got to the part where she'd been ghosted for the last month, when her mum had cracked. 'What? What kind of miserable excuse for a man is that? Coward! That's what he is! I've got a good mind to track down his mother and tell her the kind of man that she raised.'

'We haven't even got to the worst bit yet, Ma,' Keli had told her, beginning to wonder if this was such a good idea.

'Well, in that case I'm going to need wine. And a baseball bat by the sounds of things.'

Despite the prevailing tension, that had made Keli laugh again. The prospect of Gilda Clark, a respectable, upstanding woman of mature age from a picturesque village on the outskirts of Glasgow, doling out baseball bat justice to any bloke was hilarious. However, she did work as a legal secretary for one of the most feared criminal solicitors in the country, so she probably had contacts whose services could be bought. Keli had shuddered at the thought.

'Ma, before we go on, tell me you're joking.'

'Of course I am,' she'd said, coming back to the table with two glasses of wine.

She had been about to breathe a sigh of relief when her mum had added, 'I'll buy a gun. Right, go on, love.'

Keli had never felt the need for wine more, but she'd left it on the table, an ironic foreshadow of the next part of the story.

After a deep breath, she had fast-forwarded to this morning, to the text from Laurie, then the phone call, then recalled in as much detail as possible the meeting with Laurie and their conversation. Every emotion – horror, sympathy, anger, disgust, love – had crossed Gilda's face at some point in the revelations.

'And that's where we left it,' she'd finished up the Laurie chapter of the story. 'So, if she calls, then I might have to dash out, Mum.'

'I'm coming with you,' her mum had declared, puffing her cheeks out, absolutely furious. 'I want to see the look on that man's face when I tell him exactly what I think of him.'

'Did you not bring us up to fight our own battles?' Keli had chided her. 'I can do this, Mum. Trust me. It's just... well... my... my...' Oh damn, she couldn't say it. The words just wouldn't come out, no matter how she'd tried to force them.

'Your period is late,' Gilda had sighed, as she'd reached across to push Keli's hair off her astonished face.

The struggle to speak had become even tougher and it had taken her a moment to stutter out, 'H-how did you know that?'

Gilda had reached for her hand and had looked at her with such kindness and concern that Keli had almost crumbled. 'Because I'm your mother and I know you, my love. And that's the only thing that could put that expression of sheer terror on your face. That, and the fact that you haven't touched that wine. I take it you haven't done a test? You'll need to drive, because I've knocked back half a glass, but let's go right now to Asda and get one.'

'No, Mum, it's okay, I have one in my bag. That's the thing I mentioned that I have to do. I've been putting it off for a week, but Yvie persuaded me to buy it this morning.'

Her mum had pushed the wine away, got up from the table and gestured to the stairs that led to the main bathroom upstairs. There was a small cloakroom in the downstairs hall, but it was so tiny that Keli struggled to get her jeggings up without bruising her elbows, so it was no place to struggle with the intricacies of a pregnancy test. 'Then let's go, Keli Clark, because we can't start figuring out what we're going to do if we don't know what we're dealing with.'

Choked with emotion and gratitude, Keli had risen from her chair, leaned over and wrapped her arms around her mum's shoulders. 'In case I'm too busy falling apart after this, I just want to tell you I love you, Mum.'

'I love you too, my darling. Now go do that test, bring it back down, and I'll be right here ready to panic with you while we wait for the results.'

It was the push, or the comfort, or the 'all out of reasons to delay' that she needed. She'd gone upstairs and, with shaking hands, somehow managed to pee on target, and then replaced the cap and come back downstairs, holding it out in front of her like it was high-grade plutonium that could blow a crater in the earth's crust at any second.

She'd put it down on the kitchen table two minutes ago and now, that's where they were, staring at it, waiting for the verdict to appear.

Keli lost her nerve, closed her eyes, prayed to the gods of the pregnancy test to make this one negative.

'Keli...'

Her mum's voice, but she couldn't interpret the tone. Good or bad?

'Keli, you have to look.'

Still no clue. And still not opening her eyes, because it struck her that she hadn't given any proper thought to what she would do if it were positive. How would she work? How would she manage childcare and support a baby on her wages, and... She blocked herself from going any further down that baby rabbit hole.

Tress had managed to be a great mum to Buddy despite so much more adversity. Keli had her mum and dad, she had Noah, her other siblings, she had Yvie and she had Tress. She could do this. She could. So it was time to put her big-girl pants on and just look at the damn test.

She opened her eyes, narrowed in on the little box that showed the result.

'Oh Mum...' she whispered. 'I don't know what to say. Is it definitely right?'

'Well, love, I'm not one hundred per cent sure, but you're the nurse. Isn't this supposed to be your area of expertise?'

Keli shook her head. 'I've never come across a seventy-year-old who required a pregnancy test.'

'It's right. It has to be right. Doesn't it?'

For the first time, a smile began to play on her lips, as she held the test up, peered at it again, read the words in the box. NOT PREGNANT.

'I think you might find the late period and the nausea were caused by the stress of this man... what was the word you used?'

'Ghosting me.'

'Yes, that. The same thing used to happen to me. The nausea, not the ghosting. Your father wouldn't have dared. Anyway, when my stress levels were through the roof, it would knock my whole cycle off. When your sister was backpacking around Asia on her own, I felt like I had seasickness for two months. Best diet I've ever been on, though.' Gilda took a large gulp of her wine and Keli could see now how worried she'd been.

'I couldn't have done that without you, Mum. I'm so grateful.' Oh, the sweet relief. She wanted to punch the air, summon a brass band and set off fireworks all at the same time.

'It's part of my job description, my love. It's also the reason I get heartburn. Okay, I need to say what's on my mind and you're not going to like it, so do you want wine for this, or shall I just blast it out and get it over with?'

Grinning, Keli flexed her fingers, exhaled, braced herself. She'd known this was coming too. Step Two in the Gilda Clark manual of parenting.

Step One:- Be supportive at all times and stay calm in a crisis.

Step Two:- When the danger has passed, ensure child has full understanding of the error of their ways.

It was the equivalent of searching frantically for a lost child, then scolding them as soon as you found them. Keli loved listening to Noah's stories of her mum dragging him and Max out of too many dodgy situations to count, including a nightclub in Glasgow city centre that they'd managed to blag their way in to when they were only seventeen and supposed to be at another friend's house for a sleepover. Gilda had pointed them out to security, had them ejected and then castigated them the whole way home.

Tonight, it was her turn, and even though she was a grown-ass woman, she was happy to take it.

'I'll skip the wine in case I need to drive later. Okay, I'm ready. Go ahead, Mum. Give it your best shot.'

Gilda took a deep breath. 'Don't you ever, EVER...' Oh shit, the voice was getting raised. '...Give away your power or your happiness to a man again. You say you spent weeks distraught and stressed that he ghosted you? Have I taught you nothing? You're so much more than that, Keli Clark. If someone shows you who they are, then you believe them and walk away. If someone doesn't value you, you walk away and find someone who does. If someone breaks your heart...'

'I know, you walk away.'

'No, you tell me, and I'll smash their windows. And then you walk away. But you never, EVER let someone else dictate your life. Do you understand me?'

Keli could feel two fat tears streaming down her cheeks, but she wasn't sure if they were generated by gratitude or relief.

'I do.'

'And my next point of consternation – sort out your bloody contraception. You're a nurse for God's sake!'

'Trust me, Mum, I'm never having sex again.'

'Excellent decision. Celibacy is very fashionable these days. Okay. Now come help me get dinner finished before your brother gets here. I hope he's okay. I've been worried sick about that man all day.'

Glass in hand, her mum headed back to the cooker and Keli realised that she hadn't mentioned the fact that she'd seen Anya this morning. She decided not to. That was Noah's story to tell.

She was about to text Yvie with the good news when, suddenly, two things happened at once. They heard the front door opening and heard Noah shout hello, just as a text pinged on Keli's phone.

Laurie.

I think I know where he will be tonight. Can you come?

The unmistakable sound of a door closing told her that Noah had gone into the downstairs loo out in the hall.

Keli turned the handset so her mum could see it – which took

ten seconds longer than it should have, because her mum had to
find her glasses first.

'Go,' her mum urged. 'But fix your hair and get a bit of bright
red lippy on. You look like you've been dragged through a hedge
after all that fretting.'

As Keli fished in her bag for her lipstick, she felt a flash of guilt.
Noah might need her here. What if he wanted to talk? What if he
had something on his mind that he would only speak to her about?

But, on the other hand, she felt the solidarity of the pact that
she'd made with Laurie.

Noah chose that moment to come in the door.

'Hey,' she said, shoving her phone in her pocket, to free up her
hands to hug him. 'How was your day?'

'Eventful. Buckle up, I've got loads to tell you.' Keli watched him
scan the room. 'Ma, where's your charger? My phone died earlier.'

'Over there, son,' Gilda gestured to the fancy new charging
station she'd bought off eBay the week before.

Meanwhile, Keli was still trying to make a decision, so she just
blurted out the quandary. 'Noah, a friend of mine is dealing with
something and she's just texted and asked me to go over. It's no
biggie, though. I can stay if you want company.'

Her mum took her head out of the oven and stood up. 'Am I not
here? Do I not exist?'

'I mean sisterly company. Which is second best to you, Mum.
Obviously,' Keli back-pedalled, frantically.

At least Noah was still laughing.

'Honestly,' she tried again with Noah, 'I can tell her I can't
make it.'

He tossed his jacket on the chair, rolled up his sleeves as he
crossed the lounge to the kitchen. 'Nope, not having that on my
conscience. I've upset enough people today. You go, sis.'

'You're sure?'

'He's sure,' their mother reinforced the point. 'Now go. And make sure you remember what I told you earlier.'

'What did I miss?' Noah asked, puzzled.

'Nothing! Nothing at all. Just Mum giving me a lecture. Usual stuff.'

She threw her mother a warning glance, but she knew it was unnecessary. Rule number three in the Gilda Clark Parenting Manual – Never discuss your children's issues with their siblings unless granted explicit permission.

Her mum's lips would be sealed.

Keli didn't ask again. She trusted Noah was being honest, grabbed her jacket and kissed them both on the cheek.

'Call me later,' her mother called after her.

'I will, Ma. Love you both.'

She pulled the door shut behind her and practically ran to the car, in a completely different mindset from this morning.

If she'd been pregnant, she'd have had to play nice.

Now, she could do and say exactly as she pleased.

And she intended to.

8 P.M. – 10 P.M.

25

ODETTE

With trembling hands, Odette Devine reached out and knocked on Nancy Jenkins' door, hoping that she wouldn't be dead on the doorstep by the time Nancy answered. There was a searing pain in her head and she felt like it could explode at any second. Meanwhile, her heart was beating like the drum in one of those rave songs from back in the eighties. Or was it nineties? She couldn't think straight.

She'd asked Harry to stop just a little bit along the street because she didn't want Nancy to open the door and see a big bloody limo, as if Odette was trying to show off. That was the last thing she was aiming to achieve here.

She had no idea what she was going to say. Not a clue how she would be received. And she was terrified to find out, but what were the options?

She waited. And waited. No answer. She waited a few seconds more, then knocked again. This time, she battered the door like it was a police raid on a drug den. Nancy Jenkins was either deaf as a post, or not in.

Exasperated, Odette stepped to the side of the path, onto the grass of the front lawn and peered in the window to get the answer. Yes, the light was on, but that was all. In the corner, the TV was black, the fire was off and there were no other signs of life.

Bugger. The deflation and disappointment almost took the wind right out of her, and she held on to the windowsill for a moment until the light-headedness passed. It felt like she'd been in a car, racing towards a brick wall at 100 miles per hour, only to swerve at the last minute, and now her body was being flooded with a combination of relief, fear and terror at what could just have happened. And a whole load of dread, because she knew that if she were going to have a chance of making amends, she was going to have to do this all over again another time.

Behind her, she heard Calvin striding up the path. 'Not in? Right then. Let's get back into town and go for dinner. My hair and this outfit aren't cut out for the suburbs.'

Damn it. There were two choices: go back and sit in the car until Nancy came home or leave and come back tomorrow.

Her instinct was to wait. This moment was almost forty years overdue, and now that she'd finally plucked up the courage to come here, she wasn't sure she could leave without an answer. Besides, if she returned tomorrow, she'd have to find some cash for a taxi.

But then... She spotted the Neighbourhood Watch plaque on the wall next to the window and had a realisation. Security. What if Nancy's lights were on an automatic timer to make it appear that someone was home, but she was currently lying on a sunlounger on a fortnight's holiday in Benidorm? Okay, maybe not a sunlounger at this time of night, or in February, but she could certainly be sipping sangria on a hotel terrace somewhere.

'Odette, come on, darling, let's go. If Harry puts his foot down, we'll still get there before they cancel our table. I had to practically offer my body to get that reservation and I'm not giving it up.'

Odette reluctantly – oh so very reluctantly – conceded the argument. She would come back tomorrow. And the next day. And the next. And keep coming until she found Nancy. After all, she had plenty of time on her hands.

'Odette! Dear God, you're swaying all over the place there. That's the plonk from the reception earlier. Champagne, my arse. That was fizzy wine, straight from a screw-top bottle. Here, grab on to my arm and let's get you back in the car.'

Odette allowed herself to be guided back down the path, and the relief of getting back into the warm comfort of the limo was so overwhelming that tears pricked the back of her eyes.

'Okay there, Odette?' Harry asked, and she met his gaze in the rear-view mirror. 'Where to now?'

Odette really, really wanted to say home. Her head was still pounding so hard, she felt dizzy and every fibre of her being wanted to be in bed, with a cup of tea, and some true crime show about solving a murder in twelve hours on the telly. But she also recognised how much effort Calvin had gone into planning this dinner – mostly because he kept reminding her – and she didn't want to disappoint him, especially since he was one of the very few people in her life who still gave a toss about her.

'The Oyster Lounge, please, Harry.'

Next to her, Calvin muttered, 'Blessed be the fish,' visibly relieved that they were finally on their way.

Now that the rush-hour traffic had dissipated, the journey back into the city centre was much quicker than the gridlock of earlier. Calvin finally relaxed, after calling the restaurant and letting them know they were on the way. Odette took two paracetamols, then closed her eyes and let her head rest. She must have nodded off, because the next thing she knew, Calvin was gently nudging her awake.

'Okay, my darling, let's go.'

Odette's first reaction was to snap at him that she wanted to sleep longer. Her second reaction was to say that she really didn't want to do this, and tell him she was cancelling. Her third was resignation that she just had to suck it up and get on with it, and ignore the fact that she felt awful, she was exhausted, and she was still in the same outfit she'd had on all day. Oh, the shame of it. Hopefully, she could sneak in, sneak out, with as few people as possible seeing her.

'Odette! This way!' The flash of a paparazzo on the way into the restaurant squashed that hope.

Bugger. She should have known they'd be here on a Friday night. This was the hottest restaurant in town at the moment.

Putting her head down so they couldn't get a shot, grateful that Calvin had his arm around her and was ushering her into the grand entrance, she tried to blink away the pain behind her eyes and gave herself an internal pep talk. *Come on, Odette. You're a bloody actress. Just a couple more hours of pretending you want to be here. That's all. Easy. You've got this.*

Inside the foyer, a maître d' held his arms out in greeting. 'Miss Devine, it's our pleasure.'

Somehow she managed to muster a smile. Curtain up, performance under way.

'If you'd just like to come this way,' he offered, with a theatrical flourish of the hands.

Calvin slipped behind her, as Odette followed the maître d's direction. Hopefully, they'd be sat at a corner table, far from prying eyes, then she could get this over with.

Passing the main glass doors into the restaurant, he steered them to another door a little further on, to what Odette assumed must be one of their famed private dining rooms. Relief. And gratitude. Calvin had really pulled out the stops for her tonight. She flushed with shame that she'd been trying to get out of this, after he'd gone to so much trouble to give her this wonderful end to her career. Even if she still wanted to go home and put her nightdress and slippers on.

The maître d' swept the door open, then stood to the side. Odette lifted her head, resolved to make an effort to get through this. It was just a dinner. Just a quiet, intimate, private meal that...

She stepped forward, and right at that second, the whole room exploded in a cheer of 'Surprise!'

Odette lurched to the side, and only Calvin's quick reflexes caught her. In the name of all that was holy, what the hell was going on?

Three things happened in a split second. First, she scanned the room and saw that it was full of people who mattered. Or at least, used to matter to her. The head of the studio, all the producers, Carl, the director, and three or four of the other stars of the show, including that twit, Rex. Calvin's partner in the management agency. A couple of the ladies from *The Clydeside* canteen that she had known for ever. Tress, the set designer that she'd grown fond of.

The second thing was that she spotted the documentary crew in the corner, taking in her reaction for posterity.

And the third thing was that, from somewhere inside her, Odette Devine, superstar, icon, actress, found the strength to snap into character, slap on the widest grin, clutch her heart and act grateful and humble as she chirped, 'Oh my goodness, what a shock. Thank you. Thank you. Thank you all so much for this.' She turned around, threw her arms around Calvin and gave him the most vociferous hug, her gleaming smile still on her face as she whispered, 'I'm going to bloody kill you.'

'Yes, well do it tomorrow, darling, because tonight, I wasn't going to let this pass without real champagne, wonderful food and the kind of send-off that Odette Devine deserves.'

As he said that, a chill ran from the top of Odette's aching head, all the way down to her palpitating heart.

The truth was that Odette Devine might deserve all the acclaim, the cameras, the champagne, the applause.

But Olive Docherty deserved none of it.

26

TRESS

Tress was so relieved that Odette was sitting next to her at the huge round table. This definitely wasn't the quiet, intimate date that she'd been expecting. When Rex had picked her up at the house, her whole body had been trembling with excitement. Or perhaps fear. It had been impossible to tell, because all she could think about was that she was going out. On a date. With an actual man. And a very loud voice in her head was telling her to turn around and go straight back home and spend the night with her son, even though he was in the very caring hands of Nancy, and was fast asleep, with no idea whether she was there or not.

Was this the guilt that all mums felt? Or was it just apprehension as to how this night would go, and, more importantly, how it would end? Sex, was the obvious answer. Rex had kissed her long and hard when she'd first got in the car, told her how beautiful she was, that he couldn't wait to spend this night with her. She wasn't sure if he meant dinner, or the overnight part that might come next.

After releasing her from the lip lock, he'd put his foot down on the accelerator of the Ferrari and they'd roared off down the street,

Tress praying that the noise wouldn't wake up Buddy. Rex had swerved to overtake the black limo that she'd spotted earlier, now leaving her street just ahead of them, and in two minutes, they'd been on the motorway and speeding back into town.

'I hope you don't mind, but there's a work thing that I just need to drop in on first. Odette's management team have organised an exclusive party, just for her closest friends and the top execs at the studio. I only need to stay for an hour or so, and then we can duck out and I thought we could go check out the new suite at the St Kentigern? It's a penthouse on the top floor and the management have asked me to do a couple of posts to promote it. Five minutes' work, for a stay in a ten-thousand-pounds-a-night suite. Not bad-going.'

A swanky suite. In a hotel. Just the two of them. He was definitely thinking sex. She'd inhaled deeply, trying to calm her nerves. Of course, she could say no. Walk away. But was this just fear of getting back out there and having a relationship again? Of making another mistake? Was Max Walker looking down on her right now, still finding a way to influence her thoughts and keep her to himself? Sod it, she'd cross the sex bridge and all the potential pitfalls, regrets, and 'don't sleep with co-workers' ethics when and if she ever got to it. First, she had to concentrate on enjoying herself with a gorgeous man, who was proudly taking her to an important event.

'Won't it raise eyebrows that you're there with me? I mean, with the studio bosses?'

Rex had shaken his head. 'Nope, that's why it's perfect. You're friends with Odette. For all they know, that's why you're there. And anyway, I couldn't care less. What are they going to do? Reprimand me? I'm the biggest name they have now.'

Tress had decided not to share the thought that had just come back for another lap around her mind. They might not reprimand

Rex, but what about the effect that dating someone on the show could have on *her* career? He clearly hadn't thought about that. She should have said something. Objected. Mentioned that not insignificant concern. But actually, his first point was probably valid, and the thought of a lovely tribute to Odette had won her over. She'd decided to just relax, go with the flow and enjoy herself. Although, it had been a definite struggle to force the knot of anxiety in her stomach to loosen enough so that she could breathe properly.

They had reached the city centre in the shortest time that Tress had ever completed the journey, and Rex had veered to a halt right outside the restaurant. He'd jumped out of the car, thrown the keys to a young, wide-eyed guy at the valet parking stand, then opened the door for her to get out. She'd taken two steps onto the red carpet that stretched to the door, when the flashes began.

'Rex! This way! Who is your date, Rex? Can you tell us her name?'

Rex had stopped for photographs, but Tress had just kept on walking, face burning. Thankfully, the maître d' had spotted her coming and swept the door open to let her through, while Rex had spent a few more moments giving the photographers the shots they wanted.

Not the calm, chilled-out start to the night that she'd hoped for, but at least now she was sitting next to Odette, and weirdly, there was a sense of relief that it wasn't just her and Rex in an intense, intimate setting. Argh, she really had to get over the fear of this stuff. She was a grown woman. She was allowed to date. And later, she would be perfectly within her rights to have wanton, bendy sex with this gorgeous man, should she choose to do so. In the meantime, she was going to eat, drink and celebrate her friend.

'Would you like some water, Odette?' Tress asked, picking up one of the very expensive blue bottles that had already been placed on the table. She'd seen this brand of H_2O in a magazine once and read that it cost £30 a bottle. For water! They'd clearly never heard of a tap.

'Yes, please,' Odette replied, and Tress noticed she was looking a bit pale and tired. Not really a surprise. It must have been such an overwhelming day for her.

'There you go,' Tress slid the full glass towards her. 'You must be exhausted. You've been on the go since first thing this morning.' It was easy to forget that Odette was almost seventy, because she was so vivacious and seemed to have boundless energy. Tress thought again what a loss she would be to the show. This would have been such a wonderful opportunity for the writers to come up with a storyline that encouraged the support of older women, but, of course, giving her a brutal death would get much higher ratings.

'Och, I'm fine, but thank you,' Odette reassured her, but Tress could see the tightness across her eyes and wasn't convinced. 'It's just been busy. Anyway, I'm so glad you're here. I know you don't often leave your son, so I feel very honoured that you came.'

Tress didn't have the heart to point out that she was only here as Rex's plus-one. Although, if she'd been invited, she'd definitely have accepted. Odette obviously hadn't been consulted on the guest list.

'I don't, but he was already sleeping and he's with his aunt tonight, who is one of his favourite people in the world, so even if he wakes up, he's in good hands. Although that didn't stop me thinking about turning back all the way here from Weirbridge.'

Tress felt her eyes inexplicably tear up, and she had to mimic a small sneeze to cover it up. What was wrong with her? Her emotions were all over the place. Odette wasn't the only one who was having an overwhelming day. Maybe doing this tonight hadn't been a good idea. She'd thought it would stop her drowning in the memories of what was happening one year ago right now.

She checked her watch: 8.47 p.m. This time last year, Buddy had been exactly thirty minutes old. And she was about to hear Noah tell her that Max was critically ill in the building right next to where she'd given birth.

'Tress...!'

Odette's voice cut through her thoughts, and came with a bump to the elbow that suggested Odette had been trying to speak to her and Tress had been too lost in her own mind to realise it.

'Sorry. I was in another world there.' A world that was beautiful and perfect and horrific and painful all at the same time.

Odette was leaning close to her now, whispering, a very strange look on her face. 'Did you say Weirbridge? Is that where you live?'

'Yes,' Tress nodded. 'Have I never mentioned that before?'

'No. I would have remembered because I used to work there, a million years ago. In fact, I was just there earlier, trying to look up an old friend I haven't seen in decades, but she wasn't in.'

Tress got closer, enjoying the conversation, allowing it to distract her from the flashbacks to the past. 'Really? Who's your friend? It's a tiny place and everyone knows everyone, so I'll get you the inside gossip on whoever it is.'

Tress was so engrossed, she almost overlooked that Odette was even paler now.

'A lady called Nancy. Nancy Jenkins.'

Rex and Calvin, sitting on either side of her and Odette, both turned to see what was happening as Tress gasped, chuckled and exclaimed, 'No way!'

Odette chided them both with, 'Back to your conversations, boys, nothing to see here,' and when they obliged, she leaned closer to Tress, so only she could hear. 'You know her?'

Tress heard the tremor in Odette's voice and guessed that Nancy must mean a lot to her. Not surprising, really. Nancy was the kind of friend that no one would want to lose touch with. Another thought cut right across that one – why had Nancy never mentioned that she knew Odette? She didn't have time to ponder that because Odette was waiting for an answer.

'Yes! Odette, Nancy is my next-door neighbour. More than that, she's like my surrogate mum, the person who takes care of Buddy and me like we're her own. In fact, that's who is babysitting him right now. That's incredible! What a small world. Did you say you were there tonight?'

'Yes. Right before we came here,' Odette nodded, almost robotically, a strange, faraway look in her eyes. Definitely tired. Poor woman. Hopefully this news would cheer her up.

'Oh, this is just too funny. Nancy wasn't at home because she was in my house, helping with Buddy while I was getting ready to come out.' Tress pulled her phone out of her bag. 'Let me call her right now and tell her you're looking for her. Wow, Odette Devine for Nancy Jenkins,' Tress joked.

'No,' Odette interrupted her urgently.

Tress froze, shocked at the vehemence in Odette's retort. Damn, there was definitely a story here. Something must have happened between these two. Tress was sure it was nothing that couldn't be fixed, though. Nancy was the most lovely and loyal friend a woman could have. Yes, she was fond of saying she bore a grudge until the end of time, but Tress didn't always believe that. There was a forgiving heart in there too. Just as long as the person in question hadn't committed some terrible betrayal of Nancy or hurt someone she loved. 'You don't want me to call her? I'm sure she'd love to hear from you,' Tress assured Odette.

'No!' A pause. 'I mean, yes. Call her, please. But don't say it's Odette Devine who wants to speak to her. Tell her it's Olive Docherty. She'll understand.'

Tress was just about to make the call, when, on the other side of Odette, her manager, Calvin, stood up and commanded everyone's attention, before launching into a gushing tribute to Odette and her career, going back decades and recounting a dozen hilarious anecdotes while the waitstaff served their starters. He gestured to the table to eat while he continued to speak. When he offered a toast to his friend and client at the end, Tress picked up her phone again, but was cut off for a second time, when Calvin passed the torch to the head of the studio, who waxed on for another twenty minutes, right through the arrival of the main courses.

To her surprise, Rex stood up next and spoke of his adoration for the woman who had played his mother for two years. 'Odette, it has been the honour of my career and I hope you know that I will be here for you always. We love you.'

As he raised his glass for everyone to follow, Odette blew him a kiss and Tress felt her heart swell. When he sat back down, Tress felt his hand on her thigh under the table and wondered if the flush she could feel rising up her neck was visible to everyone in the room, especially Calvin, who had just brushed right behind them on the way to the loo. She tried to distract herself by picking up the phone with the intention of finally calling Nancy, but was thwarted again when Elliot, the producer of Odette's documentary, stood up.

He was on a little raised stage that Tress hadn't even noticed in the corner of the room and cleared his throat as a projector screen came down from the ceiling and filled the wall behind him. 'Ladies and gentlemen, as you know, I have been following the life of Odette for quite some time now. When I pitched my idea for this documentary to the studio, I told them that it was going to be the chronicle of a star and the kind of story that would show who Odette Devine really is. I think I've achieved that. But I'm fairly sure that the story I'm about to tell isn't the one that you expected. The programme isn't finished yet, in fact we were still shooting today as the curtain fell on Odette's career. But for the last few days, and the last couple of hours, we've been working in the editing suite, and we've put together a little preview. I'd like to show it to you now.'

He paused, stared straight at Odette, and went on to speak in a tone that seemed incongruous to the rest of the adulation that had been heaped on Odette tonight.

'Ladies and gentlemen, this is The Real Odette Devine. Or should I say... The Real Olive Docherty.'

The lights dimmed. The room went quiet. And beside her, Tress was sure that she heard Odette whisper a strangled, 'Noooooo.'

27

NOAH

Over home-made chilli, rice and roasted vegetables, Noah had spilled the story of his day to his mum, who had managed to let him get to the very end without passing judgement, which he knew must be killing her. Gilda had made her feelings about Anya very clear after the accident. In the months that Anya was healing at home, she'd told Noah that she'd support whatever choice he made, whether to try to find a way to repair their marriage or not. However, as soon as he'd confessed that he didn't see any way back, she'd almost combusted with relief and thanked the gods for helping him see sense. 'You're too big-hearted, Noah Clark. I've no idea where you get that from, but it'll be the end of you if you're not careful.'

Noah knew exactly where he got it from. Despite her latent fury at her daughter-in-law for breaking her son's heart, and her own sense of betrayal that Anya, someone she'd treated as one of her own for the twenty years she'd been part of the family, had caused devastation to them all, his mum had never lost her compassion. Anya's own parents lived in the USA, and had only been able to visit for a couple of weeks after the accident, so Gilda had continued to take care of their daughter, prepare her food, help her shower, talk to her at any time of the day or night. She said she was doing it for Anya's mother, just as she would expect Anya's mum to step up if the roles were reversed, but Noah knew that wasn't the whole truth. She'd done it for him, to help with the load, to support him at the lowest point of his life. She was exactly the kind of parent that he hoped he'd be one day.

Although, not any time soon, given today's events.

When he'd got to the end of the saga, he'd put down his cutlery, leaned towards her. 'So what do you think, Mum?'

'I think you need to get your elbows off the table,' she'd chided him, and he knew it was to lighten the mood and make him smile, before she went on, 'Are you sure you want to let Cheska go, son? You've been so close over the last few months.'

He couldn't read her reaction. Was she telling him he was making a mistake or was she testing his resolve?

'I'm sure, Ma. To be honest, she's right. I'm never going to be the person she deserves and that's not fair on her. She should have so much better.'

'Not better, just different,' him mum suggested. 'For what it's worth, I don't think you're wrong. Cheska is a gem, but I can't help thinking that if there was going to be anything serious between you, you'd have realised that before now. And as for Anya...' Of course, her lips pursed when she said her name. He had a feeling she'd have that reaction to her former daughter-in-law for the rest of her life. 'I think that we handled ourselves in a way that was right and decent after the accident.' Remarkably sage and magnanimous, he decided, until she went on, 'But I'm glad you closed down any suggestion of letting her back into our lives because I never want to see that woman again for as long as I'm breathing on this earth. The thought of her makes me want to throw this pitta bread at the wall. And why haven't you eaten any of it? You'd better not be avoiding carbs again, because I've told you that wreaks havoc with your bowels.'

He'd decided not to remind her right at that moment that he was a trained medical professional who was well informed as to the impact that his nutritional intake had on his body. He'd got up, put his plate in the dishwasher, and then kissed the top of her head.

'Thanks, Ma. I love you, you know?'

'I know, son. Anything else on your mind?' she'd asked and he could see she was fishing. Sometimes he thought she knew him better than he knew himself. But the only other thing on his mind wasn't up for discussion. Not yet. Not until he'd worked it out for himself. And not until he'd spoken to the person that it affected most. Not until he'd seen Tress.

'No, Ma, I think two major incidents are enough for one day.'

He knew she didn't believe him, but he also knew she'd wait until he was ready to tell her what was going on.

Now that he'd brought his mum up to date, it was time to do something about it.

'I'm going to shoot off. I want to pop in and see Tress before it's too late. Just check in on her, make sure she's still okay.'

'Give her my love and can you take that gift over there for Buddy. It'll save me lugging it along to the party on Sunday. I was going to pop it round earlier, but Keli...' She paused and he detected a hesitation, before she came back with, 'Keli and I got carried away chatting and I didn't get a chance.'

He laughed when he saw the present – long, with a succession of bumps along the top. The wrapping game from the women in Buddy's life had been a vibe today. 'That's either a train, a caterpillar or a set of speed bumps.'

'Busted. I heard Nancy and Val were going for the nature

theme, so I joined in. That child is going to grow up to be David Attenborough.'

Noah gave her another hug, then, caterpillar under his arm, headed out to the car. It was a five-minute, two-street journey to Tress's house, but he sat outside for a few minutes, his internal monologue arguing with itself.

What was he doing? What was he thinking? There was no way that he was feeling the things that he thought he was feeling. It was just the emotion of the day. The pain of the memories. The uncertainty of the future. It would all subside after today was over and they could put the first anniversary of the accident behind them. It had to. Because what if he said or did something that destroyed Tress's trust in their friendship? He couldn't bear that. He couldn't live with himself if he caused her a single second of pain or anxiety after all she'd already been through. No. He definitely couldn't. This wasn't the right time. The realisation he'd had as he sat in that park today could just stay locked in his head for now, maybe forever. And also, it was fricking freezing, so unless he wanted to die of hypothermia and add to the long list of reasons that today would always be significant, then he'd better get inside.

He let himself in as always, and heard noises coming from the lounge – heavy breathing that definitely didn't sound like it was a situation that would welcome a spectator. Oh shit. What the hell was going on? If he went in there and Tress was with Rex, then...

Another sound. Music? Then a gunshot.

Noah pushed open the door and there they were...

Nancy and Val, side by side on the couch, cocktails in hand watching a steamy sex scene on *Outlander*.

Nancy jumped first. 'Jesus Christ, Noah Clark, you could have given me a heart attack there.'

'Especially when this lot have already got her pulse going like a train,' Val quipped, gesturing to the screen.

'She's right,' Nancy conceded. 'What I wouldn't give for those men in kilts to storm my fortress...'

The two of them dissolved into gales of laughter that were totally infectious.

Noah plonked himself down on the couch next to a chuckling Nancy, who reluctantly paused the show so that they could give him their attention. Or maybe so that they didn't miss any of the raunchy bits.

Val regained her composure first. 'This is why I came round here. Our Michael was over watching the footie with his dad, so I could stay there and watch twenty-two men chasing a ball or come here and watch this. Nancy Jenkins, don't you dare make a filthy innuendo about men and balls. You're better than that.'

Nancy mimicked locking her lips and throwing away the key.

'Anyway, Noah, Michael said they're meeting for five-a-sides on Thursday night and they need you.' Michael was Val's son, and now that Don was in the late stages of Alzheimer's, he spent a few nights a week with his dad.

'Tell him I'll be there. Is Tress upstairs?' he asked, assuming they'd come round to keep her company.

The two women glanced at each other, and something passed between them, before they both, like synchronised swimmers, turned to face him again.

'Did you not get her message?' Nancy asked. 'Or the photos I sent you?'

'No, I... Shit.' He fished into his pocket and pulled out his phone, seeing now that it was still on the home screen that required a password before it kicked into action. He'd charged it at his mum's house, but he'd left there in such a hurry to come here that he hadn't even looked at it.

He did now. The instant he put the password in, it sprang to life, in a succession of beeps. He immediately zeroed in on the notification that said, 'Voicemail: Tress Walker.'

He clicked on it to listen.

'Hey, Noah, it's me. Just checking in with you to see how your day is going and how your chat with Anya went. Maybe you're still having it. Anyway, everything is fine here. Don't worry about calling me back, because I know you're going to your mum's for dinner. Oh, and that advice you gave me earlier? I took it. I'm going out with Rex tonight. Only mildly terrified. Actually, that's a lie. Definitely majorly terrified. I'll buzz you later, but if you need me, just call. Love you.'

Every pore in his skin prickled into a goosebump and his gut received a boot that almost doubled him over. 'She's out on a date? With Rex?'

Oh fuck. Oh fuck fuck.

He knew that Nancy and Val were staring at him, and he couldn't bear the scrutiny, didn't want them to see the reaction that was probably written all over his face, so he distracted himself by staring back down at the phone.

One new text – from Nancy Jenkins.

He opened that, and damn, a second swift boot, to the windpipe this time. A photo of Tress, all dressed up, looking incredible, her head thrown back, giggling. And a comment underneath that said, 'Shania sent this.'

Noah raised his gaze from the screen to be greeted by two pairs of eyes staring straight into his soul. He opened his mouth to speak, but the words were stuck. If he said it, there was no going back. But they knew. He could see it in the glint of their eyes, in the questions in their raised eyebrows, in the expectant expressions that were encouraging him to spit it out.

'I love her,' he whispered.

The statement clearly didn't live up to their expectations.

'Sorry, son? My hearing isn't what it used to be,' Nancy challenged him.

He shook his head, unable to stop the grin. He bloody loved these two as well.

'I said I love her,' he declared, louder, stronger.

'That's better. Say it like you mean it,' Val chuckled. 'And it's not a newsflash. We were just waiting for you to realise it.'

'Am I crazy, Val? What about Tress? Is this the last thing she needs?'

'Nope,' Nancy countered, 'We reckon she feels the same. We're just waiting for her to realise it too.'

'I mean, we're not entirely sure,' Val piped up. 'We reckon it's a solid seventy/thirty. In your favour.'

'Eighty/twenty,' Nancy argued. 'But what about Cheska, son? Have you, erm, spoken to her about this?'

'Cheska is going to America,' he sighed, then it struck him immediately that neither of them looked remotely surprised about that. 'Hang on. You two knew?'

Val had the decency to give an apologetic shrug. 'Sorry, love, but we did. She told me one night a few weeks ago when she was over helping with Don, but she asked me not to say anything until she'd told you yourself. You two want different things. I'm glad she had the courage to chase her dreams. She's a lovely lass, and she's going to make a huge difference to a lot of people's lives in this new job.'

'And that's why...' Another apologetic shrug, this time from Nancy. 'That's why we were laying it on thick with the Shania stuff. We just want you and Tress to be happy. You two belong together. It's plain as day. Just don't know why it's taken you so long to see it too.'

'I get it now, though,' he sighed. What had started as a revelation after some soul searching on a park bench now felt absolutely right – he just wasn't sure what he should do about it.

Val leaned forward, like she was about to share a valuable secret. 'But the thing is, Noah, you're never going to find out if you're sitting on that couch. So if you really do love that lass, then I suggest you get out there and you find her and you tell her, before she does something stupid with that arse from the telly.'

28

KELI

The lobby of the St Kentigern had been a bustling hive of tourism and revelry when Keli had burst through the doors like her buttocks were on fire.

Not even the prospect of seeing Ryan sodding Manning could dampen the wave of relief that she was riding. She wasn't pregnant. There was no doubt that there would be a time in her life when she'd be ready and excited for the opposite to be true, but right now the exhilaration of seeing those words on that stick felt fan-flipping-tastic. She wasn't going to have a tie to him for the rest of her life. She owed him nothing. Needed nothing from him.

She never knew that emotional freedom could feel this good. And yes, it was going to be a long time before she had sex again, and no, she would never, ever make a mistake as stupid as the one she'd made that had put her in this position in the first place. From now on, there would be two condoms on standby at all times. And bubble-wrap pants. Nothing was getting through those suckers.

It had struck her on the drive over that she could end this here. Walk away. Never see him or think about him again, but no. She'd made a commitment to Laurie and she wasn't going to back down.

It was a sentiment reinforced by Yvie when she'd called her with the update. There had been gasps at every piece of information. Not pregnant. Gasp. Then lots of happy sweary words. Actually, they were just normal sweary words, but the tone in which Yvie said them made it clear she was punching the air. Keli had gone on to tell her about the meeting with Laurie. Gasp. Recounted everything the other woman had told her. Gasp. Got to the bit about the plan to track him down. Gasp. Read out the text she'd just received from Laurie. Gasp. Then ended with the fact that she was on her way to meet Laurie at that very moment. Gasp.

When Keli was done, Yvie checked she had the absorbed the correct information. 'Hang on, let me get this straight. You're going to meet this woman at the St Kentigern, because she has found out where this bloke is going to be tonight, and you are going to go find him and confront him? Together?'

'That's about it,' Keli had confirmed, as she'd swerved the car off the motorway and onto the slip road that led directly into the west side of the city centre, just ten minutes away from the St Kentigern Hotel.

Keli had heard a rustling in the background, movement, and Yvie's words had faded in and out as if she was exerting herself while she was still on the phone.

'Yvie, what are you doing?'

'Pulling on my boots. I'm leaving now. I'll be at the St Kentigern in fifteen minutes. There is no part of me that is going to miss this or let you do this without me.'

Keli was beyond grateful and touched by the offer, but she wasn't going to drag anyone else into her mess. Besides, there was a very vital component to this story that Yvie was not aware of, and it would shock the life out of her. Keli had made a point of telling no one Ryan's identity, but she was past that now. To hell with his privacy. Bugger her promise to him that they would keep their relationship strictly private. After what he'd done to her and Laurie, he didn't deserve it. Still, she resisted. 'Yvie, I'll be fine. Laurie will be with me and what's the worst that can happen?'

'You get arrested or shot. Or you somehow create a situation that leads to his demise and then you'll spend the rest of your life in prison and I'll have to come visit you every week. And, trust me, the thought of having my very generous curves manhandled in a search by a burly prison officer makes me so embarrassed my Spanx are curling up.'

'Ouch,' Keli had exclaimed.

'Exactly. And anyway, Carlo won't be back from the restaurant until after midnight, so I'm home alone and looking for mischief.'

Keli had laughed. 'Yvie Danton, I love you. Just so you know.'

'Right back at you. Although I would have appreciated a bit more notice because getting these boots on is a workout.'

'Apologies. Next time I decide to do something totally fricking insane and irrational, I'll let you know in plenty of time.'

'Fabulous. Okay, I'll text you when I'm there. See you in ten.'

Yvie and Carlo lived in Merchant City, a cosmopolitan, trendy area of Glasgow that had designer shops and some gorgeous bars and restaurants. Carlo's dad had owned an Italian restaurant there for years and Carlo had worked there until he'd bought his own place. Keli had sent up a silent prayer of thanks that her pal was so close by, then another one for a parking space.

Her wish had been immediately granted, as she'd slipped into a space, just a couple along from where she'd parked earlier. She'd jumped out, taken a deep breath, then ran up the imposing stone steps to the entrance of the grand building.

Now inside, there were people milling around everywhere. Checking in. Checking out. Men in suits and ladies in fancy outfits going into the bar. Blokes in shorts and women in leggings and trainers sitting in the lobby chairs reading guidebooks to give them inspiration for the next day's trips.

Keli scanned the whole area. No sign. She texted Laurie, who immediately replied.

Room 202 – come up.

Keli fired back.

Just waiting for a friend, be up in ten.

It didn't even take that long before Yvie breezed through the door behind her. 'There was an Uber right outside the house,' she explained. 'Is it wrong that I'm excited by this and living vicariously through your misfortune?'

Keli hugged her. 'Absolutely. But I'd do the same for you. This is why we're friends.'

She checked Laurie's text again for the room number, then they made their way there – lift to the second floor, turn right and the room was two doors along.

Laurie opened it on the first knock. Keli had wondered if it would be awkward, or if there would be any embarrassment, but there was none. She introduced Yvie to Laurie, who seemed perfectly happy to have another person along for the ride.

'Wow, this room is amazing,' Yvie said with very obvious approval. 'If you two want to go ahead, I'll just stay here, watch TV on the biggest bed on earth and eat Pringles from the minibar.'

Keli nudged her. 'Focus, my friend. Mission first.' She steered her over to the two chairs at the table by the window, while Laurie wrapped her long legs under her on the edge of the bed next to them.

'So, can I just check if there's a plan? Are you going to speak to him? Public shaming? Just so I know when to run,' Yvie asked.

Laurie answered for them. 'I think I just want him to see us. I want him to know that he's caught. That we know. That we could use the information at any point to wreck him. Not that I would, but I just can't stand to see him glide through life thinking that he can do anything he pleases to people and get away with it. To be honest, that's the way it's been for him for years.'

Yvie seemed happy with that explanation, so Keli got things moving. 'Okay, so where is he going to be tonight and how do we know?'

Laurie reached for the iPad. 'He sent a text earlier to a photographer that we know. It lays it all out.'

Keli saw Yvie's confusion and knew she'd have to tell her, but Laurie had put the iPad on the table and she had an overwhelming compulsion to read it first.

Her eyes scanned down the words in the blue box on the right-hand side of the screen. They were in inverted commas, as if they'd been taken from a speech or an article, but as she read on, Keli realised that they were something else. Facts. Explanations. Hints. The bones of an article that any celebrity journalist would be able to spin into a story. More than that, they could twist it into a narrative that made the main character look like the greatest kind of guy.

It read...

Hi mate, we'll be there just after eight. I'll be driving the Ferrari, so you'll be able to get a good shot of me getting out of the car. Here's the script you can use later, after you get the shots.

Rex Marino was spotted tonight at the Oyster Lounge in Glasgow, attending the VIP dinner for close friends of Odette Devine, the elderly actress recently bumped from The Clydeside.

Marino was accompanied by Tress Walker, the set designer

on the show. Sources say that Ms Walker's husband was killed in a tragic car accident on this date last year, leaving her to bring up their baby son alone. Marino has put his personal life on hold to support her through this difficult time.

'It's typical of him,' a friend close to the actor stated. 'Despite his fame, he's the most decent guy you could ever meet and he's always the first one to drop everything to help anyone who needs him.'

Rumours have been circulating that Marino will be the next star to leave The Clydeside, *but in his case, it'll be for Hollywood. It has long been rumoured that he is being tipped to join the Seb Dunhill spy thriller franchise, following the reported retirement of Zander Leith.*

When asked, Marino would not confirm or deny the rumours, saying, 'I have several offers in the pipeline so it's just a case of deciding what direction is the best fit for me. I'm excited about what the future holds.'

'Bastard.' Keli felt the first shock at the name of the other person in the story, then rage building with every line. The utter and complete bastard. No. Just no. Even if she wasn't already about to rain hell on him, she'd be doing it now for messing with Tress and exploiting her grief and loss. 'Tress is my friend. She works on *The Clydeside* too – that's how I met Ryan in the first place. Oh shit, she knows nothing about any of this and she's been through enough crap.' Suddenly, her mum's suggestion about a baseball bat seemed too lenient.

Poor Tress. How the hell did she get wrapped up in this? The narcissistic prick was clearly using her for publicity, just as he used every single person he came into contact with. She could see that now. It was all about him. It had always been that way and everyone else was just a pawn in his plan.

Yvie was still sitting at the table, reading the words on the iPad again. 'Hang on, hang on. I don't get it. Can someone explain to me what Rex Marino has to do with any of this?'

'Rex Marino's real name is Ryan Manning. That's who I was seeing. Laurie's boyfriend too.' Keli conceded with a sigh.

'Well shag me sideways,' Yvie exhaled, incredulous.

It felt strange saying that aloud, even though Keli had known from the moment she met him that he was Rex Marino, the actor. It was impossible not to, given that they were at a party for *The Clyde-side's* 40th Anniversary and there were posters of him everywhere. He'd told her his real name on their second or third date, and that's how she'd known as soon as Laurie called this morning and used that name that she was genuine.

So much made sense now. She'd thought he'd insisted they kept their relationship a secret because he was all about his professional image, but obviously it was because he was dating Laurie. Now, however, he was exploiting a night out with Tress because it made him look good and he could brush that off to Laurie as a work thing. This was next-level manipulative, calculated bastard.

'How long will it take us to get to the Oyster Lounge from here?' Laurie asked, getting to her feet, grabbing a jacket and her bag.

Keli was right behind her, car keys in hand. 'Ten minutes' walk. But if we take the car, we'll be there in five. Time to go let Mr Marino know he's about to be the star of our show.'

10 P.M. – MIDNIGHT

29

ODETTE

Odette had heard the term 'life flashing in front of her eyes' many times. Now she understood it. Here it was – the truth, the whole truth and a few things that were absolutely nothing like the truth.

The preview of the documentary opened with the camera on her most recent ex-husband, Mitchum Royce, with the narrator, Elliot, on the voiceover, saying, 'Here is just one of the men that Odette tried to silence. Before making this documentary, we were forced to sign an agreement stating that none of Devine's ex-husbands would be interviewed in the making of this programme. However, respected businessman, Mitchum Royce, has agreed to speak up, after discovering that his marriage to Devine wasn't in fact legal.'

The camera zoomed in on Mitchum, looking unshaven and dishevelled, a state that Odette knew for a fact was an act. The man was a former banker with wardrobes full of suits, and he'd spent thousands of pounds of her money in Savile Row when they were together. He'd also raided enough from her bank account to afford a fricking razor. 'I gave up my career to support her and I tried my best, but she was a compulsive shopper,' Royce began. 'Spending my savings like she was Elton bloody John. She rinsed me dry and as soon as it was all gone, she was off and on to the next sucker.'

A murmur went around the room, as jaws fell open and people began to nudge each other, to whisper and shoot sly glances in her direction.

'That's not true. He's lying. He took everything from *me*,' she said to no one, anyone.

She searched the room for Calvin, but he'd nipped to the loo and he wasn't back yet. The only person who seemed to be listening to her was Tress, who reached for her hand, and Odette heard her murmuring to Rex on the other side of her, 'Rex, tell them to turn that off right now. This is a hatchet job. Make it stop.'

Odette didn't look, but she knew there was a smirk on his face by the tone of his voice. 'Fuck that, this is priceless. We'll be all over the papers tomorrow.'

'You don't mean that. Don't let this happen to her.' Tress wasn't letting it go and Odette was touched that she was desperately trying to come to her defence.

'Not my problem,' he retorted with his trademark arrogance.

'You're an asshole,' she heard Tress hiss in response, 'and you can get your hand off my fucking thigh.'

Odette barely even blinked. His response wasn't a shock to her. He'd always been a smarmy little shit.

One of the canteen ladies from *The Clydeside* studio spoke up, told Elliot to switch it off, but Elliot ignored her, letting it play on. Short of wrestling him to the ground, there was nothing much else she could do. She registered the irony that the studio execs, the cowardly bastards, just sat there, intrigued, while the only people who were sticking up for her so far were the ones with the good hearts, but without the power.

At that moment, Calvin walked back in, saw Odette's face, saw Mitchum on the screen, gauged the temperature of the room and jumped immediately to the absolutely correct conclusion. 'Get that off, Elliot. I don't know what you're playing at, but get that off.'

'Sit yourself down, Calvin. You'll miss the best bit,' Elliot sneered.

Odette felt like she was in a parallel universe where nothing was as she thought. Mild-mannered Elliot now shot a look of malevolence towards her, and a realisation hit her like a thunderbolt. She recognised that expression. That mannerism. Not from him, but from someone else. It was something in the eyes. Something she'd seen before, a million years ago. Or rather, forty years ago to be exact.

The image on the screen changed, and Odette was back, the light unflattering and her eyes bloodshot from crying. She knew when that was filmed. This afternoon. In her dressing room. After she'd spectacularly melted down at the end of her final scene.

Elliot's voice again, interviewing her, posing the question he'd asked her in their last session today. 'Okay,' he could be heard saying, 'let's wrap this up with one final question. I've read several different accounts of how you got the role on *The Clydeside*. I'd love to hear the true story straight from you.'

On the screen, Odette gave a bashful smile and began recounting her well-rehearsed version of the truth. The voiceover returned, telling the audience that everything they were about to hear, was in fact a lie.

'And now, for the first time,' the voiceover went on, 'you are about to learn the truth of the despicable things Odette Devine did to claim a career that should never have been hers.'

Odette whimpered.

A thunderous Calvin was marching towards the TV screen to switch it off, when a new face appeared.

That's when Odette knew she'd been right in her realisation from a few seconds ago. On the screen next to where Elliot was standing, their faces only a few feet apart, was a woman she recognised, and when they were side by side, the resemblance was so much more obvious. In fact, it was so strong, they could only be mother and son. It had to be.

So this was it. Karma. Justice. This man was seeking revenge for what Olive Docherty had done to his mum. The truth was going to come out now and there was no way to stop it. May as well face it and the inevitable punishment that she rightly deserved.

'Calvin, leave it,' she barked, to the palpable astonishment of everyone in the room. Appalled glares shot in her direction, before eyes darted straight back to the TV, unwilling to miss a second of this. 'Let it play,' she told him, calmer this time.

He spun around, his expression asking a silent question: *Are you mad?*

Maybe she was. But she was tired too. Tired of the lies. Tired of waiting for it to catch up with her. Tired of wondering if every awful thing that happened to her was a result of some messed-up karma she'd brought on herself by her actions all those years ago. Tired of having nothing left to lose.

What did it matter if the story came out? Let it happen. Her life was over anyway. Her money was gone. Her fame would be next. There was no family and very few friends. Sod it. Let them do their worst, because it was warranted. She had it coming. And maybe the woman who was on the screen in front of her deserved to have her moment in the spotlight. The one Odette had stolen from her four decades ago.

'We should stop this,' she heard one of the producers say to Carl, the director of the show. 'There could be legal issues for the studio.' Only interested in their own skins. Scumbags, every one of them.

Carl brushed it off with, 'Too late. Better that we know exactly what's there so we can lock this down or milk it. This could be TV gold.'

Odette had never wanted to kill anyone more, but it would have to wait.

Eyes back to the screen. The lady staring back at her was about the same age, with the skin and eyes of someone who'd shared too many nights with a packet of cigarettes and a bottle of booze. There was a hint of a slur when she started to speak.

'There were three of us who went to the audition. Of course, she wasn't Odette then. She was just plain Olive Docherty. Anyway, me, Olive and…'

Calvin came back to his seat, whispered in her ear, 'Whatever this is, you don't need to listen to it. I can get you out of here right now.'

Odette shook her head. No. She'd been running from the truth for forty years. It was time to stand still.

The woman was still speaking, but Odette didn't need to listen, because she had been there, and she knew the truth of how it ended. The phone call. That Monday morning in 1983.

She'd heard Alf's voice and known immediately who it was. 'Aye, erm, yes, hello. This is Alf Cotter. Can I speak to Fiona Jones?'

It was a split-second decision. A sliding door. A fall off a cliff, straight into hell.

She'd cleared her throat, raised her voice, copied the cadence and pitch of a brogue that she listened to every day. 'This is Fiona.'

'Fiona, like I said, this is Alf. I've got some news for you. What an audition that was. And, if I'm being honest, it came down to you and one other lass. But I'm offering you a part. You start next…'

There had still been time to do the right thing. She could just tell Fiona that Alf had called to offer her the part and Fiona would never be any the wiser. A loud voice in her head had told her to do that… but she'd ignored it.

'I'm sorry, I've changed my mind. I don't want to be on the show.'

'What?' A confused pause. Clearly Alf Cotter had never had that response before.

'I'm sorry. My boyfriend wants to move to Spain, so I'm going with him.'

'Fiona, I don't think you realise what I'm offering you here. This is the opportunity of a lifetime. Shit like this doesn't happen every day.'

'Yeah, still not fussed, to be honest. I never wanted to be an actress anyway. I only came along for a laugh. Sorry if I wasted your time.'

With shaking hands, she'd slammed the phone back down on the receiver, almost dislodging it from the wall.

Then she'd stood there, and stared at it. It was down to two, he'd said. Fiona had been number one. Was there any slight, tiny, miraculous chance that she could be the second on his list? If she was, she'd find out soon enough, because they'd all given him the same number so they could be contacted at the pre-set time.

The clock on the wall ticked. Thirty seconds. A minute. She knew the girls out in the dinner hall would be wondering where she'd got to. Still she didn't move.

Another minute. And another. Still staring.

Suddenly, Maggie, the head cook, had burst through the door. 'Olive! What the hell is the hold-up? It's like feeding time at the zoo out there. Get yourself back out and get to work or you'll be on the dole queue by the end of the day, poor Vi's niece or not!'

She'd felt the flames in her cheeks, the twist of pain in her chest, as she'd mumbled, 'Sorry, Maggie,' and begun to move. She couldn't lose this job or she'd starve. Hell, she was near starving already.

The thought had flashed through her mind that at least Nancy hadn't got the part either.

And that's when the phone had rung again. To Maggie's very obvious exasperation, Olive had snatched the receiver up, this time lowering her tone so that she sounded completely different from the voice she'd used earlier.

'Hi,' she'd said, because it was all she could manage.

He'd opened the call with exactly the same words as last time. 'Aye, erm, yes, hello. This is Alf Cotter. Can I speak to...' He paused and she'd heard the rustling of paper, as if he was checking something on a list.

Who was it? Her or Nancy? And if it was Nancy, did she have the bottle to pull the same stunt twice?

'Erm, aye. Can I speak to Olive Docherty?'

She'd almost fainted. 'This... this is Olive.'

'Aye, Olive, I've got good news for you, lass. I've thought long and hard about it, and my gut is telling me that you are Agnes McGlinchy, so...'

Olive Docherty had put her hand over the receiver, set her eyes on her furiously gesticulating boss. 'Maggie,' she'd whispered, still blocking the microphone so Alf couldn't hear. 'You can stick yer job.'

When the call ended, she hadn't even stuck around to tell Fiona or Nancy. She'd just grabbed her jacket, her beat up handbag, swapped her work shoes for her boots and charged out the door without so much as a backwards glance.

Destination – whole new life.

Before the first show aired, her management had advised her to change her name to something more memorable and Odette Devine was born. Olive Docherty was left in the dinner hall of Weirbridge Primary School. If the first character she'd created was Odette, the second was Agnes McGlinchy. And now, forty years later, she was listening to someone tell the world that the job should never have been hers.

'The thing was,' the woman on the screen spat the words with bitter anger, 'I would never have found out if I hadn't met Alf Cotter in a bar years later. He was an old man by then, barely bloody alive, but recognised me. Said I was the only person he'd ever called who'd turned down a role. Asked me if I was just home visiting from Spain and of course I had no idea what he was talking about. It soon came out, though. I thought about going public then, but who would believe the ramblings of an old man and a wannabe that never was? Well, I'm telling the world now, and I don't care who believes me because it's true.'

'Is it, Odette? Is it true?' Calvin asked her, whispering in her ear.

Before she could answer him, the room lurched, spun, and she felt entirely discombobulated. It took every bit of her strength to speak.

'Calvin, can you get me out of here?' She managed to push herself to her feet, then paused, leaning on the table.

'But is it true?' she repeated Calvin's question, loud enough to reach the ears of everyone in the room, before delivering the answer everyone was waiting to hear.

'Every bloody word.'

30

TRESS

Tress jumped up to help Calvin support Odette out of the room, ignoring the atmosphere of astonishment that had settled around them. She was appalled. Those people were supposed to be Odette's friends and colleagues and yet everyone except Calvin and the canteen ladies had sat there and lapped up the scandal, including that cretin, Rex Marino. Urgh. This was a world that she didn't want to be a part of. In that moment, it didn't matter to her what Odette had done – she wasn't going to witness a pile-on and the public humiliation of an elderly lady who was clearly not in the best of health.

Odette held her head high until they got outside the door of the private dining room, when her legs almost collapsed underneath her. Luckily, the manager was chatting to the maître d' at the front door and immediately came to their aid.

'Come this way. My office is right here.'

'No, it's okay. We'll just wait outside for my c—' Odette began, but Calvin interrupted her.

'Odette, darling, Harry will be at least ten minutes by the time he gets here from the car park. Let's just go in here and you can have a seat away from the piranhas while we wait.'

Over the top of Odette's head, Calvin gave Tress a worried glance, and her first thought was that she wished Noah was here. Her second thought? She still wished Noah was here. He'd know what to do and he'd take care of everyone and everything, he'd sort the whole damn situation out in a heartbeat because that was who he was.

Unlike that absolute arse next door.

What had she been thinking, going on a date with that guy? Or not thinking?

She'd been so determined not to let the memory of Max and his actions take this day from her that she'd given it to another narcissistic dickhead instead. Was she never going to learn?

Tress felt her throat tighten with the urge to cry and shook it off. Right now wasn't about her. It was about this poor woman who was now sitting on a chair in the manager's office, looking like every drop of blood had been sucked out of her. Which, she supposed, it had, by the vultures in the other room. They'd lapped up every second of that exposé, no doubt trying to work out how each of them could capitalise on it.

Calvin had his phone out of his pocket now and was calling for Odette's car, so Tress knelt down on the floor beside her chair.

'How are you doing there, Odette?'

The older woman shook her head slowly. 'I don't know why you're still speaking to me. Didn't you see what I did?'

Tress nodded, giving her hand a gentle squeeze. 'I saw. But I don't like to make judgements on just one side of the story.'

'It's all true,' Odette said softly, sadly, her voice barely above a whisper. 'Biggest regret of my life. Actually, that's a lie too, because if I could go back, I don't know that I'd change it. I'm not a good person, Tress.'

'Well, none of us are perfect.' It wasn't that she was letting Odette off the hook for whatever she'd done, but she still didn't understand the full picture. All she knew was that she wasn't going to walk away from her right now.

The conversation from earlier came back to her, right at the same time as a name she'd heard uttered in the documentary preview. What had the woman said? *'There were three of us who went to the audition. Of course, she wasn't Odette then. She was just plain Olive Docherty. Anyway, me, Olive and our pal, Nancy…'*

Tress was getting cramp in her legs, so she got up, grabbed the office chair and wheeled it over, so that she was sitting next to Odette, instead of kneeling on the floor. 'Wait a minute, has this all got something to do with why you were looking for Nancy?'

Odette nodded. 'I didn't have the nerve to look for Fiona, because she was the one that I did that to. Took away her dreams. But I thought if I could find Nancy, I could ask her what happened to Fiona, find out if her life had turned out great. Fiona was from Weirbridge too. Nancy always knew the story on everyone back then, and I didn't doubt she'd still know it now. She was the only person I could think of who might be able to tell me where Fiona was and if she was happy. If she was, then maybe I could convince myself that I wasn't as evil as I thought. Maybe my karma would sort itself out, once I knew she was okay. Turns out she wasn't. Like I said, it was cowardly.'

Tress wondered what Nancy would have done if Odette had turned up at the door. She valued loyalty above all else, but she wasn't cruel – she'd probably have invited her in for tea and broken out the caramel wafers while she listened to what Odette had to say.

She searched around for her bag and realised it was still next door. Bugger.

'Listen, Odette, I'm just going to nip back through and grab my bag. My phone is in it and then if you still want me to call Nancy, I will. Even though you know the answer to what you were trying to find out, maybe it will be nice to hear the voice of an old friend again.'

'I'm not a friend now, though. I dropped every single one of them as soon as I got the part. Too ashamed to face Fiona. Too scared I'd get found out. Like I said, I'm really not a good person.'

'Well, I'll make my own mind up about that,' Tress told her, getting worried about the streams of tears that were sliding down Odette's face.

Odette's hand seemed to tighten on hers, and for a moment, Tress thought that she wasn't going to let her go. Then she released her with another sad smile. 'It's okay, pet. You go back through to the party. I think your date is still there.'

'I think I told him to fuck off right before I came in here.'

Odette sniffed, wiped away the tears and collected herself. There was a tiny glint in her eye as she said, 'I thought I heard you say that, but I wasn't sure.'

'You were right to warn me about him, Odette. Why do I never see the clowns? He's the first guy I've dated in a year, and I picked someone as vile as him.'

'I picked four of them, pet. All that stuff about wisdom coming with age is nonsense.'

'Thanks,' Tress said with a warm chuckle, 'I'll bear that in mind. I'm thinking a convent might be the way to go.'

She was just trying to keep Odette talking, keep her focus away from the fact that Calvin was now hitting his phone on the desk, saying, 'Buggery bugger bastard. What the hell is wrong with this bloody phone? I've got four bastarding bars!'

Yep, her phone was definitely required here. 'Okay, I'll be right back.' She stretched up. 'Calvin, I'm just going to grab my bag. I'll come back and sit with you until the car comes.'

He gave her such a look of gratitude that she got a tug straight in the heart strings.

Out of the office, across the entrance and into the private dining room and... Shit. She'd expected it to be empty. Thought that they'd all have gone home when the guest of honour was shepherded off. But no. Elliot was nowhere to be seen, but the rest were all still there, quaffing the free booze and dining out on the gossip.

Over in the corner, Rex was now schmoozing one of the producers, who was flicking her hair back and laughing as if he was the most hilarious man she'd ever met. Tress didn't even care. All she wanted was to retrieve her bag, make sure Odette got away safely, and then get out of here, go home, kiss her boy, get into her pyjamas and maybe call Noah to see how his day was going.

She still hadn't spoken to him since his meeting with Anya. What if... what if... She tried to shut that thought down, but it kept coming back, bringing a sickening shudder of dread every time. What if seeing Anya had reignited something in him and he'd realised that he wanted to take her back? They'd been the happiest couple she'd ever known, so compatible and genuinely in love – and yes, she knew how ridiculous that sounded given what had transpired. What if seeing her had reminded Noah of all the good things they'd had together, and he decided to give it another shot? Somehow, she'd managed to find a way to live without Max. She wasn't sure she could survive without Noah in her life.

She rewound that thought and changed it. She would survive – she'd realised over the last year that she was tougher than she could ever have believed. However, her life, and Buddy's life, would be so much less without him.

Rex spotted her as she scanned the room for her bag and made an immediate bee-line in her direction. 'Hey, you're back. I was just speaking to Cindy – she thinks that they can do some really creative things with my character over the next few months.'

Tress spotted her bag, over the back of her chair, and pulled it up over her shoulder, ignoring Rex Marino, not through petulance, but because she honestly couldn't look at his face for a second longer than necessary. Had he not heard what she'd said to him earlier?

'Look, I know you're pissed off with me...' Okay, so he had heard her. He was just choosing to ignore what she'd said because he was just so thick-skinned that he didn't care. 'But honestly, Tress, that's just the way this business goes. Dog eat dog. And it sounds like your pal, Odette, knew that from the outset.'

Tress had taken a step to walk away, but now she rounded back on him. 'You know, you might be right. But I've known people like you before, people who just live for themselves, for their own agendas, and don't give a single thought to how anyone else feels.'

'And I bet they had great lives,' he countered, grinning, still acting like this was all a game. 'How did it work out for them?'

She clamped her mouth shut. Don't say it. Do. Not. Say. It.

'He died.'

She said it.

This was who Rex reminded her of, so it made perfect sense. She'd loved Max's confidence, his charm, his determination to embrace life, and somehow, then and now, that made her overlook the flaws.

Lesson learned. Once was a mistake. Twice was a relapse. There wouldn't be a third time.

This time she was walking away relatively intact.

He reached out, touched her upper arm to try to block her from leaving when a voice behind her spat out, 'Ryan, take your hand off her before I break it.'

Still staring at Rex, Tress had never seen anyone go from smarmy to horrified so quickly.

Who the hell was Ryan? And why did she recognise the voice

that had just spoken? It was so out of context that it took her brain a few seconds to put it together, but yes, it was definitely... 'Keli!'

As Tress said it, she turned to see that Noah's sister was right behind her, and she had no idea where she'd come from. Oh, and there was Keli's friend, Yvie. And another woman who was staring straight at Rex, like he was something she'd scraped off her shoe.

'Keli, what are you doing here? Were you in the restaurant for dinner?'

'No, I came to see him,' Keli explained, nodding to Rex, who mumbled, 'No way. Fuck. This is a total set-up.'

'Hey, Tress,' Yvie chirped, giving her a wave that was wholly out of keeping with the sudden frostiness in the atmosphere.

'How are you doing, Ryan?' the stranger said, the stare of her piercing blue eyes locked on his face.

Again, who the hell was Ryan?

Keli noticed her puzzlement. 'Rex Marino is his stage name. Ryan Manning is his real name. Doesn't quite have the same Hollywood ring to it.'

Tress had no idea what was going on here, but she could sense that whatever it was, Rex slash Ryan wasn't going to come out of it well.

'Tress, I need to tell you something...' Keli began, and Tress could feel her anxiety. That opening line, and the tension in the air, led to the obvious conclusion.

'That this guy is a piece of crap and I should stay well clear of him? Way ahead of you there.' That felt so good to say, and Keli's visible relief made it so much sweeter.

'Bitches,' Rex slash Ryan hissed under his breath.

Tress caught it, but just smiled and shook her head.

Keli was still back on Tress's previous comment. 'Pretty much sums him up. This is Laurie, his girlfriend of three years. I had no idea about her, so that's why I dated him for three months, until just after New Year.'

Tress's chin dropped. 'This was the secret guy? Noah and I drove ourselves crazy trying to work it out. We thought it was someone at the hospital.'

'You two know each other?' Rex slash Ryan was visibly confused, but he didn't wait for an answer. He had obviously decided to pick the person who meant the most to him to try to salvage at least one relationship. 'Laurie, babe, I thought you were...'

'Away this weekend so you could do whatever you liked? I see that. I hear it's a common occurrence.'

'No! Don't listen to them.' He nodded to Keli. 'She was just infatuated, and tonight, with this one, that was just work.'

Tress stepped back, unable to listen to his drivel any longer. There were a whole load of dynamics at play here and she didn't want or need to be part of it. 'Keli, I'm going to leave you to it. I've got a friend next door and she needs my phone to call someone... it's a long story.' Tress hugged Keli, gave her a kiss on the cheek. 'Thank you for trying to save me. I'll call you tomo—'

She didn't get any further because right then she heard something that sounded like a low, desperate scream and then everything happened in a heartbeat.

Calvin appeared in the doorway, ashen, shaking. 'Someone call an ambulance,' he shouted, panic raising his voice. 'It's Odette. She's collapsed.'

Tress, Keli and Yvie began to run.

31

NOAH

As Noah hit the motorway, it began to rain in that 'zero to torrential' way that it often did in the West of Scotland. There could be a sudden heavy shower, but a kilometre down the road it would be dry as a desert. Wipers activated, he switched the radio on and then turned it up so that he could hear it over the clatter of the hailstones bouncing off the windscreen. He immediately recognised the voice of Chris Stapleton and realised the radio was still on a country music station. On his way back from work last night, he'd picked up Nancy and Val from their Zumba class. Nancy had been in charge of the tunes, so, of course, she'd immediately gone for this channel and a few minutes later her and Val had been raucously joining Carrie Underwood in threatening to take a baseball bat to some bloke's headlights. The memory made him smile, and Chris Stapleton was singing one of his favourite songs, so he let the music play. If ever he needed good vibes and tunes about love, it was right now.

Was he doing this? Was he really going to see Tress? And what was he going to say? Nancy had told him that Tress had texted to say she was in the Oyster Lounge in Glasgow, so he'd just jumped in the car and decided to go there.

Shit, this wasn't his wheelhouse. He didn't do spontaneous. That was Max. He didn't do rash and impulsive. That was Max too. But he did do faithful and that was something his mate hadn't managed. Noah wanted to ask him why. He wanted to hear Max explain everything to him, but that could never happen. Max had left a million loose ends of questions and pain when he'd gone, and Noah still thought about that every day of his life. No closure.

Without thinking, he hit a button on his phone and then heard it ring once. Twice. Then the answering machine clicked in...

'Hi, this is Cheska. Sorry I can't take your call...'

He waited for the beep.

'Cheska, it's me. There were loads of things I didn't say today, and I need to do it now before you leave. First, I'm sorry. You're right. I'm not in a place where I can choose anyone over Tress and Buddy, but that's not because I didn't love you, it's just because they're my family. It's non-negotiable. And I know that made me a shit boyfriend and I'm sorry because you deserve so much more than that. And the other thing... thank you. Thank you for being with me for the last few months. Everything I want to say sounds like a cheesy song lyric and I know you'll be rolling your eyes because you hate that soppy shit, but we've been mates for twenty years and I don't want to lose that. So if you want to... if you could find a way... Ah fuck it, Cheska, don't throw away our friendship. I'm always here. And if you want to spend the next twenty years calling me to remind me that I'm the tit that let you go, then I'm good with that. Start as soon as you like...'

Another beep cut him off and the line went dead. He didn't mind. He'd said all he had to say to her and he just hoped now that she'd keep in touch.

Just one more loose end.

He used the buttons on the steering wheel to scroll to her name on the dashboard screen, then pressed 'call'.

It was answered on the first ring.

'Hello?' Her voice still stabbed something inside him.

'Anya, it's me.'

'Have you changed your mind?' she blurted. 'Tell me you have.'

'I'm sorry.'

It went so quiet he thought for a moment that she'd hung up.

'Are you still there?' he asked, and he heard a sob at the other end, before she spoke.

'I'm still here.'

'Okay. Listen, you need to know something. I'm in love with Tress. I needed to tell you that because you need to let the guilt go. And the regret. And the idea that if we got back together then it would all work out. It won't, Anya. Not because I'm still angry, or resentful, or because I hate you, because none of that's true. It could never work with us again because I love Tress. It's just taken me a long time and a really fucking crazy day to realise it. So let all the guilt and regret go and be happy, Anya. I really mean that.'

Closure. Everything on the table. The final line in the chapter. The last goodbye.

He heard a sigh, then a sadness in her words. 'You know, in a strange way I think I knew that already. When did you get together?'

'We haven't. I'm on my way to tell her now. Some things happened today that made me realise how I feel. I was never great at this stuff.'

'You were. You just didn't know it. And I was too stupid to see it.' At the other end of the line, a sad laugh. 'Good luck, Noah. And, for what it's worth, I think she might feel the same way too. You deserve each other – and I mean that in only good ways.'

After they hung up, he turned the music back up as the song on the radio switched to another one he recognised. Nancy and Val had belted this one out too last night.

He tuned it out, his thoughts consuming him again. He could do this. And if it didn't work out, if Tress didn't want the same things, then he would just have to find a way to figure that out too. They'd been through worse.

That thought kicked off some subconscious plea to get the ghost of their past on side and he murmured, 'Come on, Max, let me do this. Let me make her happy.'

At that second, two things happened. A bang. And then a jolt so violent he lurched to the side.

The last thing he heard as the car began to spin was the voice of Shania Twain.

32

KELI

The second Keli clapped eyes on Odette Devine, she knew she was still alive, but she was definitely unresponsive. Instinctively, she and Yvie dived to the floor. One on either side of her, they immediately snapped into the diagnostic protocols that they used on an all too frequent basis at work. Pulse. Pupils. Rule out heart attack. Choking. It was all done in rapid succession and Keli had a provisional diagnosis in seconds.

'Call an ambulance,' she instructed the man who had screamed for their attention. 'Tell them you need it now. Two nurses on scene. Probable stroke.'

'Oh God. Oh God. Oh God,' he kept repeating, furiously stabbing at his phone, his hands shaking, before launching into, 'She's had a terrible day. So much stress. She's been on the go for hours. I should have taken her home...'

'I've got it, Calvin. You sit down. Take a breath. I've got it.' That was Tress and Keli saw her pull out her phone and knew she'd get it done.

Keli made eye contact with the manager, who'd come running

into the room behind them. 'I need you to wait at the front door and show the paramedics in as soon as they get here.'

As he left, she glanced at her watch, noting the time: 11.05 p.m. on a Friday night in the city centre. There would be a few ambulances on the busiest streets, getting ready for the usual weekend medical emergencies, so they might just get lucky. The pubs hadn't begun to empty yet and the nightclubs hadn't begun to fill up, so hopefully one of the paramedic teams could get to them quickly.

She heard Tress speaking slowly and precisely, giving out all the required information. Woman. Sixty-nine years old. She told them everything Keli had asked her to say, then gave them the name and address of their location.

'The ambulance is on its way,' Tress told them, then Keli saw her put her arm around the distraught man, talk to him, try to calm him. 'They're both nurses, Calvin. She's getting the best care she can get right now and the ambulance will be here soon. And it's Odette. You know how strong she is.'

'She's coming round,' Yvie said, strong and calm, and Keli thought, as always, that there was no one she would rather be in this situation with. They'd worked on so many patients together, that they had almost an intuitive knowledge of their roles in every emergency.

Odette began to mumble, but the words were incoherent. That and the slight droop at the left side of her mouth told Keli that her diagnosis was almost certainly correct. Odette didn't open her eyes, but she began to make sounds that were escalating in distress.

Keli had her fingers on Odette's wrist, monitoring her pulse. 'Odette, my name is Keli and my friend holding your other hand is Yvie. We're both nurses and we're going to take really good care of you. I know this is frightening, but the ambulance is on its way and we're going to stay with you and look after you until it gets here.'

Keli had no idea how much, if anything, the woman could understand, but she kept speaking in the hope of calming her.

Eyes still closed, Odette made some more incoherent sounds, so Yvie took over the conversation, trying to reassure her.

'Odette, don't try to talk. Your friends are here with you too. Tress is here and...'

'Calvin,' Tress interjected with an answer to the unasked question.

'And Calvin is here too. You're going to be okay, Odette. We're just...'

As Yvie carried on with soothing words, Keli turned to Calvin and Tress. She needed as much information as possible for the paramedics. After the first symptoms of a stroke, they only had a window of a few hours to halt or reverse the damage, so it was crucial that they find out everything they needed to know. 'Did she show any signs of being unwell today?'

Calvin shook his head. 'She was tired, but I just thought she was overwhelmed with the emotion of it all. In the car on the way here, she said she had a headache and she took a couple of paracetamol. She wanted to go home, but I talked her into coming here, because it was all arranged and... Oh God, I caused this. I caused all of this.'

'Calvin, you need to stop.' She saw this all the time. The adrenaline. The panic. The self-reproach and the guilt that people jumped to in a situation like this. 'I need you to stay calm. You didn't cause this. If anything, being here was a good thing because there's a good chance this would have happened anyway and at least here, we can act on it, take care of her.'

In her peripheral vision, Keli saw his expression change as he computed that and understood the significance of it. Of course, she had no idea if this would have happened anywhere else, but she did know that having two nurses on the scene administering instant care beat having an elderly lady lying on the floor of her home all night after suffering a stroke.

'Now I'm going to ask you more questions and I just need a yes or no.' Sometimes it was as important to focus the loved ones as much as the patient. 'Did she mention any tingling in her hands, her arms, anywhere else...?'

Keli went on, asking every question she needed a definitive answer to, and Calvin rallied as his mind was occupied, giving clear answers.

When the door opened a few minutes later, she had all the information the paramedics wanted to know as they worked quickly and efficiently to get Odette onto the stretcher. As they wheeled her out of the office, Keli saw immediately that the inevitable crowd had gathered, presumably the people who'd been at the party tonight.

And, of course, there was no show without a leading man.

As Keli walked alongside the stretcher, still holding Odette's hand, she saw Rex slash Ryan's reaction and immediately knew what he was about to do. She took in his glance at the photographers and members of the public with their cameras out, just a few feet away on the other side of the glass door, swollen in numbers due to the ambulance and rumours of an incident. She read his instant calculation as to how he could use this moment, saw his lightning-quick dash to the other side of Odette's stretcher.

He got there just as the doors were blasted open and the stretcher was wheeled towards the cavalcade of paparazzi.

Keli did what any other medical professional would do and eliminated any potential hazard from the quick and efficient transportation of her patient. And yes, it may have been slightly motivated by personal reasons and the fact that when they were together, he'd told her many times how he couldn't stand Odette.

As the stretcher went through the doors, Keli made her request heard. 'Could someone remove this man, please?' she said loudly enough for the assorted photographers to hear. 'Sir, this is not the moment to be hijacking a situation for your own attention-seeking purposes. Save your bad acting for the television.'

The shock made him take a step backwards, and somehow that resulted in a missed footing and the next thing he went flying and face planted on the pavement behind them.

He bounced back up immediately, but the damage was done. A cavalcade of flashes went off like strobe lights as a dozen cameras caught the moment. Keli had a feeling that Rex, not Odette, would be the headline from this moment.

Out of the corner of her eye, she spotted Laurie chatting to one of the photographers. Laurie made a 'I'll call you' gesture and Keli knew she'd be fine.

They got Odette into the ambulance, and Keli and Yvie automatically took a step back. Too many medics in one vehicle just caused confusion, so it was time to let the paramedics do their work. Besides, if Odette woke up again, it would help to have her friend there to calm her down. Calvin was about to climb in with Odette, just as a large black car pulled up and a driver jumped out, concern and confusion in every line of his face.

'Harry, follow us,' Calvin directed. 'Bring Tress and the nurses.'

In the car, Keli texted the one person she knew best in A&E to give them the heads-up that they were on the way in. The paramedics would have radioed forward with all the relevant info, but she put all she knew in the text too – every little bit of info and judicious action helped.

After she pressed send, she looked up and saw Tress was resting her head back against the seat, eyes closed, as if trying to shut out everything that had just happened.

Keli reached for her hand and squeezed it. 'How are you doing there, Tress?'

To her surprise, Tress's eyes were full of tears when she opened them. 'I'm just so glad you two were there. I don't want to think what would have happened if...' She stopped.

'If Rex Marino hadn't been a lying arse-nugget and we hadn't gone there to chew him out?' That came from Yvie, who was both lightening the mood and trying to cheer Tress up. 'I still can't believe you were shagging him and didn't tell me.' That was directed at Keli, but Tress jumped on to it.

'Erm, I could have done with that information too. Would have saved me wasting a whole night of babysitters.'

'I'm sorry,' Keli said meekly. 'He told me we had to keep it under wraps because of his career. Said he didn't want our private lives to be public gossip and have to deal with the intrusive publicity.'

The two other women raised their eyebrows at the same time, inferring the obvious.

'Yeah, yeah, I know now that was crap and he'd sell his granny for a story.'

Tress's eyes widened. 'I just realised where you met him. It was my fault, wasn't it?'

Keli couldn't argue. 'The party at the studio. You invited me and Mum because Mum was desperate to meet Odette. I met him at the bar, he asked me for my number, but I didn't tell anyone because I didn't think he'd call, but he did.'

'Hang on – didn't he see that you were there with Tress? That would make it a ballsy move to ask her out now.' Yvie made the point, but Tress nodded in agreement.

Keli thought about that for a moment, rewinding everything in her head. 'No. I just said I was there with my family. He didn't ask and we never really spoke about it afterwards because he never met my family or friends. I guess we were just in our own bubble. Sounds pathetic now. I'm sorry, Tress...'

'No need... I've seen how he plays the game. Perfectly understandable.' Tress gave her a sympathetic smile. 'What happened next?'

'We dated for three months, I thought I loved him, he ghosted me and... well, here we are. And, weirdly, I feel absolutely fine now.'

'Yep, me too,' Tress agreed, sitting up straighter, as if full of sudden resolve. 'I just want to make sure Odette is okay, then go home, call your brother... In fact, I'll let him know what's happened now.' Tress picked up her phone and called, then almost immediately mouthed, 'Voicemail,' before pausing for a few seconds, then, 'Hey, Noah, it's me. So the date was a bust and loads of other stuff has happened. I'm with Keli and we want to tell you about it, so call me back. Love ya.' Tress hung up, slipped her phone back in her bag, and then noticed that Keli and Yvie were staring at her. 'Why are you looking at me like that?'

Under normal circumstances, Keli would keep her nose out of it, but sod it, tonight was anything but normal. 'I just think...' She paused. No. She shouldn't say anything, but suddenly a couple of comments her mum had made about Noah and Tress were making sense to her. The way they spoke to each other. The connection between them. It was more than friends. She could see it.

Yvie didn't have the same level of restraint. 'You and Noah would be perfect together. We love Cheska, but the rumour in the hospital is that she's going to go off to some swanky new job in America.'

'Is it?' Keli asked, astonished.

'Oh. Sorry. I heard that today,' Yvie replied. 'I knew there was something I meant to tell you but you kind of stole the thunder with the whole celebrity boyfriend thing. Anyway, Tress...' She refocused. 'I wish you'd get it together with Noah, because that would be the perfect romcom ending to this story.'

'No,' Tress flinched as if she'd been slapped. 'No. I can't. You're wrong.'

'But why? What's wrong with my brother?' Keli tried to make it sound like a joke, but she did want to know the answer.

Tress thought about it for so long, Keli gave up on getting a straight answer, until finally Tress said, 'Not a single thing. And that's why I could never risk losing him.'

Before Keli could ask anything more, they all juddered forward as the car came to a stop in the drop-off zone right by the ambulance bay at Glasgow Central. Keli snapped straight back into work mode, sprinting from the car, so she was ready in case the paramedic team unloading Odette needed her. In all the time she'd worked at the hospital, this was the first time she'd arrived via the A&E entrance.

'Take Calvin to the waiting room and I'll come get you,' she told Tress, as she and Yvie fell in beside the stretcher.

They'd only gone a couple of steps when the doors burst open and Dr Cheska Ayton, the A&E chief, rushed out.

'I got your text,' she told Keli. 'Listen, on you go inside, go see Noah.'

Keli didn't understand. Why would Noah be here? He wasn't working tonight. She'd seen him earlier at their mum's and he didn't mention that he was coming back here. Was there some emergency on his ward and he'd been called in? Or had he come to chat to Cheska on her break? Yep, that must be it.

Tress got to the relevant question before her. 'Noah is here?'

Cheska stopped, her gaze going to Tress, then back to Keli.

'He was brought in an hour ago. There was an accident on the motorway.'

MIDNIGHT – 8 A.M.

33

ODETTE, TRESS, NOAH AND KELI

Keli and Tress both took off at a sprint, through the doors that Cheska had just opened, down the corridor and into the central nursing bay on A&E. Heart thudding, fear squeezing her chest so hard she could barely breathe, Tress fell behind Keli, realising that she'd know where to go, all the while, screams filling her head. *No. No. No. Not again. Not again. Not Noah. Not Noah. Not him.*

Keli slammed to a halt at a board with a whole lot of numbers and names on it, searching frantically for something... 'There! Cubicle Six. This way.' She gestured to a couple of the staff over at the nursing station and they waved her on. No need for ID checks when you were a nurse at the hospital and your doctor brother had just been brought in.

She grabbed Tress's hand and they ran along the corridor, ignoring the moans and conversations and drunken yells coming from behind the curtains that they passed.

Tress was trying desperately to make sense of it. Why was Noah on the motorway? Last she heard he was going to his mum's for dinner? This didn't make sense. Maybe he was called in? But usually he'd text her to let her know that. And why couldn't she breathe? And when were they going to get there? And WHERE THE HELL WAS HE?

Keli jarred to a stop, their panicked eyes met, and she knew they were both thinking the same thing – please don't let this be bad.

Chest heaving, fear running through every vein, Tress gave an almost indiscernible nod, and Keli threw back the curtain and...

And...

And...

He was lying on the bed, eyes closed, one side of his head packed with a dressing, a bandage wrapped around it. Noooooooo.

Tress heard a strangled gasp, realised it came from her, then watched as his eyes flew open and he jolted his shoulders off the bed, only to exclaim with pain and flop back down again.

In two steps, she was at his side, his sister next to her, just as he exclaimed, 'Ouch, shouldn't have done that. Head rush.'

Tress didn't understand what was happening, even more so when Keli, panting beside her, blurted, 'Bloody hell, you just about gave me a heart attack, you absolute idiot,' then, holding on to the side of Noah's bed, began to laugh.

Tress frantically searched both of their faces for answers. 'I don't get it. I don't understand.'

'He's fine, Tress,' she spluttered.

'You're fine?'

Noah opened one eye. 'I'm fine. Although, right now, my head doesn't think so.'

Tress still wasn't getting this, but Keli pointed to a board above his bed that simply said 'OBS'. 'He's on observation. Suspected concussion?'

Noah winced as he nodded. 'I had a blow-out in the car. Doing sixty or seventy when it spun out. Thankfully, there was no one behind me, so no collision. Cracked my head against the side window when it happened but managed to steer it almost to the hard shoulder. Years of watching *Fast & Furious* movies. Anyway, the traffic cops got there pretty quick and brought me in. I'm fine though, so don't you dare call Mum. Cheska is just being extra cautious and keeping me here for observation for a few hours. I think she's just doing it as a punishment.' He was obviously joking, but Tress still couldn't wrap her head around what was going on.

'Punishment for what?'

'We're not together anymore.' This time, he managed to get both eyes open, and as they looked up at her, Tress felt her legs wobble underneath her. It was all too much. Today. The anniversary. The excitement of going on a date. The disaster it turned out to be. Rex turning out to be a narcissistic, cheating dick. Odette taking ill. The utter terror of the last ten minutes. And now seeing Noah here, and the heart-shuddering relief of knowing he was okay. It was all too much.

She slumped into the chair beside his bed.

'I think you're going to have to start at the beginning,' she told him.

* * *

After reading her brother's chart, looking at the ten perfect stitches in the wound on his head, taking his pulse, his blood pressure and sequestering a flashlight from a colleague to check his pupils, Keli had satisfied herself that Noah was fine. Possible concussion, but otherwise okay – although Cheska was right to keep him in for a few hours just to be on the safe side.

Now he was partially sitting up, his fingers intertwined with Tress's as he recounted the story of his day and Keli decided to go and give them some space.

She had meant what she'd said in the car. Not that she held out much hope for them getting together. Both of them were too cautious, maybe too scarred, to take a leap of faith and she understood that completely. It would take her a long time before she even contemplated getting into another relationship after the mess of the last one. Compared to Tress's marriage to Max, tonight's disaster with Rex slash Ryan didn't even make a blip on the radar.

She waited for a pause in the conversation before butting in. 'Okay, not that I don't love you, Noah, but now that I'm sure you'll live, I'm just going to go check on Odette.'

'Will you let me know how she is please? And, Keli, if you have a minute, will you make sure Calvin is okay? I took off and left him back there because I was too busy panicking about this one,' she gestured to Noah.

'You were panicking?' Noah asked her, a smile playing on his lips.

'You two are a nightmare,' Keli deadpanned. 'And I'm the youngest. I'm supposed to be the hopeless one.'

Shaking her head, she left the room, pulled the curtain behind her, ignoring the soft sound of her brother laughing in her wake.

She checked her phone and saw that there was a message from Yvie.

In the staffroom. Come find me when you're done.

Keli occasionally popped down to have lunch with Cheska on this ward, so she knew exactly where the staffroom was. When she got there, Yvie was the only one in the room, sitting at the table, nursing a mug of tea and scrolling through her phone.

'How's Noah? Cheska said it was a minor head wound and that they were just keeping him in for observation?'

'Yep, I should probably have waited for that little nugget of information before Tress and I went racing off to find him. That's one way to get my ten thousand steps in for the day.' She flopped down on the seat opposite her friend. 'How is Odette?'

'They're working on her now, but we got her here quickly, so hopefully the prognosis will be okay. We'll know in the next couple of hours.'

Keli remembered Tress's request. 'And Calvin?'

'Much better now. His husband arrived, and he's waiting with him. The poor man is shattered.'

Keli understood the sentiment. Her fear had been way too real when she'd been told that Noah was hurt. 'That's good. Wow, this feels like déjà vu from this morning. You. Me. Sitting at a staffroom table.'

'At least the pregnancy conversation is over. I still can't believe you were shagging Rex Marino and didn't tell me.'

'I'm sorry about that,' Keli said sheepishly.

Yvie rolled her eyes. 'Forgiven. Could you imagine being stuck with him as a baby daddy? He'd either spend his life dodging responsibility, or there would be an *OK!* photo shoot with Daddy and baby every fricking week.'

Nope, Keli decided, she wasn't going to try to imagine that because the fear of how close she had come to that reality still made her shudder. Once burned, now going nowhere near a heat source until the end of time.

'You're not wrong,' Keli chuckled, before going on, 'You know, we didn't even get to confront him properly. Odette fell ill and the whole situation got abandoned, but I don't even think I care. He's honestly not worth another minute of my time. I'd have liked to have seen him squirm waaaaaay more, but I'm done. I don't even want to think about him again. Hopefully Laurie can move on too. She deserves so much better. Ooops, talking of Laurie...'

She held up her buzzing phone to let Yvie see that there was an incoming FaceTime call and Laurie's name was flashing on the screen. Keli answered it and held it out to the side, so that they could both lean into the frame. Laurie came into view and Keli could see that she was in the bar at the St Kentigern.

'Hey, how's Odette?' was her first question and Keli thought again how lovely this girl was. Rex slash Ryan didn't deserve her.

'I'm not sure yet, but she's in good hands, so hopefully she'll be okay. How are you? Tell me you didn't let him sweet-talk you into hearing him out.'

Laurie's laugh was raucous. 'Nope, I'm currently having a cocktail on his account though, so there's that. He'll go fricking nuts when he gets the statement in this month. Big mistake giving the girlfriend a credit card. I've never used it before, but I'm making up for it now.' She held up what looked like an espresso martini to the camera, making Keli and Yvie laugh. 'Anyway, I'm calling to see if you've looked online in the last half-hour?'

Keli shook her head, with a rueful grin. 'Nope. Been slightly tied up with lifesaving emergencies.'

'Okay, well first of all, meet Sy.' She swerved the phone around, and Yvie whistled under her breath when she saw the aforementioned Sy.

'I'm binning Carlo if there are specimens like that in the world.'

Long hair, wide smile, Brad Pitt in *Kalifornia*. 'Sy is a photographer mate. I asked him to do me a favour and come to the restaurant tonight, and he did.' They watched as Laurie leaned over and stroked the side of Sy's face.

'Is it wrong that I fancy them both?' Yvie whispered, making Keli laugh again.

'Definitely not. I think I feel the same.'

Laurie's attention came back to them. 'Anyway, he recorded everything that happened, and we might have loaded one of the videos up on social media. And it, erm, might be going viral. I think

Rex Marino might have finally encountered a publicity stunt he didn't like. Or leak.'

Keli chuckled. 'I'm loving the sound of this.'

'Me too! Okay, need to go. Sy and I have, erm, plans. Can I give you two a call tomorrow? Definitely think we should hang out... you know... not just when we're hatching devious plans.'

'I'd like that,' Keli told her, just as Yvie piped up with, 'Absolutely! But just as long as you dress ugly. And bring Sy.'

Laurie was still laughing when she ended the call.

'Shit, I didn't even ask where I'd find it online,' Keli said.

Yvie was already tapping on her phone. 'Ah, I don't think you're going to have any trouble with that. Oh my God, look.'

Yvie turned her phone and Keli saw a post with the headline 'REX MARINO – HAS HE NO SHAME?' Underneath, the text of the post read:

Meet the latest NHS Hero! Rex Marino tries to exploit Odette Devine's tragic collapse for publicity but is DENIED in brutal fashion by NHS hero, an off-duty nurse who intervened to help the much-loved actress. Sources close to the actor confirmed that he intensely dislikes Devine, yet tonight he did this...

'Oh no...' Keli pressed play on the video.

It was the scene outside the restaurant earlier, crowds in the street, the whole scene illuminated by the street lamps and the flashing blue lights of the ambulance.

Suddenly, the restaurant doors slammed open and there was poor Odette coming towards them on the stretcher. Rex Marino jumped into shot, grabbed her hand, just as the woman beside the stretcher proclaimed in a thoroughly unimpressed fashion, 'Could someone remove this man, please? Sir, this is not the moment to be hijacking a situation for your own attention-seeking purposes. Save your bad acting for the television.'

The camera caught his mortified expression, then his stagger as he missed his step and went sprawling. People around him in the crowd laughed and that's where the clip ended.

Yvie had to wipe away tears of amusement. 'Holy shit, you're famous! I mean, *we're* famous, because I'm there looking deadly too, but you got the speaking part and you're fricking brilliant. He'll be mortified.'

Shallow as it was, Keli didn't have an iota of sympathy for him. He'd manipulated the media for years – it was bound to come back and bite him at some point. He deserved everything that came his way.

However, she didn't have time to revel in the enjoyment, because right then, Cheska came storming through the door.

'How is Odette?' Keli blurted.

Cheska shook her head. 'I don't know yet. We've done everything we can, so now we just have to wait and see what happens.'

* * *

Noah listened in as Tress, with the phone on loudspeaker, called Nancy, and filled her in on where they were, quickly assured her that Noah was fine, and told her that she was going to stick around until he was released.

'Oh sweet Jesus, I think I just aged ten years. Are you sure he's okay? What can I do? Do you need me? Val is still with me here, so one of us can stay with Buddy and the other one can come over...'

Noah spoke up to reassure her. 'Nancy, I love you for offering, but I'm okay. Honestly. It's just a bang on the head. I had much worse that time I fell off your roof when I was a kid.'

'Aye, well, you shouldn't have been up there in the first place, you daft bugger. Putting a flashing Santa on my chimney. What the devil were you thinking? It was March!'

Noah didn't feel this was the right time to point out that, as always, it had been Max's idea and he'd just gone along with it. Besides, he was laughing too hard and it was making his head ache.

Tress took over the call again. 'Are you sure you're okay to stay over? I can come home if not. You've done enough for me today already.'

'Nonsense. And don't be coming home. Me and Val are on season 7 of *Outlander* and we're doing a bint watch.'

'You mean "binge"?'

'Nope, I mean "bint" – it's much more fun. Right, well, I tell you what then, if I don't hear from you beforehand, me or Val will come and pick you up from the hospital in the morning since I take it your car is totalled, Noah?'

'It definitely is,' he winced. He hadn't even thought that through. He loved that car. And being in it while it spun out of control had been bloody terrifying. But he wasn't going to relive that moment or consider the other potential outcomes if he could help it. He was fine. He was relatively uninjured. Tress was with him. He was just going to stay in the moment and stay focused on the present, not the past. 'But we can get a taxi...'

'I'll not hear of it,' Nancy demanded, and Noah knew better than to argue.

'Nancy, there's something else I need to tell you,' Tress jumped in. 'Have you paused *Outlander* because this is going to take a minute?'

'Val, hit that button, and come listen to this,' Nancy bellowed. They then had to wait five minutes while Nancy filled Val in on everything Tress had just told her about Noah's accident, eliciting almost identical responses of horror, relief, concern and offers of visiting.

'Okay, Tress, we're ready,' Nancy informed her.

'Well, remember we saw that big car in the street earlier, when Rex was collecting me? It was over next to your house. We thought it was someone visiting the neighbours.'

'Aye... oh, you know who it was! Was it Rod Stewart? I said to Val, I had such a feeling that's who it was. Didn't I, Val?'

'You did, Nancy. Go on, Tress, who was it?'

'It was Odette Devine.'

Silence on the other end of the phone. Noah wondered if someone had broken in and gagged them, because he'd never heard both of them fall silent at the same time. He caught Tress's gaze and they both shrugged in confusion. Or at least, he thought Tress was confused, until she went on...

'It's okay, Nancy, I know you're not her biggest fan and I know you were friends when she was younger.'

Noah's forehead wrinkled in surprise, then he took a sharp breath as the movement hurt his head.

'Aye, until she ditched us all when she got famous,' Nancy chirped, and Noah could tell it was through pursed, disapproving lips. Nancy couldn't hide her emotions if her life depended on it.

'Well, she was looking for you tonight, and wait until I tell you why...'

Noah rested his head back on the bed and listened as Tress recounted everything. She told them about the documentary, about the phone calls forty years ago that had landed Odette the part, about how she'd lived all these years with regret, how she'd tried to find Nancy tonight because she was finally ready to try to right her wrongs.

For once, Nancy listened until the end of a story and then there was a pause, before she gave her verdict. 'Blow me sideways, that's unbelievable. Well, I'll never be happy that she ditched us all and swanned off in her swanky cars and fancy house... But jings, it just shows you. She's been miserable all these years and there was us thinking she was living the high life. I was just saying to Noah earlier, you never know what's really going on with folks, do you?'

Perhaps he was overthinking it, but Noah heard an implication in her voice that he chose to ignore for now. This wasn't the time or place.

'I guess you don't,' Tress agreed. Before going on to tell them about Odette taking unwell at the restaurant.

'Thank God Keli was there. She's a marvel, that one. How is Olive now?'

'I'm not sure, but Keli is going to let us know.'

'Och, you never know the minute. That's why we have to snatch every second of happiness. Talking of which, did all those goings on ruin your date?' Nancy asked, and this time Noah could hear the cagey optimism.

'Nope, Rex ruined the date before that even happened. Val, the things you suspected about him the other day – you were right. He was a complete dickhead.'

'I don't know why you doubted me, love,' Val said, chuckling. 'Reading people is my superpower.'

Nancy backed her pal up with, 'Aye, you knew that bloke in the bakers was the one stealing knickers off the washing lines before the police caught him.'

Noah shook his head, laughing, until he was reminded once again how much it hurt.

'So it's all off then?' Nancy asked, with unmistakable hope.

'It's all off.'

'And what do you think of that, Noah?' Val asked, this time the hint so obvious it was flashing like the Santa they'd put on Nancy's roof. In March.

'I think that I need to go, because they'll be back in to check on me soon.'

The two at the other end of the phone seemed to find this amusing, and this time, Tress gave him a questioning gaze.

'Okay, son – we'll see you in the morning. Tress, we're here if you need us, doesn't matter what time.'

'Thank you. I love you both so much.'

'Aye, same here, pet. But just one thing... Ask Noah why he was driving up to Glasgow tonight. Cheerio.'

* * *

Tress took a minute to absorb that one.

'Why do I feel like there are powers at play that I don't know about here?' she asked Noah. 'Did they send you to wreck my date because Val didn't trust him? Or were you coming to check on me? Because, Noah Clark, I don't need to remind you that I'm a grown woman who is perfectly capable of making her own colossal fuck-ups.'

She was trying not to be annoyed, but embarrassment was tipping her close to the edge. Embarrassment and all sorts of other emotions that she didn't even want to contemplate right now. When she thought she'd lost him...

Nope, not thinking about it. Not tonight. Tonight she was just going to be grateful he was still here.

'I was coming to wreck your date,' he said, the admission making him very clearly uncomfortable.

'Noah! Why would you do that? You're usually the voice of reason and the only one that can talk sense into Val and Nancy...' They both knew that was true. 'Oh no. They've sucked you over to the dark side. You're going to wake up tomorrow morning with a Zumba habit and an opinion on everything.'

She was probably letting him off the hook too easy, but again, she didn't care. He was here. That was all that mattered. Because if she'd lost him...

Damn, why couldn't she stop her mind wandering there?

Enough. Back to the present. Back to everything being okay.

Or was it?

She still hadn't asked him about what had happened with Anya and she wasn't sure that she wanted to right now because she wasn't ready for him to tell her something she didn't want to hear.

'I didn't do it for them,' he said, really quietly.

His head must be hurting again. No wonder. That was some injury. If it had been worse, he could have been so badly injured or even...

BLOODY HELL! Why couldn't she stop this? It was like her brain was trying to torture her by throwing up the worst possible scenario at every turn. By making her feel what it would be like if anything took him away from her. Any more of this, and she was going to climb in there beside him and bang her own head until a concussion made these thoughts stop.

'So why? Oh, wait, I get it. You found out that Keli used to date him and he was awful to her. Thank you. If the roles were reversed, I'd probably come charging up to see you to give you that kind of information.'

'Nope, I didn't know that either.'

'Then why?' And why was her heart thudding? The panic was over. He was okay. He was here. She was here.

'Because after Cheska and I split up today, I needed to speak to you.'

Oh. She'd forgotten he'd said that earlier and she hadn't even asked him about it.

'Noah, I'm so sorry. I breezed right over that earlier with everything that was going on. I'm a crap friend. Are you devastated? Why did she end it?'

'Technically, she didn't. It was my choice.'

'But why? You were great together.'

He sighed. He must be regretting it already.

Her brain pinged. Wait a minute. The girls said something in the car about a rumour Cheska was leaving? She hadn't paid much attention because she had her mind on other things and anyway, she figured if it were true, Noah would have mentioned it.

'Because she got offered a job in Seattle and she asked me to go with her, but I couldn't. I said no.'

Wham. Tress was fairly sure that some invisible force had just kicked her right in the throat.

'Why would you say no?'

'Because... because...'

Oh damn, he could barely get the words out. They were doing this now, whether she wanted to or not. She decided to jump right in and do it for him.

'...Because you and Anya are going to try again?'

His head jerked back. 'What? Ouch. What? No! Oh damn, that hurt. No! Why would you think that?'

'Because events of the last year have made me prone to short bouts of acute pessimism and fear and that's the worst thing I could imagine happening right now?'

Tress immediately kicked herself for saying that. She shouldn't be putting her needs on to him. They'd made a pact to support each other no matter what and...

He was speaking again. 'Tress, I'm not getting back with Anya. I said no to going to America with Cheska because I can't leave you and Buddy.'

Something deep inside her kicked up an instant reaction. 'You can.'

'What?'

'I said you can,' she said forcefully. Nope, she wasn't having this.

No way. A tsunami of irritation and annoyance made her teeth clench, so it took real effort to get the words out. 'Noah, you are not going to give up your chance of love and happiness because of me. I'm not having it. We both know how life can change in a heartbeat, and what it costs to lose the person you love, and I won't let you go through it again. I couldn't live with myself. So pack your fricking bags...' She was shaking inside, and she knew that grief, and sadness, and utter devastation were going to make her throat close in about two seconds, so she practically yelled the rest. 'And go to Seattle because we'll be fine without you.'

'No!'

'Yes!'

'Oh fuck it.' He took a deep breath, blew it back out again. 'Tress, I'm not staying because I think you can't survive without me. This isn't some messed-up martyr thing. I'm staying because I love you.'

Oh God, he was killing her here. 'I know,' she croaked. They'd proved how much they loved each other a thousand times over the years. He was the best friend she'd ever had. 'And I love you too. But I can't let you lose out on real love, on big love...'

'Tress, my big love is you!'

She jumped with shock at the force in his voice.

'You are my big love. That's what I was coming to tell you tonight. I love you. I'm *in love* with you. You are everything and I don't want to live a single day without you. I want us. The whole thing. And I'm absolutely bricking it telling you all this because if it costs us our friendship, I don't know what I'm going to do. But I have to tell you because...'

'Kiss me.'

He flinched and then immediately winced again. 'Ouch, fuck. What?'

She had no idea what she was saying, but the words were

coming out of her mouth and she was going with them. 'I said kiss me. Because every time Rex Marino kissed me it felt sexy and good...' His facial reaction to that told her it would be a really smart idea to get to the point here. 'But it felt awkward. And I kept telling myself that it was because I wasn't ready, but now, I think it might be because...' She was going to say it. She was. Somewhere on the periphery of her mind, she already knew it, had done for a while now, but she'd been too scared of losing him to grab it and go with it. But now... 'I think it's because I'm in love with you too. So kiss me.'

The smile, those eyes, the sheer joy as he reached up to...

Ouch. He flinched with pain again.

'Sod it, you leave your head on the pillow and I'm going to kiss you,' Tress said.

She leaned down, let her finger trace a line along his gorgeous face, kept her eyes locked on his, and she kissed him. It felt warm, and sexy and heart-thuddingly incredible...

And it didn't feel awkward at all.

EPILOGUE
ONE WEEK LATER

'Well, there she is, the most demanding diva in the whole of Glasgow Central Hospital,' Calvin declared with a wink, as he came through the doors of the ward, laden with flowers and chocolates. 'Ladies, we've got a wee treat for you all too for putting up with her. Freda...' he said, before plonking a huge vase of flowers on the lady in the next bed's trolley table, 'Here you go, and there's some Ferrero Rocher for you too.' He crossed the room. 'Janet, there's yours, and Vera, here's your flowers and you get a fruit basket because last time you told me your diabetic chocolates were rancid.' Apparently, someone called Emily had been in this bed before her, but she'd been discharged the morning after Odette had arrived down in A&E.

Vera hooted with laughter, and Odette shook her head. The spectacle of this man. She couldn't love him more.

Finally, he got back to her, and he pulled a chair closer to her bed, next to Harry, who was already sitting there, reading his paper.

'Just so you know, you cost me extra Botox this morning and I'm adding it to your bill. I was positively haggard. Anyway, how are you, my love?'

How was she? Alive. That was the biggest bonus. She'd woken up last Saturday morning and been terrified. She was in the hospital. She was confused. The right side of her body was stiff. She couldn't make her mouth work properly and her words wouldn't come.

Two nurses called Keli and Yvie had been the first faces that she'd seen, and they'd told her that she was in a private room on their floor of the hospital and then explained everything that had happened. She'd had a stroke, but she'd got to the hospital quickly and they'd managed to give her an injection that would hopefully minimise the effects of it. They were right. After twenty-four hours, she was feeling so much stronger. After forty-eight hours, her speech was better and the stiffness was less too.

But that didn't help how she was feeling. Miserable. Worried. Sad. Once this documentary came out, everyone would hate her anyway. What was the point of still being here? Her future wasn't going to be worth living.

Calvin had been up to see her at visiting hours, Tress too, and lovely Harry had come every single day, but the rest of the time she'd stared out of that window at a world she truly didn't care about. One that didn't care about her.

That's when Keli had breezed back in and told her they were moving her to a ward. She knew what it would be like. Her worst nightmare. The lack of privacy. The judgement. Forced conversations with people she didn't know. And it had been exactly that... for about half an hour. Then she'd got chatting to Freda, a lovely woman from up north, in the next bed, who'd introduced her to Vera and Janet across from them and she wasn't sure they'd stopped talking since. What a laugh they'd had too. And a few heated discussions as well. The debate over whether the Beatles or the Rolling Stones were better had lasted for two days, and in the end, they'd agreed to disagree.

All the awful stuff would still be wating for her when she got out, but for once, she was living in the moment and just taking it day by day. For now, 'alive' was going to have to be good enough.

'Feeling stronger every day,' she told him. 'Doctor McVitie said this morning that there's no reason I won't make a full recovery.'

He looked way too satisfied with himself. 'Good, because I don't want to get ahead of myself, but you've had an offer for panto at the King's this Christmas.'

'What? You're kidding.' The King's Theatre was an iconic Glasgow venue and the Christmas shows there were attended by thousands.

'I never joke about money, darling. I've given them a provisional "yes", and we can get all the details ironed out when you're feeling better.'

'Calvin, I don't want to do it. I can't face what's coming and it'll be worse if I'm still in the spotlight.'

'Yep, about that... Nothing is coming. The studio slapped a restraining order on Elliot and his team and if it any of it ever sees the light of day, they'll be eating beans until the end of time. Much as the piranhas would take any publicity they could get, they didn't want any negative stuff to take attention away from the new direction of the show and all the new talent they're bringing in. Actually, "talent" is a stretch. That lot couldn't act their way out of the backside of a panto donkey. They make Rex Marino look like Robert Downey Jr. Plus, they're worried that they'll get sued for failing to protect you that night. Duty of care and all that. I may have suggested legal action was pending, so they'd like you to know that they offer profuse apologies for Elliot's actions. And if all that wasn't enough, new information has come to light that calls the documentary findings into question.'

'But they were true,' Odette argued. 'And I'm not going to call that woman a liar. I've done enough...'

She didn't get to finish the point, because right then a face she hadn't seen for forty years came through the door.

'All right, Olive? It's been a minute, pet. Yer looking well, considering you've been through the wars.'

Odette promptly burst into tears. 'Nancy...'

'I was just telling Odette about the new information,' Calvin said, and Odette slid into a well of puzzlement.

Nancy pulled up a chair, on the opposite side of the bed from Calvin and Harry, opened the grapes she'd brought with her and popped one in her mouth. 'Do you feel strong enough to talk about this, Olive?'

She nodded.

'Right, well, the bottom line was that Fiona wasn't being strictly truthful with that story of hers. I was with her the night she met Alf Cotter in a pub. It was a few years after you got the part of Agnes and deserted us, but I'll come back to that one later,' Nancy said archly, making Odette smile despite the anxiety of the conversation. 'The thing is, he did call her that morning, as you know, but he wasn't offering her Agnes McGlinchy. He was offering her a different part. A much smaller one. Mavis Burney, a part-time assistant in the corner shop. And, aye, she was raging that you'd pretended to be her and hadn't told her he'd called – we worked that out quick enough – but she was even more raging that you got the bigger role. In fact, that night we met him again, he told her he had another small part up for grabs. She was so offended, she told him to stuff it up his arse and then copped off with a football player. I think she married him actually, right before he got dropped and was never seen again. So, you see, Olive, yes, you should have told her that he called, but the reality was you were always supposed to be Agnes. You're not completely off the hook, but yer not that much of a cow after all.' Nancy winked, chuckled and then popped another grape in her mouth. 'Anyway, she goes to the Wooden Spoon in the village for a bacon roll every morning, so if you want to square this up with her face to face, we can make that happen.'

Odette thought about that. She'd told a lie that had hurt Fiona. Then Fiona had told a lie with the intention of hurting Odette. For now, she was going to call that even.

'Not yet. Harry says that when I get out of here, we should go on a driving trip and I like that idea,' she said, blushing as their gazes met and he gave her a typically understated but affectionate smile. The truth was, she more than liked it. This last week had been a change for them to face each other when they were talking, rather than Odette staring at the back of his head. Maybe that's why she'd never realised before how handsome he was. Or how kind. Or how much he cared about her. When she got out of here, that was the top thing on her new to-do list. And maybe it was the drugs, but she felt a wave of giddy excitement every time she thought about it.

'Don't worry, Nancy, I can do the Heimlich manoeuvre if that grape gets stuck,' Keli told her, as she breezed into the ward.

She saw the colour on Odette's cheeks and knew that putting her on this ward had been the best thing she'd done all week.

Well, that and going out for dinner with Laurie and Yvie. Laurie had filled them in on the news that she'd moved out of Rex's apartment, and she was seeing Sy now. Apparently Rex had begged her to come back to him, especially after he'd been crucified in the press after the viral video and then received the news that he'd been written out of the show until the fuss died down. The storyline was that Hugh was being hunted by police after topping off Agnes, and had gone on the run, last seen on a flight to Malaga. He'd released a statement saying he was taking time off to pursue opportunities in Hollywood, but no one was buying that, because it had been compounded by a mass of dodgy stories about his lying and cheating that had been leaked in the last week and the public backlash had been vociferous.

Laurie had protested her innocence, but Keli wasn't convinced and she didn't blame her one bit. The whole publicity game was still a mystery to her, though, and something she wanted no part of. Well, almost no part.

On the back of the video, she'd already had a phone call from a morning TV show asking if she'd be willing to talk about common ailments affecting the elderly. Her manager, Calvin, was still in negotiations...

* * *

'Oh my goodness, it's like An Audience With Odette Devine in here this morning,' Tress said, as she came into the ward, pushing Buddy in his buggy.

Nancy immediately jumped up. 'I'll take my boy for a walk, and you have a seat, pet. There's already too many visitors at this bed. Keli will chase us.'

Tress shook her head, huge grin on her face. 'Thanks, but it's okay. I'm just here for two seconds, to check in on Odette and give Buddy to you.'

'We'll come and blether to you for a minute, Freda,' Calvin said, as he and Harry swapped their seats at Odette's bedside for the blue plastic seats beside the patient one bed along.

Tress had visited Odette every day this week. Over the six months that she'd worked with the actress, she'd grown increasingly fond of her, so she'd been worried when Odette left the show that they'd lose contact. Now Tress knew that would never happen, because, well, now their lives were intrinsically linked. She'd sussed out that Odette didn't have many people in her life and Tress would always welcome more people to the family that she'd built for herself. She'd never say no to a new aunt for Buddy.

'How are you today? You're looking smashing, you really are.'

'It's because I'm here,' Nancy announced with a chuckle.

'It's definitely because Nancy is here,' Odette played along.

'I'm glad, because Nancy is taking over my visiting shifts for the next couple of days and she'll be bringing Buddy too, because Noah and I...' Tress felt her neck go red and chided herself. What age was she? She should be over this by now, yet she hadn't stopped smiling in a week. 'We're going down to the Lake District for a couple of days, just the two of us.'

Just the two of them. Anya had gone back to the USA. Cheska had called her to say goodbye and to wish her and Buddy well.

So that just left Noah.

They'd spent every possible hour together over the last seven days and now she didn't even want to think about a time when it wasn't Noah and her and Buddy.

'I'll be back up on Tuesday, Odette, and Nancy, thank you. I've left everything at home ready and his day bag is under the pram. Call me if there's anything at all...' Tress leaned down and kissed her sleeping son, 'Love you, Noah Walker,' she whispered. She used his proper name more now because she liked how it sounded.

She hugged Nancy, then Odette and then blew a kiss to Yvie and Keli as she passed them on the way out. Then she got into the lift and smiled at the woman staring back at her in the mirror. The one who was totally loved up.

* * *

In the hospital car park, in the new Jeep he'd bought yesterday to replace his mangled one, Noah watched his girlfriend run towards him. He'd been here all morning because he had a few things to sort out on the ward, and then he'd dropped into the farewell lunch for Cheska. They'd hugged, said goodbye and wished each other well. And they both knew they meant it.

Tress jumped into the car, leaned over, kissed him, and it lasted way longer than was appropriate for a hospital car park. He didn't care. He couldn't get enough of her and she felt the same way. How did he get this lucky?

'Ah, you've finally seen sense,' his mother had said when he'd told her. 'I thought you two would get together eventually. To be honest, in the early months after the crash, before you started seeing Cheska, I thought you and Tress might get together then. Perhaps that would have saved some heartache.'

Noah knew different. Like he told anyone who would listen, this wasn't a movie. Or a song. Or a romcom. This was their lives. If they'd got together immediately after the accident, they'd never know if it was convenience, or grief, or the desperate need to use romantic love as a crutch.

Now they knew.

They'd made it through the worst that could happen, they'd healed, and they had built new lives together. And then they'd still chosen each other. This was who they were meant to be. Noah. Tress. Buddy. Their family.

'Ready to go?' he asked, when they finally came up for air.

'Ready to go,' she said, more beautiful than she had ever been.

And as they drove off for their first holiday together as a couple, Tress switched on the radio and laughed as a familiar voice filled the car. She was still the one...

Shania Twain was with them too.

ABOUT THE AUTHOR

Shari Low is the #1 bestselling author of over 20 novels, including *One Day With You,* and a collection of parenthood memories called *Because Mummy Said So*. She lives near Glasgow.

Sign up to Shari Low's mailing list for news, competitions and updates on future books.

Visit Shari's website: www.sharilow.com

Follow Shari on social media:

facebook.com/sharilowbooks

x.com/sharilow

instagram.com/sharilowbooks

bookbub.com/authors/shari-low

ALSO BY SHARI LOW

My One Month Marriage

One Day In Summer

One Summer Sunrise

The Story of Our Secrets

One Last Day of Summer

One Day With You

One Moment in Time

One Christmas Eve

One Year After You

The Carly Cooper Series

What If?

What Now?

What Next?

The Hollywood Trilogy (with Ross King)

The Rise

The Catch

The Fall

Boldwœd

Boldwood Books is an award-winning fiction publishing company seeking out the best stories from around the world.

Find out more at www.boldwoodbooks.com

Join our reader community for brilliant books, competitions and offers!

Follow us
@BoldwoodBooks
@TheBoldBookClub

Sign up to our weekly deals newsletter

https://bit.ly/BoldwoodBNewsletter

Made in United States
North Haven, CT
04 January 2024

46573647R00176